D1469045

Field
Guide

Field Guide

A Novel

GWENDOLEN GROSS

HENRY HOLT AND COMPANY

New York

Henry Holt and Company, LLC
Publishers since 1866
115 West 18th Street
New York, New York 10011

Library of Congress Cataloging-in-Publication Data

Gross, Gwendolen, 1967–
Field guide : a novel / Gwendolen Gross.—1st ed.
p.   cm.
ISBN 0-8050-6492-3
1. Women zoologists—Fiction.   2. Fathers and sons—Fiction.   3. Missing
persons—Fiction.   4. Rain forests—Fiction.   5. Queensland—Fiction.
6. Bats—Fiction.   I. Title.

PS3557.R568 F54 2001
813'.6—dc21

00-037019

First Edition 2001

Designed by Fritz Metsch

Printed in the United States of America

1   3   5   7   9   10   8   6   4   2

For J and J

Prologue

Annabel heard them even before she hiked off the dirt road and into the rain forest—the clamor of bat calls and complaints blurred like the sound of falling water. She looked down the road to be sure no one was watching as she stepped over the drainage ditch and into the woods where she'd tied an orange marker to a sapling's lower limb.

Using her compass for direction, Annabel slogged through the stingers and wait-a-while vines. The blue sky flashed through the canopy's defining lines like stained glass. She knew she was close because of the loamy scent, the sharp guano tang. The air was the texture of pudding, and condensation ran through her hair, mingling with sweat. She was rushing; she had just the afternoon for survey work before she had to meet her ride back to Townsville.

It crescendoed, the bat symphony, the cackle and screech, the scream and cry, sounds becoming distinct voices, and then she saw the black shadows like strange fruit in the trees. From the canopy, through the leaves and snake-thick vines, a pair of eyes stared down at her. More forms became distinct, fanning in the heat so their wing-membranes were backlit by skylight. Tens, then hundreds. The bats turned toward her, their eyes framed by the gray fur of their namesake spectacles. They looked, and she looked back, wonder filling her to her fingertips.

She stopped to observe a pair in the main clearing, a large male and female, their feet close on a wide branch. Lying on her back on the forest floor, she watched through binoculars as they preened themselves, licking their own torsos with long red tongues. The female scratched her belly with a wing, then leaned in and licked the male. He licked her back. They stepped closer to each other on the branch. In her notebook, she scribbled "sex, or affection?"

February 13, 1996
Pteropus conspicillatus, *spectacled flying foxes.*
Focal site: remnant rain forest patch N by NE of Beatrice River, Atherton, N. Queensland, Australia.

6:48pm *Fullest tree ≈ 420 bats. 1 couple (m1, f1) dominates most prominent branch: f1 stretches, unwraps.*

6:52pm *m1 closes on f1. f1 screeches.*

6:55pm *Sky gray. m1 stretches. Camp restless—100s wings opening.*

6:58pm *Liftoff. First m1; f1 follows. Mass exodus. Sound thickens w/scent—huge bat cloud.*

7:22pm *Bats departing ≈ 23 per minute. Off to rob orchards: swoop, grab a mango, bite, & drop. Fruit farmers hate them. A big mess, but spreads seeds.*

7:27pm *Camp starting to sound settled <100 bats.*

*7:38pm   1 bat alone on branch—wounded? He licks & licks
          at leg, folded against body. What got him—another
          bat, snake, eagle? When he finally drops to floor,
          rodents, composters & parasites will eat him in a few
          hours. Will others notice he's gone?*

*7:54pm   Almost dark. Rats searching for fruits & flesh. <50
          bats.*

8:08pm   ≈ 2 bat calls/minute.

*8:32pm   Camp's quiet. Mostly empty. ≈ 10 bats left, sick
          guy.*

8:48pm   I think he's the only one left.

Annabel pulled back her binoculars and looked up at the
theater of sky. She breathed in the green scent. The trees
where they'd roosted were stripped bare. In the thick days
of the rain forest, everything climbed atop everything else
for light; now night began, the hunters waking to start
their work. Through the hole in the canopy where the
fruit bats camped, Annabel considered the daylight's
embers, stirred into sparks of February stars.

Part I

One

You could fly into Townsville, the small university town on the northeast edge of the island-continent, but Annabel took the student's cheap route; there'd been two buses, five airplanes, and a van ride. She grew numb to discomfort after the traveling-hour tally reached the twenties. She'd left on an icy January morning in Chicago and emerged, dry-mouthed and sticky with the sour stench of airplane air, into a balmy Australian summer night. When she arrived at her dorm, she flopped onto her futon and fell asleep.

Someone was yelling, a few hours later, *wake wake wake,* the accent Australian. Annabel, still dressed, wandered into the hall, where a half-dozen others were stumbling toward the door. They were herded to a van for a ride to the lake and the dawn chorus. There was a picnic under a shelter, strange hard biscuits, the sky still dark. Then they sat by the lake with a professor, Professor Goode, who had a wide pinkish face and one dazzling blue eye, the other brown. He whispered the names of birds, common first, then Latin, as they started in occasional bursts, then began to flood the pan of the lake and the forest with squawking, hooting, whistling.

The professor's voice was warm, quiet, and distinctly Aussie. At first the calls were spare—a rustle, a short honk. The laugh of the kookaburra, like the chimp from the old Tarzan movies. Then a flock of parrots crossed the lake, raucous and flat, screaming their echoes across the water and flying in dark yellow-and-blue bands over the tops of the eucalyptuses.

"Pale-headed Rosella," whispered the professor. "*Platycercus ad—*"

A frog made a rippling bellow before he could finish the Latin, and Professor Goode smiled. "Frog," he whispered.

Annabel laughed quietly at his puckish expression. Soon the sounds were a flood, and his commentary was hard to hear, too many birds to follow.

It filled Annabel with pleasure, the quiet canvas and the strange colors of the sounds, the not knowing everything. At home she'd identify them: black-capped chickadee, cardinal, tufted titmouse. The birds here had the wild names she'd been reading in the guidebooks, and the wild sounds to go with them. She made a grid in her notebook and ticked off a tally of birdcalls in five-minute segments: 4:55, two kookaburras, a rainbow lorikeet, three sulfur-crested cockatoos. The tick marks quickly clustered as she tried to keep up.

The sounds subsided into background as the separate rays of sunlight blended into a room full of light. Annabel could see the professor's face now, intent, as he let a handful of soil from the bank slip though his fingers. He'd said the birds' names as if they were friends. There was something Annabel recognized in him, in the way he listened, attention absolute. Maybe it was that he wanted everyone else to know, to hear the details of the dawn chorus's complicated music. He knew it well, but still he listened with amazement in his expression, the two-colored eyes focusing on the feathered sources or toward hidden perches. She liked it when he looked at her; his wonder shot through her. Her own eyes were tender and tired.

She'd counted the calls of fifteen species of birds; she'd seen the dull dormant form of an orchid—a ball of dead-looking roots—and a startled, hissing, blue-tongued skink. Coming back around the lake, Annabel walked into a web and rattled a spider as big as a dinner plate, who made for her face. The front legs brushed her cheek before she backed up and slammed into the man behind her. It all had a groggy, dreamlike feeling. Annabel wanted to shake it off, the thickness, but even the rain-forest air was dense in her lungs. Jet lag, she reminded herself, doesn't rub off. It has to fade.

When they came back to James Cook, there was another meal, outside at picnic benches with the rest of the graduate students, whom Annabel thought she ought to be meeting, but she felt too slow to say much. Her roommate, Sabrina, introduced herself to the men, her voice low. She was wearing a V-neck tank top, and smelled of some syrupy eau de toilette, instead of forest and sweat and lack of sleep.

"Hey, roommate," Annabel said.

Sabrina grimaced cutely and pretended not to hear. Fine, Annabel thought, I don't like you either.

Annabel was shrinking. An apple in a very hot oven, wrinkling. Pungent.

She sat down next to the man she'd stumbled against that morning, Markos. Even sitting, he was tall, and his skin was the almost-translucent freckled variety peculiar to some redheads. Annabel looked at the freckles on his chin, wanting to connect the dots with a pen.

"What's your field?" she asked. "Animal, vegetable, or mineral?"

"Mmm," said Markos. "Oh, uh, vegetable." He waved a carrot stick at her, then took a bite. "Epiphytes. You?"

God, am I boring, thought Annabel. "Bats," she said. Bats aren't boring, though—bats get a bad rap, but they fly and cross-pollinate. Annabel looked at the pier, with its two barnacle-crusted fishing boats, the program's small research ship beside them. The other pier was where the ferries for Magnetic Island docked, and the yacht that shuttled tourists around the bay. Soon I'm out of here, she thought, soon to my bats.

"Sorry," he said. "It's because of all the travel, or whatever, but what's your name again?"

Boring and forgettable, she thought.

"Um, uh, Annabel."

"You almost forgot?"

"Oh, jet lag."

"Oh. Markos." He ate the rest of the carrot. "Truly groggy. Going back to dorms. Speaking in staccato." He laughed at his own joke.

He's more entertaining to himself than I am, thought Annabel. "I'll walk with you."

Clearly, she thought, this isn't going to be a social coup, but at least I won't be distracted when the work starts. Soon, she thought, hearing the word with each step, soon.

They walked back along the path, not uncompanionably, Annabel hoped, but quiet in their own capsules of sleepiness and thought. Parrots were fighting over fruit at the base of a mango tree; there were the smells of warm fruit, rot, and sea. The sun was flat and hard; even the late afternoon sun was potent, but good against her tired skin.

At the dorm house, there was a line for the showers. When she was finally under the spray, Annabel soaped and washed, scrubbing the travel grime. Then she settled in on her futon, trying to sleep as the sun waned against the window shades. All she could picture were the crabby, jet-lagged faces of the other students, their tired expressions and pale skin like hers. She tried to conjure the layers of the rain forest, from floor to canopy. She started with the thin soil at the bottom, imagined the vines reaching up into the lower trees, the sharp palm fronds starting at her height, cutting light into triangles, then higher, where the orchids' dazzle of purple and orange split the browns and greens. She looked up behind closed eyes to see more epiphytes filling in the rare spaces where the sun wove its fingers through the tops of the trees. And bats; in her version, there were bats camped on the branches. She hadn't seen them yet, but she knew they'd be there.

The next afternoon, she sat on a chair with a split cushion and a single rolling wheel, typing an E-mail message to her sister in Connecticut. The other side of the world. The Australian university had arranged the computer trailer for the graduate field-science program—she was short for the setup; her feet didn't quite reach the floor. The trailer smelled of mold and eucalyptus, and already it seemed familiar: the odor, the metal-framed window stuck open a few inches, the burst of green and yellow light from outside, the sound of her own breathing and key-clicking. She could imagine working on a final draft of her research project here, knowing something about her bats that no one else knew—some profile of relevance about their daytime activities assembled from thousands of observations—pointillistic dots that looked like nothing up close, but became a picture if you stepped away. She had faith in that discovery, a sense of pleasant possibility, belief that her efforts would be meaningful.

Now Alice, Annabel thought, might not always have faith. Her sister was always steady in action—her sturdy strides down the aisle at her wedding, her march forward in marriage, the regular relationship with their parents, her job—but Annabel thought maybe faith ran through Alice in uneven veins. Annabel had her own doubts sometimes, looking up close at too many dots. What could she honestly have to say, one human, watching bats?

Sender: (Annabel Mendelssohn)
AMendelss@ausnet.jcooku.tvl.edu
To: AEMendel@biosci.com
Subject: Hello! Hello!
Wednesday, January 17, 1996

Alice, my dear, hello from Oz. Do you know if Mom is on-line yet? Are you still calling her every week?

Arrived, got the James Cook University standard visitors' housing—it's a real house, but incredi-

bly cramped, or might I say COZY. Got a roommate
who appears to be a monster of vanity, but I
should give her a chance anyway, right? I'm sure
you would. But she's already stacked up hair
sprays and toxic-waste face paint and removers and
curlers and thong underwear and a whole sequined
pile of nightclothes in her corner, and it's
spreading. Environmental Ethics and Soil Science
201 are really chichi classes, I plan to wear my
stilettos. Two dozen grad students, and I get her.
Okay, maybe I'm crabby from jet lag. You know I'm
not a TOTAL snob.

Other than the roommate, I've met a few decent
people in the program. One guy, Markos, went to
West High around the same time Kevin did . . . I
don't remember his last name, though. Did I
tell you they had us out on a field trip already?
We recorded dawn chorus in some tiny strip of
rain forest. Saw a bandicoot, rainbow lorikeets,
roseolas—weird marsupial, amazing parrots, but
it's hard to fully appreciate anything on only two
hours of sleep. So, more later. Let me know if you
get this.

Love, Annabel

p.s. Is it snowing? I'm on my second summer!!
(Don't be too jealous.)

   Annabel pushed her disorderly reddish hair behind her
ears. She wasn't sure she should've said all that about the

roommate, but she had to confide in someone, she had to talk with Alice somehow, and E-mail was free. She had friends who would write from Chicago, and she had a phone card she ought not to use because of the expense. Alice was essential, though, Alice was her anchor, sometimes irritating, sometimes soothing, but always there. No one else could understand her history without a sense of sympathy—at this point she didn't want sympathy. Sometimes all she wanted was to talk, or write, about the present, even though Robert intruded into her daily life as if his timeline hadn't ended. She imagined him looking at her roommate, a quick look of lust followed by disgust. Robert's face had revealed him the way sky revealed weather. And he changed as quickly, too—you could watch the overcast of his displeasures dissipate in seconds for the clarity of purpose.

Robert would have loved it here, Annabel thought, the flat blue of the water, the parrot cacophony. But he'd have been impatient for the work to start. She was here for the bats, but first she had to wait out the formalities of class work and proposals, hurdles to keep her from starting the real search, field data, breaking down behaviors into numbers and percentages, then reconstituting the data to make a whole greater than the sum of the parts. The clean satisfaction of observations kneaded into truths.

She'd left her Chicago lab job, impatient for what her brother had called the real work: the field, putting her hands on life. She'd had a taste of it, but she was impatient, waiting for the meal of her own research.

Jet lag made everything overstimulating and slow—the too bright light, sharp smells. The lake they went to, in

that rain-forest patch, haunted her. The other students had
talked about hitching a ride back to go swimming, but she
looked at it and saw floating hands, bloated faces. Alice had
warned her that you couldn't just leave your history.

Alice had missed work for two days. The flu clogged up
her eyes, nose, chest, and perception. Everything looked
slightly blurred at the edges, smudged by a careless finger.
Her body felt like an oversaturated sponge, leaky, swollen.
Sometimes Alice thought her size was perfect: against
Kevin in bed, she was water to the cup of him. She was
voluptuous and foreign to herself—the curve of her own
ankle, her shoulder small under his arm when they were
touching each other, wrapped. Sometimes she liked her
shiny brown hair, cut short and neat. Her eyes almost the
same deep shade. But today her hair was strings, she was
puffy, swelled with her own discomforts. She was the
wrong size for the couch, the robe she wore; she smelled
of the overused, overwarm bed, and her hair tangled with
the bad air of the flu.

Her sister, Annabel, was in the Southern Hemisphere,
doing real science, and it was summer for her. Sometimes it
seemed like Annabel's energy surrounded her like perpet-
ual summer.

Outside Alice's small Tudor house, her cave, it was January in suburban Connecticut—the trees were stripped and
their gray arms matched the sky. Alice parted the insulated
curtains to peek at her empty street. Even the cars looked
desolate. If only it would snow, paint everything bright
white to reflect the feeble light and wake the landscape of

parked Volvos and Fords crusted in road salt, gray sidewalks and lawns, colonials and capes sitting squat on their modest lots. A gray bird landed on the nude dogwood in her front yard and didn't sing. Alice let the curtain settle shut.

She coughed, lay on the couch, and turned the TV on and off, hoping each time to find something distracting. She hated being out of work; she felt guilty, as if she were playing hooky.

But she was genuinely sick, and her phone rang a lot, with questions from the office, her boss, with disgruntled *where did you put*s and *what did you do about*s. Alice gritted her teeth. He was annoyingly kind, and annoyingly help-less without her. She heard her own voice whine like a leaking accordion—she told her boss where, what, that she was feeling a bit better, that she'd be back soon.

If she thought too hard, everything started to hurt, col-ors, sound. There was a familiar pale taste of metal in her mouth. What was she doing now, one of her family's sur-vivors—handmaiden's work, grants administration, instead of real science, like Robert. She could have taken up where he left off, or started her own, like Annabel.

But she had Kevin. She had a home, she had a sweet steadiness in her days.

Alice coughed and put a lemon drop on her tongue to chase the metal taste. She turned the TV back on to watch the *Wheel of Fortune* contestants buy vowels so they could guess incorrectly, greedily, at clichés. If only she could leave Connecticut winter for a week—the sameness of the sky, rushing in from the aching cold to the inside's artificial light. In the thickest green of sweaty summer, Alice thought she longed for winter, but what she imagined then was a white coat on her house, the burnt blue sky, sweet fireplace warmth on her cold face. It wasn't like that in real January—winter was dead leaves still mounded in the gutter and old air from the sealed containers of house, car, work.

She loved their house, a three-bedroom Tudor with warm slanting walls and a fat chimney. Over the bridge from her parents in New Jersey, it was close enough for a day trip, but not so close they could happen by without warning. They'd been able to afford it because it had only one bathroom, and because the retired social worker who was moving out had rejected six offers already on the basis of not liking the potential buyers. She liked Alice and Kevin—liked their bright faces, she said. She also told them she expected them to fill the house. As it was, one bedroom was theirs, one was a guest room, and the third was an office.

She leafed through the supermarket ads, hoping to discover a stranded postcard from her sister. It had only been about a week since Annabel left Chicago for Australia, but Alice wished she had some word from the sunny other side of the world. Really, she would've liked her to come over, bake cookies, give the house extra noise and energy, the way she had as a kid. It was never like that as adults; Annabel wasn't truly lit with unending enthusiasms, the way Alice imagined her from a distance.

When she returned to work, Alice had fourteen voice-mail messages, three handwritten phone messages, and twenty-two E-mails—many of which were duplicates of the phone messages—about meetings she'd already missed, office charity funds, and one that informed her she was out sick and wouldn't be available until Monday. It was Monday, and she wasn't feeling so available. She shut her door.

Sender: (Annabel Mendelssohn)
AMendelss@ausnet.jcooku.tvl.edu
To: AEMendel@biosci.com
Subject: Hello?
Saturday, January 20, 1996

ALICE? Did you get my message? I'm much more
coherent now, I've slept a little. I was kinda
crazed before. LET ME KNOW IF YOU GET THIS.
Love, A.

Sender: AEMendel@biosci.com (Alice Mendelssohn)
To: AMendelss@ausnet.jcooku.tvl.edu
Subject: Re: Hello?
Monday, January 22, 1996

Dear dear Annabel,

Yes, I got your messages. I've been incognito in
that boring suburban way: with the flu and out of
work. Kev took good care of me, though.

That roommate—ugh—maybe once you all get really
dirty in the field she'll let go. Maybe she's a
female impersonator; have you seen her without her
clothes?

Have your classes started? The dawn chorus sounds
wonderful, I'm jealous. I didn't want to say it, I
wanted to let it pass, but right now, in this

stuffy office that smells of politicking and rumors
of cutbacks with no real science in sight, I
really wish I were in your shoes. It's not just
the weather (and yes, we have old drooly snow. It
was lovely coming down, but have I been out to ski
or play?), it's being here, the job. Not the Kevin
part; he's still bliss, yup, wouldn't give that up.

Mom is worried about you. I'll bet she has E-mail
access, but I doubt she'll use it. She'll probably
mail you those soapy blue throat lozenges intended
for me, and I'll get the pocket-money check.

Tell me more; any interesting people? When do you
get to your research? Let me live vicariously
through my little sister.

Love, A.

Yes Annabel, Alice thought, I'm still calling Mom every
week. I won't feel silly for it either; it's not as if I'm trying
to prove anything. I just like knowing where everyone is;
someone has to do the job of keeping track.

T w o

Annabel was watching mudskippers emerge from the mangrove swamp. Bug-eyed, mud-colored things; she looked at one and thought, Do *you* think you're an evolutionary marvel? She slid her cheap underwater camera out of her backpack and snapped a shot.

The first group project was essentially finished, rough observation work, which Annabel thought was quite below graduate level. The mudskippers breathed in water, they breathed in air, they were basically one up on humans. The sun patches that came through the trees felt like flames, but she didn't shed her long sleeves and run into the inviting ocean on the other side of the mangroves.

Sabrina was with her, and two other American graduate students: Maud, an older woman who seemed to take the surprises and discomforts of the program in stride, and Lars, a dark, quiet man who'd left a lab job in Minnesota. It appeared that all the women were after Lars already. Annabel was disgusted, but she was flirting a little, too.

Maud said, "God, it's hot. Why is it we can't swim?" She scratched at the sleeves of her blue-striped button-down man's shirt. The tails were muddy.

"They told us, *Cubomedusae*," said Sabrina. The record keeper for their group, she was labeling Maud's mudskipper diagram.

"That's right, they said that. And do you guys know just what *Cubomedusae* are?" Maud wasn't embarrassed by what she didn't know. Annabel took note, because she usually was.

"Box jellyfish," Lars said. His eyes were closed, as if he were listening to some glorious private music.

Maud murmured. Her thin lips were dry—Annabel imagined lip balm smoothing over the uncomfortable cracks. Her hair was back in a braid, and the wisps around her face looked dry, too, as if in the heat of this place, she was slowly roasting.

Annabel said, "Where do they get off, anyway, being so deadly, and invisible. Seems like overkill to me. I read the sign at the entrance to the park—says if you're touched by ten centimeters of tentacle, you're history. I just wonder why something so deadly *is*."

"Because it works," said Lars. He opened his eyes. They were very blue. Big deal, Mr. Blue Eyes, Annabel thought, wishing she didn't think that he'd been clever.

"Big prey, maybe," said Annabel.

Maud murmured again. "Oh, yeah."

The mangrove-swamp camping trip took two days. Ten minutes to get drenched by drizzle and swamp muck, and then too long, Annabel thought, to study the salt tolerance of mangroves and the breathing mechanisms of mudskippers. One of the professors gave her a Ziploc bag with silicate powder packs, to keep her camera and money and passport from molding in the relentless spore-filled damp. Her hat already had a thin, permanent mold scar.

Mosquitoes, which the Australians called *mozzies,* clouded and bit each evening. There had been leeches in the thick, wet forest campsite. As soon as she stepped from the tent platform she'd noticed one stretching off a leaf toward her, two-thirds in the air like an acrobat. Annabel didn't consider herself squeamish. She felt mildly superior to Sabrina, who squealed, who practically dunked herself in the leech-and-tick repellent one of the professors offered, toxic stuff that was banned in the United States. But after Annabel discovered them full and fat in four places between her toes, she put away her sandals for hot, protective boots. The skinny beasts were ubiquitous, begging blood from every twig and leaf. At first the bites stung a little, then they itched, but mostly, blood kept running out after she'd pried the satiated leeches off, leaving a spotty trail as she walked, making a mess in the tent.

Annabel was glad to come back to the house, where space wasn't *entirely* communal. Piles of laundry were waiting in line by the washer and dryer, and everyone was drying out. Annabel's skin itself felt slightly rotten. She sat on her futon, examining her wounds, while Sabrina unpacked, folding things carefully, even her dirty clothes.

"So," said Annabel. "Did *you* expect the parasite parade? I know I wasn't really prepared."

"The repellent works," said Sabrina, folding a purple bra.

"Yeah, I guess I didn't expect so *many* bloodsuckers."

"Oh, Annabel, you don't seem to mind. Actually, you don't seem to mind anything."

Annabel tried not to peel off a recent scab. She started, then patted it back down, hoping for a new clot.

"Thanks, I guess," she said, thinking, Of course I mind things. I mind you, for example, saying that.

Walking to the computer trailer, Annabel wondered whether she was really cut out for field science, if a little damp and hot and a few leeches and a cold roommate could scare her off so easily. She walked up the path through fire lilies and morning glories, saw parrots fighting again, a flock competing for a single mango on a fecund tree with piles of fallen fruit, hundreds of others still on the branches. They were like people, battling over the most visible resource, unwilling to find their own branches when one spot, a single fruit, seemed most desirable. She wasn't ready to give up yet; besides, soon she'd get to her bats. Some bats raised their young communally, she remembered. Of course, they might compete sometimes, for food or mates, squabble over territory, but could thousands of humans get along in a cave together? Or in a camp in the branches of a dozen proximate trees? No, humans needed walls between them, at least she did.

Annabel climbed the milk crate that served as a step into the trailer to see if she had any E-mail to answer yet.

Sender: (Annabel Mendelssohn)
AMendelss@ausnet.jcooku.tvl.edu
To: AEMendel@biosci.com
Subject: Alission, alicomatic,
Thursday, January 25, 1996

Banish that flu! I'm glad it's almost better, and
I'm sorry you have to be back at work, where you
caught it in the first place—and where no doubt
they have piles of stuff waiting for you, enough
to make anyone violently ill. I know you don't
hate your job, but I wish they'd let you out more.

Perfect timing, your minor envy. I was already
starting to get a little rotted and moldy and wish
for my clean old lab. We went on a camping trip,
and there were leeches, and Sabrina (my sequined
roommate) did have to let her hair down a little,
though you'd be surprised how religiously she
sticks to the dress-up routine. There's a person
under her base, powder, and blush (and not a man,
I have seen evidence), I'm trying to have faith.

Classes are beginning in earnest now. We had three
hours of lectures with Professor Goode today. He's
a soil scientist, and passionate about what he
does, though rather stuck on the jargon that makes
us sound, well, educated. I suppose that's how we
get hired, by saying "using the baseline data we
can make probability statements that render pre-
diction of domain and constitute evidence of the

sphere of influence," instead of "we do some tests
to see if the system's okay."

Professor Goode has one blue eye and one brown,
it's the first thing one notices. That and his wild
hair, and the way he looks at things, and people—
he really concentrates. He smells a little like
soil, I think, not dirty, but earthy. I'm going to
be on a project with him next week, a marine
setup, actually; we're going to take core samples
around giant clam sites to test for minerals and
pH. Giant clams!

There will be a few other grads on the project,
and one other prof. And Monsieur le Goode is definitely too old for me, Alice—I can see your worried Puritan look. He's divorced I think, or
separated, so don't fuss, I'm just looking at
those enigmatic eyes from afar.

Keep out of those politics! And go ski! And keep
writing me, I miss you. Lucky you, to have Kevin
the Magnificent for comfort and care.

Love, Annabel.

Annabel used to have a latent crush on Kevin. She remembered how, the week before Alice's wedding, he kept
appearing in her dreams—sliding his hands around her hips,
pressing her thighs apart. In the dream he smelled like a
forest, a rich, green scent. It was his good dark eyes, maybe,
or his quick laugh. He laughed at jokes, never acted superior. Like Robert did, too sophisticated for little sister's

jokes. Their father laughed hard at things he thought were funny, his big voice thumping, then trailing off into a wheeze. He didn't think many of Kevin's jokes were funny.

During the ceremony Annabel couldn't look at Kevin without blushing, abashed by her dreams' clarity. She'd focused on a single purple iris in Alice's bouquet, filling herself with purple, and pride in her lucky, smart sister and her sister's laughing man.

Annabel looked out of the small trailer window and saw Maud coming up along the mango-strewn path. Maud's shoulder-length brown braid was tight, and her face was long and oval. She had dark brown eyes, and creases around her mouth from smiling. Annabel ducked out of the trailer and caught up with her.

"Hey, Maud, what do you think of the lectures so far?" God, she thought, why do I have to ask that? Here we are living at practically the edge of the rain forest, extraordinary species all around, and I ask about the dull classroom experience.

"I don't know if I can keep up, Annabel, my math's pretty rusty."

"I'd be happy to study with you, if you want, though I'm sure you're better off than you think."

"Oh, I wouldn't be so sure." She took the lip balm Annabel proffered, smoothed her dry lips.

She wasn't better off than she thought, and Annabel found herself giving a patient lecture in basic statistics. She didn't mind so much, though; Maud was good company, and seemed to be one of the only women not caught up in pursuit of Lars. They sat on the grass by the library, where they could still hear the parrots squabbling. Halfway through the chi-square discussion, Maud mentioned a crush on Professor Goode. Some scientists we are, Annabel thought, all the way out in the Southern Hemisphere, thousands of species to investigate, and every pathetic person looking for love. Not me, please, not me, too.

Annabel, Lars, Sabrina, Professor Michael Trimble—call me Mike—from Canberra, and Professor Goode were on a small boat, getting very hot. Mike was tall and knobby—he had freckled skin and big elbows. His face was round and kind, but his mouth, wide and smooth, seemed conspicuously sexual to Annabel. Men are strange animals, she thought; their bodies give such complicated messages.

Another boat from the program bobbed like a floating bathtub on the horizon. Lars and Professor Goode were pulling up the core sample; the winch had stuck, so they were working hand over hand. Annabel had offered to help before Lars did, but chauvinism permeated the entire universe, and Lars's offer, as he arrogantly shed his T-shirt and displayed his pale skin to the potent sun, had been the one to which the professor grunted and nodded yes. That's all right, Annabel thought, I don't need to sweat more than I am already.

Besides, the professor respected her. He'd asked Annabel for suggestions on the clam study on the van ride up, and he'd listened to her ideas about the bats.

"Daytime behavior," she'd said, as he turned them onto a dirt road leading to a boat ramp.

"Gross observations first?" he asked.

"Yeah. Site mapping—"

"Good on yer," he said. He'd sounded interested, he'd paid attention.

Mike was doing a pH test. Sabrina watched Lars with quiet but obvious interest. She played with the end of her braid, then undid and redid it, blond hair glinting as it folded out into firmly sprayed waves. Annabel had thought maybe she and Sabrina would have a chance to talk, perhaps reverse the path they'd been taking.

Since the mangrove trip, Sabrina had been going to meals with other students, coming back very late at night; Annabel learned that they'd been hanging out at the pub, letting the local loggers and dairy farmers and the occasional university student buy them beer. Probably they'd been squealing at darts games, not playing, merely pretty observers. Still, Annabel wouldn't have minded being asked along, but she didn't know how she could manage to mention it now, without sounding defensive, needy, or pathetic.

She'd already read all the articles she could find on local bats, and had marked potential sites on her maps, trying not to care about her roommate, or anything but getting on with her work. Nothing wrong with civility, though, she thought.

"So," she said to Sabrina. "Have you done much marine work?"

"Actually, as an undergrad, I thought I wanted to be a marine biologist," said Sabrina.

"What happened?"

"I went out on a project—had to learn to dive, first— but then I went out on a summer project off Hawaii and got the bends, and I wanted to *die*." She was looking at Lars while she spoke, let her glance flutter in Annabel's direction a few times, like checking a rearview mirror on the highway.

"So—that was it?"

"Not *it,* exactly, but I was more interested in plants after that, land plants. And steady land."

She stopped talking, as if she'd been released. Annabel was released, too. Enough effort, she thought. Water washed the boat, muffled lapping; no one said anything.

Mike held a tube up to the sky, licking his lips as he compared the water to a color chart. Lars and Professor Goode grunted gently. A gull let loose a soliloquy on expecting fish as it circled the boat. They pulled the sample in, the metal corer thudded against the bottom, and the chain settled in a pile like a spent snake.

Annabel did wish Sabrina had asked whether *she'd* ever been interested in marine biology. In fact, she'd already thought the conversation might turn, and had prepared to answer: yes, briefly, when I learned about marine mammals as a kid, but I'd been pretty obsessed with bats for as long as I've been seriously studying. She'd even thought about telling Sabrina about her brother, that he'd been a marine biologist. But they didn't even eat dinner together, so why was she on the verge of confiding something intimate? Maybe it was the wrong instinct, maybe it was sort of a cheap attempt at closeness to tell someone your brother had died. It would be artificial, unfair to Robert, *using* his story. Anyway, Sabrina didn't ask anything.

Annabel pulled and scraped the sample out of the corer and she and Lars and Sabrina each started on their assigned tests. Professor Goode smeared zinc oxide on his nose, which was already swelling with burn.

"What now?" Annabel asked the professor.

"Now." He kicked his shoes off, into the puddle in the boat. He tossed his cap, a stained white one with a red-and-green tree logo, atop his shoes. "We swim." Professor Goode rolled backward into the water in a slightly goofy but very dramatic exit.

"Ah," said Annabel. She bit the inside of her cheek. She'd have to be brave about getting in the water; it was going to keep confronting her. In the past two years, she'd been in a swimming pool twice, but she'd avoided leaving boats and shores at lakes and oceans. She was a good swimmer. It wasn't fear exactly, but desire not to think it through, not to imagine what could happen.

"Now we swim." She took off her shoes and followed.

Alice was taking the train from White Plains to New York City to meet Kevin for dinner. Sometimes she felt pushed out to the suburbs to stay, with a simultaneous longing and revulsion when she thought about the shoving, scintillating city. Stamford, where they lived, was crowding in with new housing developments and office parks, but the street where they'd bought a house was quiet and unharassed. It was next to the Bartlett Arboretum, a green blob on the map, with a swamp walk and banks of azaleas and rhododendrons that lit up spring with blissful pink.

When she thought of living in the city, she remembered a tightness in her chest. When she was twenty-two she'd been depressed. Not a simple blue, the average cycle of it, but down enough to stop caring about things, to let things slide. She was in the last year of her graduate program in genetics. Kevin had moved in with her; they had a small apartment in Brooklyn with a big sunny window that faced a neat little backyard. It wasn't their backyard—it belonged to the two-family house on the next street. She watched a girl play there sometimes, a girl with some disorder that kept her out of school. She had to use crutches with special arm braces, and she seemed to smile all the time, crookedly.

Alice watched her in the backyard, sitting in the muddy spring grass, tracking ants as they climbed a fence post. That little girl knew something, she thought, things she couldn't articulate about gradual progress. Alice watched as she followed ants to the corner of the post, where they'd turn out onto the wire between fence posts. The girl smashed the ants, the ones she could catch, between her mittened thumb and fingers. She squashed them and then looked into her hand to see the evidence of death. That same awkward smile. The brutality of this gesture made hurt spread across Alice's chest.

She wept at night when she thought Kevin was asleep. He woke sometimes, comforted her. He was so full of school he was exhausted, but he still wanted to know what was wrong. He invented scenarios, turned on the light and tried to identify what was bothering her, whether it was her family, her school, if it could be related to the light, the weather, if it was something he had said.

Colors hurt, and light. A metal taste sat on her tongue, cold, nulling flavor and attention. After a few weeks, she ate less, and then stopped eating unless Kevin was around, because it took too much effort. She hated the packages that sealed up butter, the crusted edges on the jam jar. Eventually Kevin convinced her to go see a counselor at the university, who sat and listened even when Alice felt she was inventing things to be sad about. But she cried, she emptied the pressure in her chest.

After a few months, she was hungry after going to the counselor; she wanted to eat ice cream when Kevin met her. The weather became hot. She finished her master's degree, and they moved to Connecticut, so Alice had to drive too far to go regularly to the counselor, who had suggested antidepressants. Alice didn't want them; she was getting better. Then the sadness eased, she forgot it, even when she had brief blue periods. It wasn't the same deep well, though she knew it was always there, dormant for now. Sometimes the pale cold coated her tongue. She could mask it, though, with plums or chocolate, with Kevin's kisses.

Robert got depressed, so depressed—she didn't like to think about his dark voice on the phone. Sometimes Alice wondered whether her mother got depressed, whether Annabel did. Probably not Netta, who was transparently pleased by small things: her lilacs starting their buds, the picnic bench she built from a kit for the backyard. She knew their father had the darkness, though, long silent spells she remembered punctuating his steadiness. They didn't call it depression for him; they called it "tired." Dad was tired from work, or from traveling. He needed to be left alone.

Annabel had always been intent, like Robert, but Robert was darker, he had dangerous extremes. Alice had read that some people kept depression inside them, waiting, like brown nubby flower bulbs, waiting for the right amount of heat and rain, the right kinds of pressures, before blossoming. But Annabel showed what she felt—on the phone, when she told Alice about getting the grant to go to Australia, Alice could hear her shine, the hot energy of pleasure radiating across the phone lines through her voice. Robert was never that obvious about his enthusiasms, or his sadness.

Back in her office, Alice tapped the keys on her keyboard without pressing hard enough to send letter signals to the screen. Her mother had just called, asking about Annabel. *Ask about me*, Alice had wanted to say, but it was too childish. Thinking it made her feel petty.

Sender: AEMendel@biosci.com (Alice Mendelssohn)
To: AMendelss@ausnet.jcooku.tvl.edu
Subject: some other nonsense
Wednesday, January 31, 1996

Dear Annabel,

I know I wrote a few days ago, and you are probably wrestling giant squid or, more likely, tagging them with a minimum of disturbance to their natural behavior cycles, but I wanted to say hi again. The snow has started to melt already; there's heavy slush soaking the feet of the entire metropolitan area.

I don't want to nag, but Mom says she hasn't heard a peep from you. Maybe you could send a quick postcard? Just to make her a little less nervous?

Is there anything you miss, anything you'd like me
to send?

Tell me about those clams.

Love, A.

Annabel sat on the shore of a small barrier-reef island
between Professor Mike Trimble and Professor Goode.
She liked these two men—they knew why they were here;
they knew which tests to do and when to quit for a dip in
the ocean. There was a scraggly palm tree casting a little
shade over her, but the men were in the sun, getting red-
der. They'd finished the project, and they'd gone swimming, blissfully—there were no *Cubomedusae* out on the
reef. It took some effort to make herself go in again, but
the water felt natural, as long as she concentrated on where
she was, on the artificial currents of her own motion, the
brilliant corals, the warm hand of the sun on her back, and
the filtered light below. Annabel used her snorkel mask and
dived down to the giant clams, gorgeous shades of blue.
She took photos with the underwater camera, though the
pictures would probably look like big blue blobs.

Annabel touched the clams' open maws with her flippers and her fingers. They did close upon touch, but
slowly, elegantly, not in a snap-up-the-hapless-scientist sort
of way.

Professor Goode had brought up a plant sample with
some sand from around its roots. He set up the microscope
in the boat and stared at the slide he set, fingered the plant.
Annabel watched him from the water when she came up

from the clams. His face was intent—the deep sleep of absolute concentration—and it made him beautiful to her. He had the glow of intimate observation, and she longed to have that attention directed at her.

Lars and Sabrina were guarding the sand mound where they'd buried fish wrapped in banana leaves to cook atop hot coals. Annabel didn't care; she'd given up on Sabrina, at least for now, and the professors were excellent company.

"I'm not really a professor, you know," said Professor Trimble. "Now your Professor Goode, he has the official distinction." He tossed some sand in his colleague's direction with his toes.

"It's not the same as in the States, Annabel," said Professor Goode. "It takes a bit longer—"

"A bit longer? A bit longer? One must be venerable and ancient." Mike Trimble laughed. One of his front teeth was chipped under the smooth mouth; his knees were huge—they looked like swellings on his thin legs. Annabel liked him.

"Not much is the same here as in the States," Professor Goode continued. "We don't talk about everything, the way you do."

"What's that mean?" asked Annabel.

"You know, you Yanks talk about everything—love, honor, duty, and then there's sex and divorce, oh, and *feelings*." He leaned toward her and pulled his cap off his head, pushing it onto hers. It smelled of sea.

"You don't? And what, exactly, is wrong with talking about those things?"

"He's jealous, love," said Mike. He patted a handful of sand onto her ankle.

"I suppose I am," said the professor.

"Well, then, you're with one of those loose and loquacious Yanks," Annabel said, looking at his eyes. "Out with it. Feel free."

"I'm getting a divorce," said the professor. He looked right back at her.

Annabel shivered, silver, cool. She hadn't expected this, but it felt good to have someone trust her. And it was familiar—if they weren't intimidated, people told Annabel about themselves, secrets. She thought she must have a trustworthy face.

"Oh, I'm sorry."

Mike mumbled something about checking the food and hauled himself out of the sandpile. His footprints melted as water filled them.

"I'm sorry, too. She's had enough of me, I guess, and there was this other woman. But I was a fool to act on it. You know, fantasies are perfectly all right, but one ought to control oneself when it comes down to actual behavior."

"Hm," said Annabel. "So your wife said that was it, no chance of reconciliation?"

"We . . . well, we tried counseling. But she wanted freedom, too, said since I'd tasted it she was damned if she wasn't going to get her own."

"She sounds pretty angry."

"Oh, Annabel, she ought to be. I was a bastard." He sat back slightly, put his arms around his knees. Thinking about closing, like a giant clam, Annabel thought. She felt like she was looking right into the belly of the clam, at hidden valves and pearls.

"The worst part," said the professor, "is my kids."

"Oh? How old?"

"They're grown. Andrew's twenty already, and Leon is twenty-eight. He's gone over to the States—Leon has. Andrew's at the university in Sydney. It's not the age. It's that they won't talk to me at all. I write, I call. They're civil, of course, quick notes back on noncommittal post-cards, they're willing to say 'Hello, Father,' on the phone. Not that either one of them ever called me 'Father,' before. It's so biting."

"Maybe, well, how long has it been?" She tried to imag-ine Professor Goode with a wife and two sons. It was hard to envision him with anyone, he was so sturdy alone.

"About six months since I moved out. Since she asked me to move out. Andrew doesn't live at home or any-thing—both their old rooms are offices now, and Andrew's stopped coming home every holiday. We pay for tickets for Leon to come home sometimes. He went over to go to Harvard, for graduate studies, but he's working in a museum now. Andrew, actually, should be graduating this year." He swept his hands through the air, as if waving to these sons.

"Maybe you need to give them a while, you know, let them get over being angry. They probably feel a little betrayed, too."

Lars and Sabrina were walking toward them on the sand. Their faces looked naked to Annabel. Pink and blind, oddly obscene, like mole rats.

The professor's hands rested. "Do you think I ought to stop with the letters, stop calling?"

"Definitely not. That's how you're faithful—sorry about the pun—to them. You have to keep trying, even though it's painful, and probably a little insulting. Just keep trying. No time for pride now; they'll need you sometime, and it's your job to be around when they do."

The professor noticed Lars and Sabrina. He touched Annabel's shoulder, long enough so she could still feel it, a short caress, after he took his hand away. "You're really rather wise," he said. "For a Yank, and a youngster." He stood, spilling out a lapful of sand. "So, how's that fish?" The clam closed.

"Fine," said Lars. "But we found something really gross by the tent."

"Don't need tents out here," said the professor, following them back toward the fire.

Annabel felt small again, two steps behind everyone, shrunk like wool in the dryer.

"John," said Mike Trimble, standing behind a tent, his face screwed in a peculiar expression. "What's this?"

Annabel caught up, saw some remains, about two feet long—tailbone, picked clean, cords of intestine wrapped around and through the ribs. A few inches away, a cleanly sliced half a brain, slightly bird-pecked, worms tunneling in and out like happy garden gophers.

Acid filled her mouth, but Annabel came in close behind Professor Goode to see.

"Pig?" she asked.

"It's just a wild boar," said Professor Goode. "So move the tents." He held out his hands, appalled only by their fragility.

I'll bet he isn't even a little nauseated, Annabel thought, impressed.

·   ·   ·

There was hardly any fire left, hot ingots casting a small dome of orange light. Professor Goode was a few yards away, his whistling breaths rhythmic, vulnerable. She'd given back his hat, and he was holding it against his chest as he slept. Only Annabel was still awake, trying not to think about the boar-corpse, wondering whether the man breathing mere steps away had imagined kissing her, how his neck tasted, his chest. It was wrong to imagine him this way, she thought—he was too old, he was her professor. But she could do whatever she wanted in the safe vault of fantasy. Still, Annabel's conscience clicked in, forcing her from imaginary pleasure. She sat up in her sleeping bag and watched the ocean. It was barely lit by the moon, the green flashes of phosphorescence like lost stars in the water.

Robert was a lost star, Robert was fallen. Annabel made herself think about him because it hurt. She wondered whether addicts felt like this, alcoholics, seeking the pain that was almost pleasure. Maybe Professor Goode felt this way about his separated family; maybe that's why he'd told her.

Robert used to rub her skin to make it burn. When he was ten and she was eight they had a game—he called it The Test. If she passed, she could play with him. She had to let him give her an Indian burn, wring her arm until the skin went scarlet. She had to eat a mixture of Tabasco and sugar, a spoonful of dirt. She had to steal Alice's plastic horse, the one she wouldn't let anyone touch. No one else was allowed to do things to Annabel, though—Robert's friend Steven wanted to make her take off her shirt, said she had to let them sit on top of her. He'd tried to push her down, but Robert, his dark hair too long, almost covering his eyes, his arms scarred pink from picking at scabs, punched Steven in the stomach.

"You can't touch her," he said. "She's mine."

She used to believe she belonged more to Robert than to her parents. More to Robert than even herself, perhaps. She remembered the smell of him, as a boy, dirt and salt and crushed leaves. They had to rake the leaves in the fall—Team Mendelssohn, their mother called them, coordinating from the back porch. Alice made neat piles; she collected the reddest leaves to press in waxed paper. Annabel stopped and started, willed the leaves to stuff themselves into bags by magic.

The rake chapped her hands. She was tired, and splinters stabbed her soft flesh. Robert waited until Mom went inside and dove into the piles, whooping. Annabel followed him, but he moved too fast, she could never make it to his pile before he scrambled out again. Then, when she thought she was chasing him, he jumped back in after her—he landed on her leg and it hurt, he pinched her and then helped her up. She wouldn't ever complain about the bruises.

On the island, sand smooth under her back, Annabel wondered whether Robert had ever believed in God. They weren't taught to, though they'd each had a few weeks of Sunday Hebrew school to decide whether they wanted to study. Alice and Annabel kept going for a few months, but Robert quit after week one. Sometimes Annabel thought it was a sort of deprivation, not being taught to believe, then sometimes she thought her parents had nurtured free will in the best way possible, by not indoctrinating. But when Robert had died, almost two years ago, she'd hoped he'd believed in something, Fate, maybe, or afterlife. She liked the idea that she'd get to see him again sometime, that he'd tell his own drowning story with that dry sense of humor, make death seem funny because she'd have him back.

Sometimes it seemed as if this were still The Test, as if Robert were checking to see whether he'd made her cry. He was gone so long, so often, in the years before he died, that now she could sometimes believe he was working on another project, that he'd send her an eccentric little note or be home for Thanksgiving. He wouldn't. She made herself think it.

He was in that ocean somewhere, one of the phosphorescent glints, even though they'd hauled his body out, swollen, incomprehensible. She watched the water, trying to make it benevolent, trying to believe he was waving at her, the night-light of organic material on the surface, messages from his self-lit creatures of the deep.

Three

Leon Goode was taking his lunch break in the theater of the Transparent Woman. There was NO FOOD OR BEVERAGES ALLOWED in the theater, but he sat against the back wall near the booth, wearing his lab coat and trying not to make crumpling noises with the butcher paper as he unwrapped his turkey and Swiss on rye. Americans, he thought daily, knew how to make sandwiches; it was worth staying in this country just for the lunches.

Leon was pretending that he wanted to be in the back of the theater, that he was reviewing the show, instead of wishing he was inside the booth with Ursula Lee, the intern, fresh out of a master's program at Northeastern. Ursula was operating the Woman. She didn't run the recording; she spoke the story of the lighted parts into a microphone. "The skeletal system provides support for the entire body," she announced, and the bones blinked on. "Without it you'd be like a bag of jelly." When Leon operated the Woman he let the recording do the talking, flipping switches for the endocrine system, the circulatory system, the reproductive system with the breasts like headlights in the dark auditorium. But Ursula still had the drive to be brilliant, to entertain.

There was a lot of great acting, razzle-dazzle teaching he could do at the science museum, even though he'd passed the job-honeymoon period, but the Transparent Woman was so stiff, she'd lost her charm for him. He liked being on the stage, demonstrating the Van de Graaff generator, dipping things in liquid nitrogen, completing hand circuits with the Tesla coil. He liked petting the porcupine with his bare hands, letting the shy and squeamish touch the snake. Sometimes the kids pinched, or grew rowdy, but Leon liked them, he liked that fundamental curiosity, that malleable quality. They didn't yet believe without exception.

Ursula wasn't cleared for the classroom work yet—the lectures for visiting school and camp groups. The committee, two people who met over pizza, thought she would need at least a few months before she'd be ready. But Leon thought she could do anything; she was one of the best educators he'd ever seen. And she *loved* science, in that beautiful, geeky way he found unbearably attractive. She wore dresses under her lab coat, thin dresses to stay cool in the layers and lights. She was much more voluptuous than the Transparent Woman.

He'd seen inside Ursula's dress once, when she was taking off her lab coat at the end of the afternoon. Her top dress button had come undone, and a flash of smooth flesh beckoned Leon, for a second. A bra strap, the top of a nipple. He'd said, "Urs, your button." He'd wanted to do it for her—he'd wanted to undo the rest and slide his hand inside, to test the texture of her skin. Leon had put his hand into his pocket to hide an erection. Now just the possibility of seeing her kept him mildly excited all day, his skin electric with the possibility of touch.

Leon liked the cool of the auditorium, even the musky smell, like mice. At home it was summer, but outside, here, the last day of January, there was ice and salt smeared on the streets like a kid's cake-and-ice-cream beard. Inside, Leon was secreted from the backward Boston seasons. It was climate-controlled, dark, he could be anywhere—the movies in Boston, the movies at home.

He'd gone home in March at spring break, and thought about working up in Brisbane at the University of Queensland for the summer—northern summer, since he was on backward time. Then he found out about his dad, and decided he was better off back in the States, where he wouldn't pick fights with his father, or worse, be the one to tell Mum.

It had been at the revival movie house near the university, not even some sleazy private place where no one would see. It was almost as if his father wanted to be caught. Leon had taken Lizzie Fairfield, his girlfriend from the uni, to see a rerun of *Breaking Away*, only a dollar for students. Lizzie was working in the art library now, but she could still pass for a student. And she wasn't seeing anyone, so they'd slept together twice since he'd been home, as if slipping into an old bad habit.

Leon loved certain things about Lizzie: her hands that moved like birds, quick and anxious, when she talked. He sometimes felt as if he were feeding her when they made love, her hungry hands, her hard kisses. She suckled when she kissed, as if drinking his mouth. And he loved the smell of the backs of her knees, intensely sweet, with a tang, like dried apricots or raspberry syrup. The rest of her body was cottony, didn't have much of a smell, but the backs of her knees compelled him, filled him with longing.

They were in the third row of the movie theater, and Leon got up to get a drink of water. The extended race scene didn't excite him this time around, his fourth viewing; he'd only come because Lizzie had never seen the movie. There, in the back row, faces milky with the light sliding in through the badly sealed door edges, his dad was kissing a woman. Who wasn't his mother.

Leon exited the theater, bent to the fountain for his drink, and thought maybe he'd imagined it. In the men's room, he considered his face in the mirror as he washed his hands. His eyes looked lopsided, the left one drooping slightly lower than the right at the corner. He liked his own eyes, greenish eyes, flecks of gold in them. Lizzie liked to kiss them closed. Sleeping with Lizzie had been a mistake. Thinking that guy in the theater was his dad must've been a mistake, too—maybe he was experiencing sudden severe myopia.

Back in the theater, Leon sat down in the empty row across from the couple. It *was* his father, sliding his hand inside this woman's shirt collar. The woman—he could see the stiffness of her hair in the light—she used hair spray. Her cheek looked yellow. When she turned her head in a kiss he could see it was Lila Wallard, a woman his father knew from graduate school. She was married, and her husband, Dr. Fred Wallard, who smelled of lime aftershave, was their childhood dentist. He remembered a dinner party with Lila and Fred Wallard sitting at his parents' dining room table; he'd been about ten, and too nervous to enjoy dessert in front of his dentist. Lila Wallard had huge pale hands; she'd looked enormous holding the fork and knife as she cut her meat, easing stingy bits to her giant adult mouth. He had no idea why his father would want to kiss Lila Wallard. He strode back down the aisle to his seat beside Lizzie. It had been like driving slowly past a car wreck; the bloody images imprinted on your eyes even after you passed. The glint of sun on bent chrome, the twisted arm of a victim. Only Leon saw Lila Wallard's yellow cheek and his father's fat slug lips.

"Where have you *been*?" whispered Lizzie.

"Sorry, saw someone I knew."

"You missed the best part."

"No, I saw it coming in." Leon took Lizzie's hand and tried to pretend.

Leon went back to Boston early that spring break. His brother, Andrew, had come home for only a few days, and Leon felt distanced from him, from everyone, by his information about Dad. He couldn't stand not to let his mother know, or Drew, who came in and sat on his bed and spun out a long story about the woman he'd been sleeping with, rendering the shape of her calves on Leon's bed with his hands. Andrew had his father's big lips, a soft mouth, boyish now on Andrew. Boyish on his father, too, childish, maybe. Leon envisioned Andrew kissing Lila Wallard, his tongue pressing against her soft palate—it made him want to gag. He said he had some lab work to attend to, found a standby flight, and went back to Boston.

All summer, Boston summer, he thought about coming home, but did nothing about it. He worked in the lab part-time and took the train out to Singing Beach, where the hot sand smelled like ice-cream cones. The next fall, school began to seem futile. Leon worried that he was trying to be a scientist because of his dad, like he couldn't cheat genetics, like he had to. His grades sagged. He did obsess about Lizzie, creating rituals with her letters when they came, few, cheerful, surprisingly thin. He couldn't open them for three hours after he received them. He could hold them up to lamps, still sealed, and speculate. He could think about her when he masturbated, but he couldn't look at her letters when he did. Only the invented Lizzie could accompany him.

By January, his grades had dipped low enough for his don, Dr. Boudhali, to call him in and warn him about losing the scholarship and his teaching-assistant position. The winter afternoon sun was tapping its tepid fingers on Dr. Boudhali's desk. Leon saw a crumb in the man's graying sideburns—food, was it? Toast? A bit of bun from a hamburger? Or was it lint, or a tiny wad of paper? The don's leg shook under the desk as if he were a nervous adolescent. Leon wanted to laugh at the poor man, tell him he really had no problem hearing the truth. He imagined himself, the sunny Aussie, chirping, "No worries, mate!" Instead, he nodded politely, said he had to think about his motivations, and shut the don's door quietly behind him. He was pleased he'd said "motivations," a very American word, it seemed to him. He'd been almost weightless, walking back down the wide, echoey hallway.

Leon quit Harvard that afternoon. He called the regis-
trar and said he was withdrawing. He printed up a résumé
at the computer center and walked into the Boston
Museum of Science, one of his favorite places to wander.
They gave him an internship, then a full-time job in the
education department. It had been a year now, and he
didn't miss school at all.

The Transparent Woman show was over, and the crowd
of about twenty people wandered out like nocturnal animals stunned by daylight. The wall was cool against Leon's
back, and he could hear Ursula shutting down the switches,
getting ready to come out.

"G'day," he said, as she locked the door of the booth
behind her.

"Oh!" Ursula sounded genuinely surprised. He didn't
know how to interpret this.

"Apricot?" Leon reached over toward her with a plastic
bag full of dried fruits. Sitting, his head was about level
with her thighs. He wondered what the backs of Ursula's
knees smelled like.

"Were you here the whole time?" Ursula squeezed her
folder against her chest. She was flushed. Her small round
glasses glinted in the fluorescent lights.

"I'm not checking up on you or anything, love. Just here
for lunch break."

"So you like to see inside women's bodies while you eat."

Leon hoped this was flirting. Sometimes American
women were hard to read. Her black hair was so shiny it
withstood the dull inside light and still gave off its own. "I

like how you do her. I've gotten rather lazy—I use the tape." His fruit was still extended toward her.

"Okay." Ursula picked out a fig. "I love the seeds," she said.

Leon stood up, and was suddenly a giant. He'd liked being small beside her; it felt safer somehow, made him unafraid of rejection.

Annabel walked back to the trailer with Maud. She was tired of talking about Maud's crush on Professor Goode, but Sabrina had a friend over to study in their room, and it had seemed like they were waiting for Annabel to leave, because they were polite, but cold and quiet.

"Well, how's your species-diversity plot going?" Annabel had asked Sabrina while stuffing a book in her backpack.

"Fine." Sabrina turned to her friend. "You've got something very unpleasant *here*," she said, pointing to her left nostril. It wasn't until she'd left the room that Annabel realized she'd meant Annabel's nose. God, she thought, pulling out her bandanna, feeling the involuntary heat spread across her cheeks. Why couldn't she be a little less snide and a little more direct? Then Annabel wondered whether she was projecting, if they were really entirely normal and friendly. If she was the one who'd seemed dangerous, like unsanded wood.

"Hey, Maud." Annabel scratched at her calf, slowing down as they walked. "Do you think Sabrina and her friends are, well, a little *insular*?"

Maud laughed. "Honey, they're spoiled brats, don't worry about them."

"Ah," said Annabel. "That makes me feel better."

"You haven't been worrying about them, have you? I mean, even Professor Goode mentioned how catty they are. Just last night he said—well, I can't remember exactly, but he said something about how girls with pearls should stick to shoreline. It made sense at the time, anyway. But he adores *you,* really."

"Thanks, Maud. I needed to hear that, because she's really been a pain in the ass." She grinned. "And she wears too much makeup—oh, look." Annabel stopped them both. There was a brown tree snake in the path, fat and shimmering. "Wow," she said. "It's gorgeous."

"Wow," said Maud. "And kind of venomous. Don't go too close, honey."

"What would you say"—Annabel craned forward—"six feet?"

"I would say let's go to the computer center another time."

"Oh, he'd be scared of us if he stopped basking and woke up. Guess we ought to inspire him—" She tossed a few pebbles toward the snake. Maud yelped and stepped back. The snake curled as if winding up, then eased off the path and into the low-lying acacias and tea trees.

"I wouldn't have done that," said Maud, still holding in her arms as if protecting the egg of herself.

"Sure you would have," said Annabel, walking on.

Maud looked into the bushes before passing the spot where the snake had been. "Nope, not brave enough."

Sender: (Annabel Mendelssohn)
AMendelss@ausnet.jcooku.tvl.edu
To: AEMendel@biosci.com
Subject: cute is moot
Monday, February 5, 1996

Dear Alice:

My roommate is a pain in the ass. I'm working
on the rest of my proposal, and the project
should get me out of here for good blocks of
time. And after that, I can move out altogether.
Do a little travel. Always wanted to see the tem-
perate rain forest in New Zealand. But lots to do
first.

Markos White is a cool guy. He's been working on
epiphytes in South America. You should see the
orchids here, Alice! Most of them are dormant
blobs of uninteresting root right now, but the
occasional one in bloom is so sexy. Markos also
showed me his photographs; I think he should be
working for *National Geographic* instead of plug-
ging along with the science drones.

As for me, I'm all geared up to observe daytime
behavior of *Pteropus conspicillatus*, spectacled
fruit bats. Not much equipment required, just
notebook, binocs, tape to mark the plots, machete,
tent. . . . Next week we're going to a site where I
can get a good look at them—we're also going to
count scrub turkeys or maybe take soil samples,
depending on the professors who come along.

I've seen other flying foxes coming to raid the
mango trees behind the library at night. I'm more
interested in seeing what they do during the day
than messing with radio collars and tracking. Most
of the research is on nighttime behavior—but
there's much more to bats than flying around at
night—they probably have busy social lives, too,
you know, Parcheesi tournaments in the trees.
Mine, like most fruit bats, don't echolocate
(beepless bats!), so their other senses are
decent. Huge eyes, from the photos I've seen—
charming, Alice, they look like pups with wings.

I get the second half of my grant upon "internal
approval" of my research proposal. Which means
I'll have to get one of the profs to come out to
approve my site after I get the project going.
I've heard Professor Goode is fond of bats, so
maybe it will be him. If my friend Maud hasn't
lured him off to some island. She's getting to
be as bad as the rest of them. Alice, if I start
to act like a headless chicken because of some
man (Darwin notwithstanding), will you please
tell me?

I guess I hope those cutback rumors aren't true,
but then, if you had a big fat severance agree-
ment, you could quit the cold northeast and come
visit your sister.

Love, and hi to Kev,

Annabel

Annabel watched as Sabrina, Professor Goode, and Lars disappeared under a bridge that crossed the wide river; they were going to look for platypuses and collect soil samples. Mike Trimble started the van and pulled back onto the road to deliver Annabel to her potential site. She sat in the front seat, pulling the buckle on her backpack, tense. This could be it, where the work finally started.

After all this thinking about the bats, writing proposals, reading graphs and making lists of questions, Annabel's neck was damp with excitement and a little stage fright. What if their daytime behavior was random—impossible, she thought, but what if she made it random by disturbing them? What if all they did was sleep, and all she would have to do was to try not to wake them as hours passed? No, there'd be something. She had questions, and she had a way of watching that yielded the secrets of her subjects.

Mike parked. He stretched hard and yawned. They'd left Townsville at dawn and had been on the road for over six hours, with three stops. Mike turned to Annabel with a weary grin. "Well, we should be able to hear them from here."

He rolled down the window and let in the thick warm breath from the forest. Fruit and guano scent, the not-unpleasant smell of plant rot.

Annabel pushed open the van door and stood by the side of the road. There was a narrow drainage ditch between the dirt and the trees—a wall of green in varying shades. A strange sound warbled out of the trees, barks and calls, short high cries that reminded Annabel of an infant human. Wailing, repeated shrills. One voice overlapping another. And the persistent hum of water falling somewhere, the murmur of leaves rubbing their palms against each another.

"That's them," said Mike, climbing out of the van.

"Anywhere in particular I should go in?" Annabel started over the ditch and looked at the edge of the trees, a border, no gaps. Now she was really sweating, from the thick heat and the thrill of the odd bat music.

"I don't see anyone." Mike smiled. "Just don't string your marking tape up like Christmas decorations."

On the drive over, Mike had warned her about local greenie-bashers; some loggers felt threatened by environmentalists who came to study the last scraps of Queensland rain forest. There had been pub brawls, threats, and unexplained forest fires.

"Here." He handed her a machete. "You'll need this to cut a path, but be careful, even though it's dull. And watch out for stinging trees."

Annabel unsheathed the knife and used it to part branches. She glanced at a leaf as it brushed her arm; too late, a stinging bush. She felt the tingle as the fibers pushed into her skin. Professor Goode had pointed out one of these before—the leaves and smaller limbs had fibers that slipped inside your skin when you touched them. After the initial jolts of sting, the spots would be painfully sensitive to wet, heat, and cold for weeks. They grew only where the forest had been disturbed, and they spread in patches across this forest; this one was almost as high as a mature ficus. Maybe there'd been logging here, she thought, estimating by the weeds' height—ten years ago?

Annabel was too full of other sensations to focus on the spreading jolts of pain. She started mentally mapping the site as she pushed into the woods. The fruity smell was already becoming familiar, the tang sharper as she followed the sounds. The thick heat stuck her fingers together as she pushed forward, following the treasure map of scent and sound toward her subjects. She looked up at the understory as she passed, at palm-lilies and epiphytes: the elk-horn and basket ferns holding tight to the trunks, where they caught rainwater and took nutrients from tree rot. The trees were mottled with lichens and mosses, and she watched a quick skink catch a butterfly at an orange orchid's lip.

Annabel held back the trees for Mike Trimble, slashing occasionally at stingers, a few thick vines. She didn't want to make a mess, but if she were to use this site, she'd need some kind of path to get in. She'd need gloves, her own machete. Annabel followed the eerie bat songs, pushing through until the low foliage grew thinner. Less logging damage here, she thought, pleased.

"And pythons like it here," said Mike. She'd forgotten about him, the echo that followed her footsteps. She suddenly wanted him gone—if this was going to be her site, she didn't want someone else there her first time. She didn't respond, but held back a heavy vine so it wouldn't smack him as she passed.

There was a sudden burst of sky, an open-eye blue with thin strips of clouds. Light filtering down to the forest floor. Oh, Annabel thought, they're big, oh, they're moving. The bats were dark forms rustling in the tops of tall ficus trees, the branches stripped bare by bat feet. They grew louder as she entered the clearing, howling at her, then quieted.

"I'm not going to bother you," said Annabel, straining her neck to try to make an approximate count. At least a hundred, she thought, thrilling. Maybe two hundred, or more. The bats stared.

Mike waited at the edge of the clearing, quiet. As she sat down he whispered, "Careful." Annabel lay on her back on the forest floor, counting, memorizing the features of the bats and their camp. The bats were swinging from branch to branch, on wing-hooks and feet, hanging quiet or chattering on, upside down. Several pairs of bats were wrapped together like perfect spider-meals, black bundles with two bright heads. There was gray fur around the big black eyes in the "spectacle" shape that gave them their common name. She took her binoculars out of her backpack and focused.

"You guys are beautiful," Annabel whispered. As if in answer, a bat swung around on wing-hooks so its bottom was facing down and let loose a long stream of pee that hissed to the forest floor. Annabel giggled. The sting of leech bites drew her attention to her hands; she pulled the offenders off without looking away from the bats for too long.

"What do you do all day?" Abruptly, as if someone had flipped a switch, the light turned pale. The air was dense and wet, and then it was raining. The bats clamored, packed together. A quick squabble broke out, and Annabel watched one long pink tongue dart forth as a larger bat yelled at a smaller one. Oh, both males, she thought, noticing the black fur around the testicles. I could watch these guys all day, she decided, chart out behaviors: the peeing, huddling, the squabbles, there was almost too much to observe. Not enough time. Maybe she could start tomorrow. Maybe she didn't need to finish her course work. They were so big—that's what startled her most, like medium-sized dogs with wings—and so bright-faced, so active in the middle of the afternoon. She'd have to stay awhile so they could get used to her, stop swiveling their curious heads in her direction. Water splattered down the stories of foliage like a rhythm instrument; only a thin spray reached Annabel on the floor.

The rain was over before the bat-huddle or squabble was complete. Then a human face broke into Annabel's sky.

"Okay, lassie," said Mike. He looked distorted, huge. "We've got to meet the others. So, is this your site?"

Annabel felt numb. Of course. Did the rain induce territorial behavior? Did they take the same branches when they arrived each morning? Were they monogamous?

Annabel didn't take the hand Mike offered, but she did sit up.

"Uh-oh." He squatted and leaned in close to her face. "Leech in the eye." Mike poked at her tear duct for a while, then pulled back, successful, with a fat leech in his fingers, a grimace on his wide mouth.

"Guess I'll need a tarp," she said, standing up. Her eye stung and she wiped tiny blood tears off her face.

At the road again, Annabel turned and listened. This is it, she thought. My site. I wonder, I wonder. It was like waking up after a nap, intensely aware of where she was.

She was hot, dusty, and it looked so good.

Sabrina said, "God, aren't you coming in to swim?"

"I guess so, just a minute," said Annabel. She could do this, swim in a pool under a waterfall—there were no bodies in the water, only the churn of the water's tumble from the cliff, like a whirlpool. Annabel chewed her pinkie nail. Sabrina breaststroked slowly away, across the calm part of the lake.

"Hey, Yankee," yelled Professor Goode over the roar of the falls, only his wet head visible. "What's the delay?"

"Weather conditions," Annabel yelled back.

The professor cupped his hand to his ear, then shrugged and leaped back in.

When they used to visit her grandparents' Cape Cod house in the summer, Annabel would swim with Robert in the shallow edge of Little Sippewisset Lake, silt molding between their toes. Alice swam out to the raft, strong. She was twelve; she was starting to "develop lady features," as Grandmom put it. But Annabel was, at eight, still a girl and Robert let her climb onto his shoulders to dive off into the murk they'd stirred up with play. They came out for lunches their grandmother set up on a warped picnic table on the narrow beach. Salty cheese sandwiches. Alice cutting elegantly through the water on her swim back. Robert galloped out, his legs striped with silt, still tickling her as they dried their pruney hands and feet.

She would do it. She didn't believe in ghosts.

When she climbed along the wall under the edge of the waterfall's flow, Annabel felt like she was looking over a cliff, longing to feel the airspace around her, fantasizing about a leap. But it was safe to push off into the flow, the pummeling of the water. It was like being washed clean, succumbing to a bath. She came back to the airspace behind the faucet for breath, then slid back under the falls.

Annabel was in a lighter water flow on the edge of the downpour, trying to hold her eyes open to watch Professor Goode porpoising with the others. Annabel felt a combination of things about him now. The pure physical distance from her colleagues in Chicago gave her quick slices of intense loneliness. She was used to working with people, and while Maud was kind and nice to talk with, and Markos White was friendly, she felt like she was in her own universe—a single set onto herself, like in logic class, a circle with no overlaps, no intersections, onto any other circle.

Sometimes at night, with her roommate breathing secrets of sleep, or out at the pub, she imagined her ex-boyfriend, hazel-eyed, soft-mouthed Ethan, to help her sleep. His voice, his hands. She shut down the inevitable movie of their breakup when it came—the repeated theme of impending distance, which caused distance between them long before she left. Of course he was an invention now; her longing was not for someone real. The letters from Chicago already made the move seem permanent. Her friends' lives flowed on without her; they missed her, maybe, but lived on past her.

Alice's E-mail had solace in it, sometimes. She was no less a sister for longitude or latitude. But Alice was so controlled, Annabel suspected there were streams of belief and emotion that she'd never have access to. Here she thought she might lose her job, and she sounded smooth as a sheet. Too cool. Annabel could imagine her voice saying the same things, the same sympathetic drone, the appropriate wobbles, but no explosions of sound. She wanted her sister to bubble over sometimes, be true.

And sometimes, not in the same way as rendering Ethan of course, Annabel imagined she could talk with Robert. She didn't picture his face, but she could see his hands—he'd had a way of moving them as he talked, as if they were animals separate from the body. Robert, she knew, would understand this kind of loneliness. But that wasn't what they talked about when she conjured him; instead, she described the sites they'd been to, the mango orchard with the green band of rain forest below, the dairy farm near the bats, a long wild swath of pastures and fences, with ginger-blossom trees like bouquets sprouting from the landscape. She explained how the bats' daytime life had great potential, scientific territory that had barely been charted. She recounted how she'd climbed into the buttress roots of ficus trees to help retrieve the traps a professor used to count populations of melomys and wood rats near the university. She told him about stinging trees, and the leeches.

Robert, Annabel believed, would be surprised by none of this. He'd drink it in like a good glass of water. He'd say to go for it with the professor, to hell with reservation and convention. He'd pretend his fingers were leeches and tickle her. And even though she didn't tell him about the loneliness, bringing him into her landscape alleviated it; at the same time it was magnified by the impossibility of having him back.

When she looked at John Goode, Annabel felt like she was granted a tiny piece of Robert. She wondered whether she wanted her brother back so much she was projecting him onto any serious male scientist.

But Professor Goode wasn't her brother; he was an enigmatic, unrelated man. His intimacy made him desirable, but Annabel didn't *want* him, exactly. She didn't imagine she ought to want him, even if she overcame the ideas of age, of the power relationship between student and teacher, even if he wasn't still in love with his wife—it was more thankfulness than want. He talked with her about real things, about feelings, relationships; he'd shown her how to eat a star fruit, flicking out the sexual seeds with a knife as they sat in the front seat of the van outside the market, waiting for the other students to finish their trips to the phone booth, the post office, the dry goods store for more socks. Even as he pushed the flesh of the fruit into her lips, his fingers fat and smelling of soil, Annabel's flush of pleasure was safe, almost chaste, though the warmth spread through her chest and then the rest of her body.

When he came up next to her in the space behind the waterfall, though, she considered what it would be like to kiss him. He was saying something, but she couldn't hear him through the roar of water pounding around them. She wondered if she'd feel his lips at all, or if a flow of water would keep their skin separated by a thin layer. He yelled louder, something, she thought, about the water, or did he say "ought to"?

She saw his arm come toward her but didn't think to swim back for a breath. Then she was being pulled into the water beneath the falls. She couldn't see anything, and made the mistake of trying to speak; water rushed in and she began to cough, but she was in a swirl, underwater, and she was being held. Annabel didn't know where it was safe to come up, whether she could come up. Of course—now that she was brave enough to swim, she was going to drown. She thought maybe this was what it felt like to die, a small tug underneath, confusion. Mistakes surrounded everyday life, especially in the field. There was a constellation of mistakes orbiting everything you did; you might just fall out of your own star and into one of the bodies of mistake—death was that simple.

Her throat burned and her chest ached for lack of breath. Everything slowed, though; Annabel opened her eyes and saw the collision of water and water, bubbles, blur. She closed her eyes again and stopped moving, stopped fighting the arm that clutched her. Then there was air on her forehead, her face. Professor Goode was holding her up, staring at her.

"Oh, God," he said. "I only meant a bit of fun. Are you all right? Annabel? Can you breathe?"

Annabel nodded, but she wasn't sure she could; she was still choking. He hauled her up, over his shoulder, and carried her to shore.

She didn't want the others to see—they'd make a fuss. She felt the exposure like direct sunlight. They'll think I'm after him.

"Annabel, can you say something?" He helped her lie down on the grass. This grass, she thought, is probably full of leeches.

"Why, exactly, did you try to drown me?" She managed to change her cough to a laugh.

"Oh," said Professor Goode. "I thought you needed a bath."

Annabel looked at his unmatched eyes. Not at all like Robert, she decided. More reckless. She stopped looking at him and clambered up for her towel. No, maybe that's exactly how he is like him.

F o u r

Sender: (Annabel Mendelssohn)
AMendelss@ausnet.jcooku.tvl.edu
To: AEMendel@biosci.com
Subject: counting
Friday, February 16, 1996

Dear Alice:
I have all the research facilities to myself,
since nobody else seems to be doing any work what-
soever. Even my friend Maud has disappeared. I
wish Professor Goode was around to talk.

Don't look at me like that, I know you're giving
the message a LOOK, Ms. Alice. I'm not interested
in Professor Goode. I like him, but he almost
drowned me in a waterfall and then dragged me out.
Not very romantic. I've forgiven him—he just plays
too hard.

I have definitely decided on the bat site. I've
even finished my basic proposal, and I went into

town to get some equipment—a machete, which is very cool, and marking tape, and some secondhand waders because mine only went up to the knee. I need hip-highs to keep out the stingers and the leeches and to stay dry. On Tuesday after morning classes I tagged along on a soil survey and spent the afternoon with the bats, making gross observations. I watched them leave camp in a big bat flurry.

This is the part I love, Alice! Going into the Woods. And also anticipation, setting up long sheets of empty records to fill in. The unknown curves! You remember this rush, don't you, when you have questions and you're designing an investigation?

There's one thing to watch out for in the Tablelands: there are quite a few people who don't like environmentalists. They call us greenies, and they can get mean. It's not like I'm trying to save the mountain gorilla, but I'm glad I have the machete.

Mom sent me COOKIES. They took four and a half weeks, so they're kind of gray and crumbly, but that may also be because the package looks like it was dropped in the ocean and then retrieved with a grappling hook. Of course, I love them.

Maybe you and Kevin should BOTH come out and join me for a beer in the forest. We can have boring old Foster's or XXXX or Vic Bitter, or Toohey's . . .

I gotta go. I think I see Maud outside in the sun
by the mango tree.

Love, Annabel

Alice sighed. It was obvious, what her sister saw in the
professor. And what she pretended not to notice. Annabel
had only seen Robert's surface, and she'd wanted to be
close to him, to be like him. When they were children, his
cruel teasing made him more desirable. She remembered
Annabel when she was around four years old, following
her siblings in a stumpy toddler's jog. Robert had always
stayed far enough away that she could never catch him.
Alice, at eight, must have been in a maternal phase. She
stayed a step ahead for a few minutes, then let her sister
catch her, press her sticky, apple-scented face to Alice's
pant leg. But because she was available, she became less
interesting, and Anna cried for Robert, chased him, tear-
ful, laughing and screaming for her brother.

Thinking about it now, Alice could almost laugh and
scream, but she wouldn't let herself; she didn't have
enough breath to scream that way. She didn't have enough
energy to risk that kind of despair. And no one could catch
Robert now.

Her sister could sleep with whomever she wanted—she
could make mistakes—it was just that she didn't want
Annabel to be damaged, hurt somewhere so far away. Alice
vowed not to mention it in her message back.

The museum in winter smelled of wool and dust and grape-flavored gum. Leon walked through the lobby toward the physical-science stage—past school groups shedding mittens and crumpled paper handouts and an occasional plastic dinosaur as they clumped through paleontology and past the pendulum, toward the planetarium and artificial night.

Winter in Boston was almost like artificial night to Leon, who was used to the Southern Hemisphere. He'd found his second autumn even more luscious than the first, because he knew the trees would capture light in the opera of their dying leaves. He anticipated the sharp, tragic blue of autumn afternoons. But in the winter, this time around, he was either nervous or he wanted to sleep. At work, when he knew he might see Ursula somewhere, it was a tender anxiety that propelled him; he constantly felt as if he'd just finished jogging. The true sweating started as the muscles cooled down. But in his apartment, even when he came home early, the light had already finished, giving up before teatime.

Dinner. He was going to ask Ursula to dinner. It would be easy enough—all he had to say was *Do you want to grab a bite* when they were both in the basement getting ready to go. But somehow he wasn't there when she was leaving, somehow she slipped out before him.

He climbed the stairs, waiting for an old couple in puffy coats to pass. The man held the woman's elbow gently, as if after years of touching, he was still slightly shy. Who knows, Leon thought, just because they're old it doesn't mean they're not a new couple. His parents had cut a new notch in his vision. Not his parents: his father, forgetting everything important for long enough to lose it. Sometimes he talked to his dad on the phone now—his father was the only one who didn't at least try to calculate the time difference, so when the phone rang at four A.M. he knew it was his father, in his own next evening, wanting to chat before tea. Wanting to fix things. It was this combination that disarmed Leon. He wanted to remain repulsed, and he was until that phone woke him, his father's big voice thin across the distance, pretending to be happy.

"How's my son of the great north?" asked his father. "Staying warm?"

"I'm in bed, it's the middle of the—"

"Have you heard from Andrew? Or your mum? How is she?"

These words twisted in Leon's chest, the call around the world for old news about someone close by. "Drew's surfing. It's his new vocation, I think. At least a few weeks ago it was, we don't talk that—"

"I'm sending you something, something I got when I was over on Magnetic Island. Let me know if you get it."

Leon's father was always planning to give gifts, to send things, that he never sent. He'd talk about it for months, then forget to put it in the post. Or forget to buy it in the first place. He meant to, just as he meant to calculate the time before calling. But his impulses overtook his intentions—maybe that was what had happened, maybe that was how he'd been able to forget himself.

"A lot of people think electricity is a complicated thing," said Leon. There was a kid in the audience who was working on a heckle. Leon could tell by the sneer, but he wasn't going to let it throw him. The kid had a ripped leather jacket, shoulder-length blond hair, a pierced nose, and very expensive boots. All that effort to look torn, but the boots gave him away as indulged and bored. He had perfect hair.

"But think of it this way: it's an invisible force, like gravity. You can't see gravity, but you can see its effects. If I drop these keys, for instance, gravity forces them to the ground."

An invisible force, he thought, like all attraction. Like my father to Lila Wallard. He wondered whether they ever saw each other anymore. After his mother found out—after she heard from someone who'd heard from someone who'd told her in her own office—a patient's mother, maybe, who kept her voice low as her child dressed after Molly Goode's exam—after that his father promised to go to counseling. Drew said their father cried, though Leon wondered how Drew could know. All this hearsay, none of them there but the informant and patient, but Dad and Mum. Static electricity.

He dropped his keys. The kid whispered something to a girl, who giggled.

Leon bent to pick the keys up, and the kid hissed, "Wowie, he can drop keys. I want my money back."

"You can also see the effects of electricity," said Leon. He rubbed a balloon on his head, then pulled it away, making the strands stand. "That's static electricity," he said. "Rubbing two things together creates electricity. The balloon is attracted to the negative charge, and my hair likes the positive charge. Ordinarily, there's an equal amount of positive and negative charge, but when there's an imbalance, the charges pull together, like two ponds on level ground with a stream between—" He gestured with his hands and finished the analogy. Leather Jacket made a fake yawn, loud.

"Now that you've seen what static electricity can do for a hairdo—" Leon stepped down from the stage. He took Leather Jacket's hand as gently as he could. The kid pulled away, and Leon said, "I need a volunteer, and if this guy's too scared—"

"Just don't touch me," said the kid, strutting up to the stage.

"Now sit here—" He gestured to the plastic stool and the kid settled in. "Put your hand on this dome," said Leon. The kid made a sour face, but put his hand on the Van de Graaff generator dome. "Don't take it off until I tell you to, or this might get a bit shocking—"

The kid mimicked "shocking," trying for Leon's accent. His mother didn't even want to try counseling, but she'd submitted to two sessions. Drew told him. Drew also said she'd kicked their father out after that. Left the house and instructed him to be gone before she returned. Leon had tried to imagine his mum confiding in Drew, her hands knit together on the couch as she spilled out details. It couldn't have worked that way; his mother was too strong, too private for that. Sometimes he thought he should have stayed home for her, but more often he knew this was embarrassing, this was when she needed privacy the most. Cheerful phone calls, postcards, and privacy.

"The Van de Graaff generator," Leon said as the motor started up, "was invented down the road at M.I.T. This generator doesn't make electricity—it's plugged into a normal one-hundred-and-ten-volt socket. There's a belt inside like a giant rubber band." Leon loved that American term, *rubber band;* it sat funny on his tongue. "Which carries a negative charge to the dome—"

The machine hummed on, and Leather Jacket's perfect blond hair stood up spectacularly.

"Cool," said Leather Jacket's girlfriend. The word bounced around the audience like a mouse trapped in the kitchen.

"A round of applause for our volunteer," said Leon, as he turned off the motor.

Leon made sparks by hovering his hand close to the dome, then moved on to the Tesla coil. Leather Jacket was his biggest fan now, clapping and smoothing his hair.

"Nikola Tesla was brilliant," said Leon, as the machine warmed up. "A bit quirky, and misunderstood. He calculated the cubic contents of each meal before he ate—and would only stay in hotel rooms with numbers divisible by three—" He thought of his father's quirks, more of the forgetful school than the compulsive. Once he'd stopped at a road-cut on the highway to collect soil samples; Leon remembered the red-striped soil, the hot day. He was almost a teenager, but still young enough to get out of the car with Andrew, to climb a tea tree while their father scraped soil into vials. Mum was working, or hadn't wanted to come along. Leon was pulling Andrew up to his limb by one arm, his brother dangling like a yo-yo, waiting to be reeled in, when they heard the car pull onto the road. Dad had forgotten them, like forgetting his keys or an umbrella in the rain.

He'd come back after about twenty minutes, remembering his sons as he turned off the highway, but the wait had seemed like days. Andrew had tugged his clothes and cried; Leon had pretended he was too old to care.

"Now remember what we said about current—there's alternating and direct. The Tesla coil uses direct current to make alternating current . . ." Direct is dangerous, thought Leon, noticing a red lab coat behind the audience. Could Ursula be listening? Was her Woman show over yet? Keep focused, he thought, that Tesla coil's hot. He remembered his first few mistakes when he'd learned to do demonstrations: porcupine rash, jolts from the coil and generator, and kids trying to grab the snake's head. He'd have to be careful when he finally asked Ursula to dinner—he'd have to use alternating current.

The posthole digger was chafing Annabel's leg. Lars tore at his fingernails with his teeth, too close beside her. He smelled of vinegar, but his clothes were clean, and she couldn't help thinking he'd been one of the cheats who jumped that laundry line. Whenever Maud said something amiable, which was in periodic bursts like sun showers, Annabel twisted around to try to chat. She was jostled and nauseated, but she kept thinking how she wanted to be a responsive new friend.

It was the sixth hour in the van. Annabel wanted to drive, to take over and feel independent again. The windows let in too much dust and too little air. There was a coat of dust on the driver's seat in front of her, thick as frosting. Professor Janice Martin was driving; Mike Trimble was the front passenger, his long thin legs folded up against the windshield. There was a crack like a sideways V from a stone that flew up about an hour ago. Annabel worried for those vulnerable legs, that they might break through the windshield; she could picture blood on his calves, a vein of surprised pain on Mike's face. When she told him to watch out for the crack, though, he said, "It's safety glass, love," and grinned.

Janice wasn't exactly what Annabel had expected—she was aloof and quiet, except when she had a point to make. Annabel had read some of Janice's work on migration; she used scatter graphs, which were beautiful when they were typeset. One article had been produced in three colors, and Annabel found herself looking for faces in the graphs, thinking of the colored dots as the animals themselves. This was before Australia, sitting at her desk at the Chicago lab, feeling trapped by circumstance.

In the first year after Robert's funeral Annabel thought of finding some new career no one in her family knew anything about. Arts administration, maybe, or sports therapy, or she'd take a few more courses and try to get into vet school. But the last two were science-related, and her mother volunteered for the local chamber orchestra, so she still wouldn't have escaped family. At her lowest point, the field-studies program brochure arrived: *for science undergraduates: a master's degree, with research applicable toward a Ph.D. through a list of accredited universities.* It was like a tiny rescue canoe, creased and pushed into her mail slot with other, unimportant glossy fliers.

Students weren't allowed to drive, said Janice, her long blond ponytail pushed through the headrest. Annabel looked at the lumps in her hair, guessing they were moss or lichen. Janice had lived alone "in bush" for months at a stretch to do her research. She was a stickler for rules, and for being in control. Mike Trimble offered to take over the driving several times, but Janice, who leaned forward as if she expected animals to spring into the road at any minute, declined. She stretched her neck every so often, rolled her head, and squeezed out her shoulders, which made cracking noises Annabel could hear even over the rumble of the tires.

The road stretched out before them like a metal measuring tape, long and slightly concave. The other van—Professor Goode's—drove into a ditch. It almost looked purposeful, settling in hard on two wheels. The caravan stopped and Annabel watched the physical comedy of Sabrina, Markos, and Professor Goode pushing the two lowered wheels back onto the road while another professor steered. Sabrina didn't really push; she placed her hands on the side of the van, healing-style. Markos and Professor Goode stained their faces plum with effort and the van rolled back onto the asphalt. Professor Goode had been driving when they went into the ditch, and Annabel thought he had probably been telling a joke with his hands in the air when it happened. Or maybe he'd been slicing star fruit on the dashboard.

"Licorice?" asked Maud. She was holding some out. It was broken into little pieces and looked like tenpenny nails.

"Thanks, no." Annabel worked her face into a smile, trying.

Maud was still holding it out. "The others?"

Annabel sighed and took the handful of nails. "Anyone up there for licorice from Maud?" She leaned into Mike Trimble's domain.

"I love licorice," said Janice. "Can I put it here?" She took a handful and pressed it into Mike Trimble's lap, right where his thigh met his hip.

Annabel imagined Mike and Janice in a tent together, their bodies luminous green in the light through the rip-stop nylon. She pictured Janice's ponytail unraveling and objects flying out: a bird-wing butterfly, shedding its fabulously blue wing dust onto the hair, nail-sized bits of black licorice, fluorescent orange marker ribbons.

Annabel squinched down in her seat. She pulled back her thigh each time it pressed against Lars's. Hot flesh rubbing—how fickle the body is, she thought, that sometimes touch sends a shock of pleasure, sometimes discomfort. She banged her knee against the posthole digger again, gave a quiet "Ow." Then she settled her head on a bag of netting, bent her legs into a space between the handle of the digger and the window, and pulled the neck of her T-shirt up over her nose to filter the dust as she breathed. I'll never sleep like this, she thought as she dozed off.

At the train station, Annabel unfolded herself out of her pretzel sleep-shape.

"You've got guck in your eyes," said Lars. He smiled.

"Gee, thanks," said Annabel. Brilliant observation, she thought, glad to be free of his body.

"I'm going after chocolate," said Maud. She walked away, disturbing the red road dust to flight.

Annabel stood by Professor Goode, noticing that he was actually quite tall. The vans were being loaded onto flat-cars; they looked like miniatures on the train car—a train set atop a bigger train set. Maud set out toward the town, which appeared to have two buildings: one, the train station, with CHILLAGOE stenciled across the windows; the other building had a small square sign that read "LTD."

"That's the town?" Annabel asked Professor Goode. She touched her hair, wondering what his felt like, and thought how small she must seem from that height. She didn't feel small; she felt the warmth of talking with him, the possibility.

"There's another shop or two on the other side of the square." He pointed. "I have to settle up with our freighter, but you've got a half hour until we go, if you'd like to guide your own tour."

"Aye, aye," said Annabel. She picked up her backpack and followed the red dot of Lars's T-shirt as he walked toward the park. She wouldn't be disappointed, she thought; she'd enjoy a few minutes of being alone. Sure enough, after a short stretch of lawn, the telltale lager ad graced the awning of a pub.

This wasn't like any Australian town she'd seen so far; the whole landscape had been sucked dry. When they'd gone to the Atherton Tablelands for the first dawn chorus and that unsettling lake, and then when they went back up for the falls, they'd been in lush land, full of insects and noises. Here there was the hum of the train, and Annabel thought she could hear a hum of heat. The park was grassy, but the grass was stiff and bleached a faint green. Dust coated the streets and buildings; a tumbleweed bounced by the pub.

.   .   .

Annabel sat with Maud on the train, holding the bottle of orange soda against her face, relishing the cold. As the train lunged and started, groaning, they all opened windows and peered out. Annabel took her camera, leaned half her body out the window, and shot a photo of the red-and-white train car, the bright faces out the windows: Sabrina and Lars in one, Maud hidden in back, the top of Professor Goode's head glinting behind Mike Trimble's T-shirt sleeve. Everyone looked so happy, she thought, so uncomplicated when they smiled for a camera.

Once the dry browns and shrubby patches of green landscape started to blur, the professors and the students split off into small groups, with empty seats between them, luxurious space after the vans. Janice and Mike were chatting on the little platform at the back of the car. Lars was stretched out on a single seat. There were wet bandannas spread on the antique metal luggage racks, and the mute of the train noise covering conversations. Maud came over and sat by Annabel on the wooden seat. She fiddled with her braid, rubbing the even ends.

"You got a haircut, didn't you? Looks great." Annabel wondered how long ago she should have noticed.

"Markos did it—he's fantastic. I needed a change."

An eighth of an inch of change, Annabel noted. "Any particular reason?" She thought of Professor Goode, and didn't really want to know if it was related to the crush. Annabel had her own crush now.

"Um, yeah." Maud looked like she was made of rubber. Shiny. Bobbing.

"Oh," said Annabel.

"Aren't you going to ask me why?"

"Um, yeah. I mean, why?"

"Because I have someone starching my socks."

Annabel laughed, a big, loud Hah! "*Starching your socks,*" she giggled. A faint numbness spread in her throat—not John Goode, she hoped, looking at Maud for clues.

"I met this guy who works at the aquarium—you know, 'Great Barrier Reef Wond*ah*land.' " Maud stopped bobbing. "He's mostly a diver."

Stupid to even think it, Annabel thought, student and professor.

"And just where have you been seeing him, *underwater?*"

"One could say that," said Maud, grinning. "Neglecting my calculus. Oh, I brought you something." She pulled a paper bag out of her backpack. "It's about bats." She unwrapped a small book, *Tower Karst,* about the bats of Australia.

Annabel squeezed her arm. "Oooh," she said. "You're the best, thank you." She leafed through the book, mumbling, "Great photos. So, tell me more about your diver—"

Maud's face and arms glowed pink from sun.

"William. Well, he's worked for the aquarium since he finished his doctorate, and he's British, and he's gorgeous."

"Excellent." Bright flashes from the window banded Maud's face with light.

"And he's younger than I am."

"Excellent: women live longer, anyway."

"A lot younger," Maud paused. "A bit of a wunderkind." She was looking out the window now. "He's twenty-eight."

"Ah, excellent." Why did she keep repeating that sixth-grade word? Twenty-eight. Her age. Robert's age, too, when he stopped having birthdays. Soon she'd be older than Robert was, she'd beat him to twenty-nine. Annabel envisioned Maud and Robert, his hand on her thin sloped shoulder, spreading her hair, sorting gray from brown.

Annabel wanted to ask whether they'd slept together. "Does it bother him?"

"He doesn't care, he said."

"How old are you? I don't even know. Or really care." She knew this last part couldn't be true, since she was asking. She wanted to calculate the difference.

"Forty-two."

"Young," said Annabel. She couldn't help blushing. Fourteen years, she thought.

"He's incredible in the tanks; he's working on that encapsulated reef project." She put her arm around Annabel. "You're a good kid," she said. "Thanks for letting me be a teenager about this."

"Anytime." She remembered how Janice had put licorice on Mike's thigh, and wondered why they all struggled so hard to be older, to be serious scientists with new theories, new terminologies, if when you got down to the basics, everyone was a horny teenager. She vowed not to be jealous. She leafed through the book. Two shots of bats mating.

The research crew set up tents between termite mounds at 40-Mile Scrub. Everyone was subdued after the train ride, enclosed in their own private perceptions, but amiable, soft somehow. Annabel, too, felt enveloped by the place and the group—an atom moving despite the molecule. The termite mounds jabbed up to three and four feet high, a few even taller than the van—cracked red mud cones spaced like chess pieces on the scrubby ground. There were acacias, an occasional eucalypt, and cattle skulls.

Janice walked from tent to tent, explaining that she'd gotten special permission from the ranchers to be there and warning them not to go off alone or without bright-colored clothing. Annabel wondered whether that was to avoid being mistaken for poachers or so the professors could find them if they got lost in all that dusty same landscape.

Annabel and Maud set up the tent they'd share with Sabrina and Janice, who were on tea duty—dinner. The sky started to stripe orange, growing intense at the horizon where the dust was thickest, rising from the earth like steam. The fat tent poles slid into each other easily; Annabel remembered camping with her family in Maine. The family tents had lost most of their poles and were strung with nylon rope from tree branches. If it rained and you touched the sides, you'd get wet. Annabel always touched the sides, because Robert, who slept between her and Alice, was a sloppy sleeper. He flung limbs when he slept, and mumbled, and jiggled. Sometimes he used to wake them up, screaming a potent terror, his voice high and panicked, ripping from his vocal cords in long lines until they shook him awake. He said he never remembered anything, but Annabel believed it was a secret version of horror, something special somehow, that he kept from them.

Professor Goode came over to inspect the tent. He put a cow skull atop the green peak and shined a flashlight on each of them. He was grinning, Annabel noticed, acting young and mischievous.

"Croc-oh-dial, oh, croc-oh-dial," he sing-songed.

"Are you trying to tempt them across the scrub? I've heard they've taken to living in termite mounds." Maud tugged on his corduroy shirtsleeve. Too hot for corduroy, Annabel thought.

"Yes, I thought one might make a good bed companion." The professor winked, though he was looking at the skull. "Rather, we have the spotlights set up for a trip down to the river after we *dine*. I thought you might like to come along. Sabrina and Lars have begged off already—exhaustion."

"They must have had some particularly strenuous *research* activities today. I'm in, though." Maud was feisty, Annabel thought, more assured than usual. Or maybe it just took her a while to reveal herself, maybe they'd whittled through the dull bark to the sappy green.

"I'm in, too, as long as you promise not to use me for bait."

Annabel felt like hugging someone; the light was orange, she was hot, and her throat was dry and sore. Still, they were going out with spotlights, designed for the stage but equipped for portable generators and handheld brackets, to search for crocodiles. Catch them hunting, or at least active, unlike the slow blobs in zoos.

After dinner the four spotlighters, Maud, Professors Goode and Janice, and Annabel, piled into the truck and drove to five different sites on the river. There was nothing at any of them, just sticks in the water, unmoving trees and shrubs, and then, at the last spot, a likely plop. They pushed close to the riverbank and slung the heavy lights around, but all they saw were stones sliding down the bank. Professor Goode turned off his spotlight, heaved it off his shoulder with a grunt, and Janice followed suit. Then she stepped into the cab of the truck for a night-nap, she said.

Maud switched on a flashlight. "Going to visit a tree."

"Don't go far." Annabel watched the dark shadow of her braid swinging as she crossed the road.

"At least we can see the Southern Cross," Professor Goode said. He climbed into the truck bed and leaned back on the generator to look at the sky. Annabel followed him up.

"Glorious." Annabel leaned back, too.

"Such an odd idea that we *ascend,*" said the professor.

"Some of us, that is." Annabel was trying to figure out the sky. The constellations were different, backward, upside down. She'd noticed the difference before, but had never seen it with such incredible contrast.

"Do you think you're going?" Her voice boomed in the quiet. Insects buzzing, an owl. The river was silent.

"I'm not," said the professor. "I'm a lousy husband. I think I've failed in the father department, too. That's enough points against me on the heavenly scales. Bags of good dust are no match for boulders of bad deeds like that, I think."

"Still that bad?"

"Yeah, I've been awful. My sons don't call and they don't have much to say when I call them. I ought to do something about it, but I have this horrible pride. Anyway, I ought to stop feeling sorry for myself. It's you sympathetic Americans, you bring it out in me."

Maud thunked up into the truck bed, delivering the smell of crushed eucalyptus. She leaned back with them.

Annabel felt safe, her back on the cold metal, with these two scientists beside her. Friends, new friends, people who didn't know her past and who liked her current self. They'd both confided in her in the same day, and she was heavy with her own history. She didn't look at either of them, but started to talk.

"My brother died, almost two years ago. He was a field scientist, a diver. He died underwater, maybe the bends, maybe some bizarre mix of the tank and his own chemicals. He was my age, now. He really knew what he was doing." She paused and put a hand up toward the sky, trying to track the Big Dipper. On this side of its cup, anything you put into it would spill out. Almost two years ago, she'd said, but it was twenty-two months and three days. April 20. The date was more important than a birthday, an only instance, the end. She didn't know what time. She wished she did, so she could see if she felt anything at that exact moment of anniversary.

"I'm sorry," said Maud.

"Thank you." Her answer was pure reflex. This should be it, she thought, stop talking. But it was such a relief to tell, she kept on going. "At the funeral, one aunt came up to me, my great-aunt Maxine. No one believes what she says, because she borrowed money from a sister or something and never gave it back. But here we were at the funeral, the reception after it, when everyone mills around acting sorry and catching up at the same time—it was my first funeral. They didn't let me go to the one for my grandmother, I was too young, they said, but they let Robert, my brother, they let him go. Anyway, Aunt Maxine comes up to me and says how sorry she is, and then she puts her cold hands on my arm and whispers, 'You know some are saying it wasn't an accident.' " Annabel wanted to rub Professor Goode's corduroy between her fingers, or to feel Maud, not just hear her own quick, shallow breathing.

"So I asked her what that meant. I shouldn't have asked anything, I should have shrugged her off, or offered her some food or something, which is what we usually do when she gets peculiar on us, but I listened instead. She said that some people thought he was too experienced to get the bends, so I asked again, what did she mean, what was she getting at. It's completely the wrong thing to do with someone like that, encouraging the spleen. But she said she thought Robert had always had it in him. 'The melancholy,' she said, 'it runs in the family.' " The lumpy bottom of the truck bed was starting to make her back ache.

"And then I finally stopped encouraging her, and she stopped telling me things I didn't want to hear, but I can't get rid of the idea. I haven't even told my sister, or my parents. Aunt Maxine is absurd, of course; there was no special melancholy in him, whatever that is. God. Sorry, I shouldn't have gone on like that, I'm sorry."

She wasn't really sorry; she felt lighter, and honest. She waited for something to happen, a shooting star, for someone to apologize again. Maud reached over and put her hand in Annabel's.

The professor cleared his throat. "It's horrid to be left," he said. "I'm sure you're right—I'm sure it was an accident." He touched her shoulder, but lightly, so she couldn't feel the warmth of his hand.

Annabel waited for more. More touch, more words. She almost wanted Professor Goode to speak for Robert. She half expected that he'd know something about it, that her overlay of Robert's passion for work onto the professor's had brought the live man closer to her brother. What happened, she wanted to ask, what would have happened if you'd been on that dive?

The professor cleared his throat. "Well, so much for crocodiles," he said.

"You okay, Annabel?" asked Maud.

"Yeah," she said. Her face flamed, but still she shivered as she looked up at the cold, inverted constellations. Robert, she thought, never really told me what he felt; I drew belief from the clues of his face, from what he said and what he didn't.

Five

Alice could fill pages, listing the dangerous things he'd done. Robert swallowing live wasps, mixing acids and bases in his room, making "mystery beaker cocktails" without goggles, dissecting batteries, assembling, populating, and burning his plastic ant farm; the sharp sour stench of melted plastic and burnt ants clung to the walls of his bedroom for years. He was curious about the living and the dead—he probably became a biologist, she thought, because the insides of things interested him as much as the outsides.

Once, when she was fourteen and he was twelve, she found Robert shredding a dead bird. He tore off feathers, then pulled apart the flesh. The bird was a blue jay, struck by some house cat who was bored, probably, as soon as the bird stopped struggling. It looked dry, as if it had been parching in the summer afternoons when the sun crept below the open umbrella of rhododendrons. Alice sat on the back porch and watched her brother. He tore at the bird as if it were food, as if he were hungry and trying to get at the meat. He fingered the bones, the disarticulated wing, the spine.

"Hey, Rob, what're you doing?" She stepped off the porch.

He threw down the bird. "Shit, Alice, how come you snuck up on me?"

"I asked first, what're you doing?"

"Just nothing. Just nothing that matters to you."

"How do you know if you won't say?"

Robert jumped up the steps to the porch. He pressed one hand on each side of her cheek and she stood still, taking it. She expected his hands to smell rotten, or of blood, but all she smelled was soil, and her brother's fruity sweat smell. She didn't flinch; she wasn't going to let him win. Robert kissed her on the lips, like a man would, hard, but fast.

"Hey!" Alice squirmed away from him.

"You saw me, then, so what if you saw me. Don't spy on me, Al." Robert's voice was high, on the verge of changing. He looked at his feet.

"I just don't want you to do anything stupid," she said.

There was trouble with Professor Janice Martin's traps. Something was springing most of them, without taking any bait. She'd been working at them for two days, with her volunteer assistants, and this mystery made her irritable, unfocused. Everyone was up at the site, two or three times a day, in the brief shadow of a sharp red outcrop. The whole world was flat except for the great red ridge, with the river away on the horizon. By ten o'clock in the morning, it was stinking hot. Then when they came back at six, with dusk starting, the cold spread across them like lacquer.

Janice and Annabel were setting the evening lines down, and Annabel tried to talk with her; she thought maybe there was some way to cheer her, comfort her.

"So, this is part of a longer project?" She didn't know why she bothered with this question. She felt stupid, really, hot and tired of silence.

"I sort of went over that already, Annabel."

What a crank, thought Annabel. Here she's getting free assistance. Well, when it doesn't work out, it's hard. "Yeah, you did." She pulled at the trapline and a swift metal splinter punched into her thumb. Blood appeared in a bright dot.

"Can you hold this?" Janice thrust a broken trapdoor in Annabel's direction.

"What do you think of Townsville? I mean, have you lived there much between going into the bush?" Why, she thought, can't I stop talking? "I mean, do you spend much time—" She stopped. Heard her own voice bubbling out like a shaken beer after the top's popped off.

Janice shifted upward, so her weight came over her feet. Most of the time she was bent over; even the back of her neck was a darker tan than her face or chest. "Annabel." She looked directly at her. "You're not so good with quiet, are you?"

Annabel took this as a challenge. She said nothing.

"I'm sorry." Janice bent over again. "I'm tired of this project. I have funding for another month, that's it, and the data is so lean I don't think I could squeeze significance out of it if I had a cider press. So I've been short with you, and I shouldn't be. But real science is full of scrambling and searching, for the money to start, and then when you get down to the actual work, the clock starts ticking before you even have your equipment. You buy guy line"—she snapped at the wire—"and you've got three fewer days with the radio equipment."

Annabel sucked her bleeding thumb.

"And you can't go into a pub without being hated for your green tendencies. Or threatened, even. It's worse for women." She sighed and looked at Annabel.

"And then you abuse the poor doctorate grubs you've recruited for manual labor."

Annabel waited, but that was it. She looked over at the red rock, which was starting to glow as the sun slunk down below the horizon. The dust rose up in whirls and the gum trees looked scrawny and lost on the flat ground. I'm not going to be like her, she thought—I may get the grants, I may even teach, but I'll never forget how you're supposed to treat people. I hope.

There was a rumble, quiet at first, then growing.

"What the hell is that?" Annabel turned to Janice, forgetting her vow to say no more.

"Bloody, bloody hell," said Janice, staring at the horizon.

Annabel saw a blur of shadows. The traps clinked shut down the line, one by one, as the earth vibrated. Earthquake? she wondered. Sonic boom?

"Fuck," said Professor Janice.

The other students and professors were clustered together; they stopped untangling a rope; Sabrina even stopped talking to Lars's chest.

"Bloody cattle," said Janice.

Annabel stepped back from the trapline as a herd of cattle churned the dust into a thick, fast-moving bank. It looked like the cattle were coming directly toward them. The group dispersed, first walking fast, then running, toward the rock, the vans. Maud was up by the rock outcrop; she'd started scaling a boulder near the base. Annabel backed toward the vans, thirty yards maybe, then looked at Janice Martin, who stood staring at the cattle. When the herd came within five yards of her, she started hooting and waving her arms. The dust coated her, surrounded her, until Annabel couldn't see her at all. Then the cattle veered off, dispersed, and disappeared. Annabel and several of the others ran toward Janice. As they ran through the dust, swatting it down, they could see her, still standing. She had a wide, almost goofy grin.

"Well, someone needs to move her traps to the other side of the rock," she said. She started picking up the trap sets, pulling the line. She was laughing lightly.

Now that Professor Janice's traps were replaced, the science crew had settled into a better campsite, closer to the research and much closer to a swimming hole. Janice was mollified; she only asked for one assistant for each trek, and to fill in the rest of the time, to give them their money's worth, Professor Mike had started a bird-species assessment, for practice. They strung the fine nets in a likely flight path, and took turns checking for netted birds to examine. Annabel enjoyed her turn, for the thrill of seeing what they'd caught and, even more, for the relief of letting the terrified birds go. Mike let her hold them in a gloved hand while he measured and sexed and recorded species and key markings. She could feel the heat and heartbeat through the glove and thought about her bats, how this time she wouldn't catch anyone; she hoped to learn enough by watching and recording, to measure without the potential damage of touch.

The swimming hole wasn't technically a hole—there was a wide shallow river running in meandering bands with dips and eddies. Annabel and Maud, Mike Trimble and Professor Goode walked down the path, over a bluff, in their sandals, and then they wallowed in the water. Sabrina and Lars followed behind them; Janice was alone at her site. There was a good thick part of the river a few kilometers down, deep enough for actual swimming, but there were crocodiles there. Even at the shallow parts Mike and Janice had instructed them to keep paired, to look out for mud with eyes.

The sun baked them, so mud dried and cracked on their skin as they wallowed in their bathing suits. Sabrina was strangely friendly, asking Annabel about the spotlighting, her undergraduate work. Annabel didn't mind; she was worried that Maud and Professor Goode would stop liking her now that she'd exposed herself to them. They'd been quiet, solicitous—she felt as if she'd had a one-night stand.

Sabrina, Maud, and Annabel walked downstream. The sky looked like a thin layer of blue paint over a white wall. The heat of the sun and warm scrubland rose to meet each other, stole the moisture of breath.

"So, do you think you'll want to be a field scientist, still, after all this?" Sabrina squished a mound of silt with her toes. She had thin strong legs and had stopped wearing so much makeup since they'd been camping.

They sat on the bank.

"Funny, I never really question it," said Annabel, though she knew this was untrue. "Maud?"

Maud slid into the stream. She lay back with her hair and the back half of her head in the water and closed her eyes.

"Maud?" said Sabrina. "She looks like the Virgin Mary," she said to Annabel.

"Thanks," Maud said. "The nuns who raised me would be pleased."

"I thought you couldn't hear us," said Sabrina.

"Even better." Maud sat up, a moon cookie, brown-backed and dry and clean on the front. "We're getting bush tans. God, it's so hot. I think we've warmed up all this water. The river is as slow as my grandfather in the bathroom."

"Yuck." Sabrina squirmed.

"Shall we make our way downstream?" Annabel stood up, her head feeling slightly swollen from the contrast of heat and cool.

Mike was sitting on the opposite side of the river. He threw mud in their direction; even thrown mud looked lazy as it fell in and barely made the river splash.

"Where, I wonder, is Professor Goode?" said Maud.

"John went downstream," Mike called. "Watch for crocs."

They didn't find Professor Goode downstream. Sabrina retreated, ascending the bank as they passed Lars, who was sitting with his feet in a small pool, wearing a huge sun hat, reading. She didn't say anything as she departed, and Annabel decided she was tired of constantly revising her opinion. Why did she bother to care about Sabrina, to try to like her? And why did Sabrina make it so difficult? Proximity, small space, sharing a room and a tent with someone made a logical place for kinship. But Sabrina—she could imagine forgetting Sabrina after she went home, after she went wherever she was going next, and thinking of her only when she made some joke about the living conditions in the field-science program.

"Shall we stop here? I think we're getting awfully close to the crocodile zone," said Maud. She was rubbing her leg as if she expected leeches, but there were none here, Mike had said.

"That professor, he's gone off alone to find the crocs, I guess."

"Maybe we should go down a little farther."

Annabel didn't want to pursue him—the professor knew what he was doing—but then, she wasn't alone, looking for him; it would be a legitimate safety check, couldn't be misinterpreted. Who cares, she thought. I am a being of free will. "Okay," she said.

As they walked on, the scrub around the riverbank grew thicker, and they tramped down into the water. Annabel wondered what Maud was thinking. Conversation could swing so quickly from the important, the emotional, to the details of dinner. There was a loneliness about it, and at the same time Annabel longed to be really alone for a little bit. Outside, so much space, and they crowded together in it in their tents. Maud made a small snoring sound at night, her head tilted back. Once, she'd moaned in a sexual way;

it woke Annabel, and she felt like a voyeur, rude, as if she'd opened a door on a private scene.

The river started to get deeper, so they scrambled up the bank again. The shrubbery was thorny and stubborn.

"Should we shout, maybe? This is really too far. And we can't wade here, because of the crocs." Annabel held back a branch so it wouldn't slap Maud.

"Professor?" Maud's voice was tentative. Then very loud, and very strong, as she yelled, "Professor John Goode, John Goode, Professor?"

The sound of her shout seemed to overtake the gum tree's rustling, the growing river sounds. It was as if they had left everyone else, gone so far away they could be separated by a continent, a rift valley. A sense of adventure surged in Annabel. They walked on a little, then Maud stepped into barbed wire. She pulled a piece out of her leg, a rusty spike an inch long.

"Damn. Damn, that hurts," she said. The hole of the wound was perfectly round, like a giant period.

"Shall we forget our wayward prof? That looks nasty."

"Why don't you look around a little more? I'm going to tie my bandanna—which is a big bacteria festival from being in the river—around this stupid cut."

Annabel looked over at the river, now about twenty feet down below the bank, and wider, with shady edges where crocodiles might lurk. It was less murky here, and deep. She yelled for the professor and then she saw him, the tiny lump of a head, arms swinging up in an uneven stroke. At first she thought he might be flailing.

"Hey!" she yelled. "John Goode! Are you okay?" The form kept splashing, and Annabel thought of a crocodile tugging from below, insistent, hungry, and huge. The teeth. She pressed through the scrub and scratched her legs on thorns, yelling, watching the form. The flailing motion stopped.

"Hello?" He wasn't screaming; his voice was clear and calm.

"Are you all right, Professor?" Annabel's throat was dry, her face hot, and there were sticky stripes of blood on her scratched legs.

"Just swimming." His head went down, and he swam toward her bank—he was a sloppy swimmer. She could see his muscles working—heavy arms, but strong, intact. Close enough to speak, his head popped up again. Annabel could see the foreshortened outline of his body as he treaded water. "Much better spot for a swim," he said.

"What about the crocodiles?" She could hear her own pulse as it passed through her head. Why had they bothered to track him down? He's fine, and he's crazy.

"Ah, they wouldn't want me, I'm too stringy. Freshies don't bite—not much, anyway." He splashed. "If you want to come in too I'll keep an eye out for you. But you'd be a bit more tempting to a croc, I'd say."

"No," said Annabel. "Maud's cut herself on barbed wire."

"Ah, there's first aid back at camp. Do you need help, then?"

"No. See you later."

The professor dunked back in the water.

Back at camp, they did a better job of bandaging Maud's leg, and had hot tea, jasmine, in bags fished from a dusty tin. Swallowing the steamy liquid felt right despite the heat, the dry mud on their legs and arms. Annabel tried not to wait for the professor. Maud had said, "Forget him," as they'd worked their way back through the thorns. She'd talked about hijacking a van and driving back so she could be with William. She'd said Annabel should come, too, and they could stop for milkshakes as soon as they reached civilization. *Milkshakes,* she'd said, twice, as if she could taste them through the word. *Do Aussies know how to make milkshakes?*

Annabel thought about the shifty form of the riverbank, about how a crocodile could be there, sunning, could look like old leaves and mud. She thought about the professor's arm torn by teeth, how the veins and muscles would look exposed, then the tendons, the fat opened into the river. She moved around the campsite, getting a new rock to hold down a tent peg, wiping the dust from the tea tin with her fingers.

The others came back, Lars and Sabrina a discreet distance apart with their secret bodies and their faces pink. It was still hot. Janice pulled up in the van, bringing swirls of dust with her. She emerged in an unusual spurt of cheer, teasing Mike, laughing. Mike snapped his towel at Annabel, and Janice poured drinking water on Maud's dusty bare feet. Janice, who had reminded them to conserve water, like a mantra at every meal.

"Have you seen Professor Goode?" Annabel couldn't help asking Mike.

"You two didn't rescue John from the jaws of a croc?" Mike picked up Annabel's cup of tea and slurped from it, but she didn't mind. "I thought you went after him."

"We found him." Maud dabbed more ointment on her wound. "He was playing Great Explorer. I'm sure he'll be back soon."

"That looks nasty." Janice leaned over Maud.

Maud held her leg up like an infant. "I found some barbed wire when we were looking for John."

"Does it feel hot?"

"Yeah."

"I prescribe Tylenol and rest—" Mike procured the pills.

Annabel felt useless, as if she should do something. When she looked at Maud's pink leg, she thought about a crocodile tearing at Professor Goode's head, the ear torn off, the hair clotted with river grass and blood. She swallowed hard, trying to stay in the present, where everyone was more or less whole.

Maud napped in the van and Janice kept her company, cleaning up her site logs. Mike was in good spirits, stirring Milo powder into hot water to make a drink that tasted sort of like cocoa, wrapping potatoes in foil for the fire. They had freeze-dried fish stew with carrots from a battered bag.

"For the fresh effect," said Mike, slicing carrots.

"Don't you think he should be back by now?" Annabel felt the cold creeping up with the dark. Her legs were dry and achy from sun; her neck pulsed with minor sunburn. "I mean, even daredevils have to come in for food."

"He's not the most predictable of men," said Mike, smiling.

"Which means?"

"Oh, I shouldn't say, really. But don't you worry; he'll come good this time. It's just that he's gotten into trouble taking off before—that's the problem with his wife, I'd say."

"Oh." Annabel suddenly wanted not to care about the professor. "So, what kind of trouble have you been in, Sir Mike?"

"That's rather forward of you, my dear." Mike was still grinning. He tossed her a piece of carrot. "I'll beg off like an American and say 'I do not recall.' And then I'll ask you to check that potato over there—done?"

Annabel poked at the potato, and sparks flew up at her face.

After dinner, the group sat in a circle around the fire making pellets with aluminum foil. Sabrina lay back against Lars, and Janice started them singing "Waltzing Matilda." Then Lars, whose voice was surprisingly sweet, led some James Taylor songs, which sounded funny to Annabel with the professors' Australian accents.

Annabel remembered a family story of how Alice had wandered off on a family camping trip and was discovered sitting in a patch of poison ivy, eating the leaves. Her father recounted this story in his sturdy, cheerful voice, which knew the outcome, which didn't doubt out loud. Luckily, the story went, Alice turned out to be immune, or maybe the exposure effected immunity. Annabel was too young to go on that trip; she'd been with her grandparents, so the story was like a myth to her, her family without her, Robert and Alice as a pair of siblings. She was missing from the story, she thought, the family unbalanced, like it was again now.

Professor Goode came up the path from the river, whistling along with "Sweet Baby James."

"You have some left for your wayward mate, I hope." He took a spoon and mashed a potato into the stew pot.

"Annabel thought you'd been tucker for a croc, ratbag," said Mike, gently shoving the professor as he sat down by the fire, eating quickly. Lars was still singing, and Sabrina, her voice high and thin.

"You led Maud down the path of destruction," said Mike.

"Another one?" Professor Goode chuckled. But when he examined her wound by flashlight, he seemed to wake with responsibility.

"I'm a fool sometimes," he said. No one responded.

He settled down, lay back on a plaid blanket, and closed his eyes to the stars. Annabel looked at the smudge of stew on one corner of his mouth. There was some on his shirt, too, and she remembered how pale his belly looked in the river, vulnerable. He would seem like a kid if he didn't have that intense way of looking at things, at her, too; Annabel realized he made her feel *studied* when he looked at her. It was intimate, not entirely sexual, but not chaste, either.

Mike, Lars, and Sabrina left one by one.

"I'm headed in," said Maud.

"Me, too." Janice leapt up.

Maybe I should go, too, thought Annabel, but she stayed. She wanted the agitation of being alone with Professor Goode's careful attention, those different eyes looking at her, even if it seemed dangerous.

"My wife used to get so angry when I took my sons out," he said.

"I thought you were sleeping." Annabel poked a potato with her stick. It had been forgotten in the fire, and now it was probably a burnt lump inside the foil.

"I just had such a good time with them, playing in waterfalls, fossicking, general walkabout, and she didn't want to go so far—not that she's too tender or anything, she's tough."

"What does your wife do?"

He sighed. "Molly's a doctor. Pediatrician. Sets lots of broken bones."

"Ah."

"Including mine. And both my sons'. Though it wasn't always my fault, I swear it. Sometimes they fell off things all on their own." He laughed, privately. "She used to like the naughty boy in me."

"Yeah," she mumbled. "And now?" Annabel took her stick out of the fire and rolled it between her hands. It was too dark to see the charcoal smudges.

"Now she thinks I'm getting too old to act so young."

He rolled over, faced Annabel. She sat up quickly, afraid he was going to touch her, or even kiss her. She didn't want to cross the line, even if she wanted to edge up close to it, think about the other side.

Professor Goode stood up. "I'm tuckered," he said. "See you tomorrow. More rivers to muck about in, unless you're on trap duty." He walked off to his tent. With a slight limp. He isn't young, Annabel thought. Maybe her father's age. She tried to imagine Dr. Mendelssohn out in the bush. He'd have the whole campground ordered and labeled. But he wouldn't come this far, she thought, so far from Mom and home, his desk.

Then she thought of Maud and her new boyfriend. Fourteen years difference. Professor Goode was probably fifty. She decided not to do the math.

In the morning, getting breakfast ready at dawn before the hot hand of heat, Annabel saw half a dozen kangaroos bringing dust up behind them—the elegance of muscle traversing space. This is why I'm here, Annabel thought, I came to see them cut across gravity, great dusky red blurs. Then they were gone, and it was time to get out the muesli, pick out the pebbles that had filtered into the supplies during the long van trip.

Sender: (Annabel Mendelssohn)
AMendelss@ausnet.jcooku.tvl.edu
To: AEMendel@biosci.com
Subject: Back from the bush.
Wednesday, February 28, 1996

Dear Alice:

Guess you've been too busy at work or something, no notes from you. Or else you've gone on an unexpected trip to Bali. It's hard to picture you in your winter coat, on the East Coast USA. It's hot and humid here—they say there may be a hurricane coming, and the wind is wild. It's nice after our dry walkabout in 40-Mile Scrub. No major casualties, but god, this field stuff is wearing on a body. My friend Maud walked into barbed wire, and Professor Goode flirted with crocodiles, though we didn't actually SEE any.

We did do some cool work on a mammal survey,
though, saw echidnas, bandicoots, a wild pig. Red
roos! (Those we didn't trap!) We even did some
bird netting—butcher-birds, currawongs, a pied
honeyeater. I know they're generally okay after we
release them, but I can't help feeling bad for the
birds: they panic so much when they're netted. You
can feel their frenetic little hearts when you
settle down their wings and hold them for measuring and examination. I was sure one of those
hearts would burst from the terror—sometimes we
humans seem so much more dangerous than anything
that honestly lives outside.

I'm glad to be back to semi-civilization, though.
I have a week, and then I'm going into my study
site to set up, get approval from Professor Goode,
and start the real research.

Well, gotta put my laundry in line.

There's a phone in the office, by the way; I gave
the number to Mom just in case.(See how good I'm
being?)

Love, Annabel

Six

Rereading Annabel's message, Alice tapped a pencil on a grant proposal on her desk and thought about the puppy. Puppy-proofing: tying up cords and other dangerous chewables in the house.

When they were kids, Alice and Robert lobbied for a dog. They drew pictures and Robert named it yearly: Stovepipe, when he was interested in presidents and their hats; Marco, when he read about the explorer; and Fork, just because. Netta Mendelssohn said she was allergic, and though Alice still wasn't sure she hadn't just been allergic to another responsibility, they never had a puppy.

The compromise was two male gerbils who defied the pet shop gerbil-sexing expert and had a litter of eight. Alice was home sick on the day after they were born. Annabel and Robert wanted to be sick, too; Robert even rubbed his forehead, hard, trying to give himself a fever, but only Alice passed the thermometer test. So she was sitting by the gerbil cage, wrapped in two blankets, when she was supposed to stay in her bed. She even had the TV beside the bed on a rickety table so she could sit up and change channels, but the gerbils had been making tiny shuffling noises—they were too thrilling to leave. There was a window seat, and a round red table where the fish tank of gerbils lived.

Alice, wrapped in her blankets and sweaty with cold, watched the mother gerbil eat two of the wormy babies, sucking them into her horrible mouth like sacks of sweet pink dough. They squealed, tiny metal-rubbing noises. After school, Alice told her siblings, and Annabel cried. Robert thought it was gross but amazing. He whispered to the mother to do it again, there were six left to eat. He watched her until late at night, sneaking out of his room and into Alice's. His breath was steady as he sat, meditating on the possibilities of the body.

"It's awful," whispered Alice.

"No," said Robert. "She probably couldn't feed them all. Or else she's too closed in."

But after he gave up, he climbed into her bed to keep her company.

It was Robert who, after the gerbils were weaned, had secretly set the babies free by the blackberry vines.

Sender: AEMendel@biosci.com (Alice Mendelssohn)
To: AMendelss@ausnet.jcooku.tvl.edu
Subject: still . . . here . . .
Thursday, February 29, 1996

Dear Annabel: I feel like I've been in the bush, too. The upshot of an office melodrama is that I thought I was going to be fired, but instead I was promoted. More work, a tiny bit more pay. Hardly

enough for one dinner out to celebrate. I was all
ready to get my box of stuff and go home.

I said yes to a puppy, to an incredible, wild, and
frenetic ball of fur, tongue, and teeth. We're
bringing her home in a few days, and I need good
name suggestions. What am I going to do with a
puppy and a promotion?

What's next? Are you going into your bat haven for
more than a week at a time? Will you be alone out
there?

Love, Alice.

Annabel lay on her towel in the field behind the professors'
house, pretending to read *Tower Karst,* the book Maud had
given her, watching Professor Goode load rock hammers
and samples and test kits into the back of a battered white
hatchback. She'd come to the field to be alone and to
watch the sky split into grins of blue and white. Now that
the hurricane had passed, the weather felt especially delicious, the heavy sea moisture swept away with the unreal-
ized storm. Still, there was electricity in the air, tension.
And the other students seemed to respond: Sabrina had
snapped at her more than usual in the room this morning,
and even Maud was short with her when they passed on
the campus paths.

When Annabel looked up from her spot in the grass and
saw John Goode, she decided not to get up so he could see
her. Instead, she watched him shift heavy boxes into the

back of the car, heaving the weight with his back instead of his legs. Annabel remembered her father's instructions on lifting with the legs. He'd come to visit when she was moving into her last Chicago apartment, using the excuse of a conference, a paid-for hotel room. But he helped her shift books to shelves, and stopped her short when she bent over boxes to lift improperly.

"Lift with the legs," he said. "Or you'll be sore tomorrow." His knees cracked as he bent to demonstrate.

"Like this?" Annabel clowned, straddling a box and pretending to lift it between her knees.

Her father had seemed old to her then. For the first time, he'd looked as if he too could hurt his back, and he'd let Annabel help him hold the bed as he assembled it, instead of insisting, in his usual Superman style, that he could take care of it.

John Goode wasn't much younger than her father. He heaved a box that looked heavy enough to be full of rock samples onto the car's bumper, then shimmied it into the back. You'll be sore tomorrow, she thought. He hadn't been around much since they'd come back from the trip to 40-Mile Scrub. He gave his ethics lecture and swept out of the classroom without stopping to answer extra questions when it was over. Annabel didn't think much about where he might be going; after all, classes weren't quite over yet. She did think of what she'd said about Robert, though, and of lying beside him at the site, when he talked about his wife, when he didn't kiss her.

Annabel dug in her backpack for her camera. Professor Goode, observed in the field, she thought, as she clicked. She felt like a spy. She watched him settle hard into the front seat of his car, roll down the window, and rub his thumb along his chin. He looked at himself in the side mirror, tilting it to examine his whole face, throwing his hat on the seat and smoothing the craze of hair. Annabel, lying in the grass, imagined she could smell him, soil and musk. He wasn't much like her father. The dust swirled into the clean air as he drove away. She looked down at her book again and leafed through for a picture of the spectacled flying foxes. They'd be much easier to study than men.

Sender: (Annabel Mendelssohn)
AMendelss@ausnet.jcooku.tvl.edu
To: AEMendel@biosci.com
Subject: I'll huff and I'll puff . . .
Monday, March 4, 1996

Dear Alice:

The hurricane missed us. We tied down everything that moves and I was all set for a thrilling show—oh well. It's been dull back at base camp: there are classes, the same agonizing arguments about statistics and ethics. I believe it's important, really I do, but what idiots are going to waste their time and money making up data? Never mind, I know we've both run into cheats.

I can't wait to get back to the field. I'm going to my site in a few days, though I'm supposed to go with Professor Goode so he can check out my setup. Approve me. He missed a lecture on Friday, and we don't know where he is.

Lars likes to eat Vegemite. I think it smells like
sewage.

Your promotion: great! My selfish instinct was that
if you did get let go (not that I really believed
it could happen) you'd come out and see me. Did
you get a bigger office?

I've got another two days before I'm supposed to
go; I may give up on P. Goode and take the bus to
the Atherton Tablelands alone to spy on bats.

So send messages.

Love, A.

Annabel was late for the last ethics lecture. She couldn't
find any clean underwear—she dug through the piles and
her backpack. She'd just done laundry, though—this was
impossible, she had to get out of this place, it was making
her crazy, cramped, fussy. Finally, she found a single pair
wedged between her camping stove and Sabrina's statistics
textbook. By the time she was dressed and jogging down
the path toward the classroom, she didn't have time to chat
with Maud, who was leaving her house and strolling in the
opposite direction.

"Hey, aren't you coming?" Annabel asked. She slowed
but kept going.

"I'm not—well, I'm going to see William—"

Annabel waved. Maud hadn't been around for Professor
Goode's second absence, either, when Mike filled in with a
spontaneous dialogue on kangaroo culling as an alternative

protein harvest. Richer and more sustainable than beef cattle or sheep, they didn't create dust bowls by overgrazing. Despite the logic, Annabel learned, no one wanted to eat the national emblem. Unless they didn't know that was what they were eating.

She rounded the corner to the classroom door. There was a torn scrap of paper tacked up: NO CLASS, GO WILD.

Funny pun, Annabel thought. She sat on a bench by a hibiscus, touching the soft red anthers of a flower's stamen, exhausted from her own flight of lateness.

Professor Mike emerged from the classroom, shut off the lights, and locked the door.

"Hey," said Annabel. "No ethics anymore?"

"You could say that." Mike gave her a pale smile.

"What's the deal with our good professor, decided to ditch the doctorate grubs?"

"It's odd, Annabel—he was supposed to be back last Wednesday, and no one seems to know where he's gone. Then, you've seen our John in action, he can be diverted. Still"—Mike kicked dirt over his shoes—"he's never flaked out on the program before."

"He's supposed to come inspect my site tomorrow—" Annabel looked down, embarrassed to be so focused on herself. She thought of John Goode's face after he'd pulled her under the waterfall, full of intent and accident, his bright face. She remembered his dirty white car driving away last week. Some ethics professor, neglecting his lectures. Her own ethics, having a crush on him, wasting energy that could've been directed toward research. If she ever made it to her own research.

"I suppose—" Mike started, then straightened up, becoming older than her, professorial. "You should give him another day or two, then you may catch a lift or get a bus to Malanda. I've seen your site—I'll sign off—" He smiled quickly. "But give him another couple of days."

Sabrina had been using her hairbrush, Annabel could tell from the sticky blond strands. And last night she'd woken up because of thumping and giggling, and she'd seen Sabrina in her underwear and a T-shirt, leaning against a fully dressed Lars in the doorway. By the crack of light from the hall, she could see that it was Annabel's underwear Sabrina was wearing.

"Get a hotel room," she mumbled.

"Oh, thought you were asleep." Sabrina grabbed her sleeping bag and held it in front of her body.

"I was. Stop wearing my underwear."

Lars said, "Going, later—"

And Sabrina said, loudly, "I would *not* wear *your* underwear."

Annabel put a pillow over her head and counted sheep with Sabrina's face, then imagined leeches in Sabrina's bed, then finally she fell asleep, thinking about her bats, the site with no other humans, her bats.

Now she was in the computer trailer, rereading the few citations she'd found on the behavior of *Pteropus conspicillatus*—most of the research had been done on little fruit-eaters and the giants in New Guinea. Maybe New Guinea should be next, she thought, maybe there were some decent colleagues in New Guinea.

Maud thumped up the milk-crate step into the trailer. The barbed-wire wound was healing, the skin pulled in pink around the new scar on her leg. Her braid was undone, and her long hair was back in a barrette. She wore a cotton batik dress and sandals.

"Wow, great field outfit," Annabel said.

Maud smiled. "I've decided I'm not going."

"No seed dispersal for you after all? Can you still switch at this point—what did Janice say?"

"No, I mean, I'm not going to do fieldwork. I can get a temporary job on my visa, so I'm going to collect tickets at the Wonderland and be with William and, well, try it out. I wanted to say thanks for the statistics help, and—"

"Not going?" Annabel almost wished she were wearing the dress, that she had a boyfriend and an untaxing job— but she couldn't imagine it for long. Her well of inquiry was still there, the need to know, to look deeply, that green leechy site, the bat camp—

"You know, I realized I'm not cut out for field science. I'm not disappointed. Actually, I'm kind of relieved. Some people can do it—" Maud raised her index finger toward Annabel and smiled. "And some people were meant for other work. Not that I know exactly what that is. But I do know I'm going to take a chance on William. It's not often a forty-year-old woman finds the *boy*friend of her dreams."

"Maud, God," said Annabel. "You are brave."

"Me? You're the snake girl. Anyway, thanks for every-thing." She held out her palm, bearing small silver earrings with pale green stones. "Adventurine," she said. "Reminds me of you. Come visit me if you're around."

"Oh," said Annabel. Pleasure spread wings in her chest. "Thank you. Are you sure you—no, pretend I didn't say that."

"Good on yer." Maud pronounced the Aussie expression slowly. "You're going today?"

"As soon as I finish my laundry. Did you hear Professor Goode's still not back?"

"I did, it's odd. But then, he's not exactly predictable." She touched her scar, making an unconscious connection.

"I guess not. I'm going without him if he doesn't show up—he'll probably appear right in time for my grant money to run out." She sighed and embraced her friend; the soft hair spread across Maud's back like a kelp forest. She looks relieved, Annabel thought, beautifully relieved.

After Maud had gone, Annabel gave her E-mail one last look before her trip.

Sender: AEMendel@biosci.com (Alice Mendelssohn)
To: AMendelss@ausnet.jcooku.tvl.edu
Subject: RE: Huffing
Tuesday, March 5, 1996

Dear Annabel:

Puppy keeps us up at night, but she's adorable. Keeping my mind so numb I haven't had time to really process this promotion. They fired two people in the publications department who hardly took time off to breathe. There's a rumor about a woman who keeps notes on everyone. I'm too disgusted to relate it.

I want to name the pup Pavlov, and Kevin wants to
name her Comet. When I hear Comet I think of a can
of cleanser.

What's the deal with your professor? Has he come
back yet?

Love, your staggering sister, A.

Annabel wrote back,

Alice: PAVLOV, without a doubt. Why didn't we ever
have a puppy? Didn't you ever beg for one? Surely
Dad would've given in to you? I'm afraid Professor
Goode is missing. It's very odd, but I'm going
without him.

She typed in her Poste Restante address in Malanda and
tried not to let that familiar image fill her head—Robert,
underwater, his open eyes, empty face, Robert's body
when Robert was gone.

S e v e n

Sender: AEMendel@biosci.com (Alice Mendelssohn)
To: AMendelss@ausnet.jcooku.tvl.edu
Subject: me again
Friday, March 8, 1996

I hope you don't mind my writing about Robert.
I've been thinking about him, and I do talk about
it with Kev, but he'll never be able to understand
it viscerally, do you know what I mean? I'd never
tell him that, but it's true.

I have this bracelet from when Rob first went to
Africa, I think he sent you one, too. He told me
that he traded a T-shirt for a whole mess of them,
that he tried out his Swahili and asked the kids
he traded with where the beads came from, and they
said "the coast," and he asked where before that
and they said, "the boats," and he said but before
that, where did they come from before that, and
they said, "from God." Did he ever tell you that

story? I wonder, Anna, whether he believed in God.
I'm not sure I do myself.

Robert's with me right now, right under the surface, and I can't really feel him and he's all I
feel. I'm not sure what to do about it, except
write you.

There's more, too—the way he died—it's something
we should talk about, even though it's horrible.
Sometime, when you're home

Alice hit the delete key, twice, to be sure the message
was gone. She shut her office door and sagged back in her
chair. Headache. She touched her temples, which were
tender. Maybe she was getting a migraine. Robert had had
migraines. In college he took medicine—ergot—which he
said took him on a trip that made him forget more than
the headache.

He'd called her once while it was still affecting him and
said, "Alice, did you ever see objects melting, did you ever
notice that objects are no more solid, really, than liquid, if
you just slow them down in time?"

"Robert," she'd said, cradling the phone and wishing he
wouldn't call when he was like this—she'd be awake for
hours, wishing she could fly out to Stanford in time to
bring him down safely. It felt dangerous, the calls, the medicine, and the way it made him sound. And there was
nothing she could do over the phone, except to say,
"Never noticed. Robert, please stay in bed until objects
get solid, okay?"

Alice went to the bathroom and turned the tap to hot, running her hands under the water, trying to wake herself somehow with heat.

When Robert died, Kevin had known he needed to hold and listen to her, wait for her to be ready to talk about it. She'd landed on him like an island in the ocean of her family; they'd all been lost in surprise and grief. But Kevin had known Robert only a little, met him at the wedding, at a few family events. He didn't understand how her brother had connected the elements of Annabel, their mother, their father, and Alice couldn't explain, especially not *after*.

Alice, feeling lost in her own childhood house, stayed for a few days after the funeral; Kevin had gone back to school. Her mother returned to her practice, filling herself with other people's wellness and ills, but her father was like a ghost in the house. He sat at his desk, staring at the same issue of the *New England Journal of Medicine,* not even bothering to open it.

Alice was caught; she didn't know how to be alone with him. For her mother, wrapping food after dinner was a gesture of grief; she touched Alice whenever their bodies came in close proximity. But her father was dangerously quiet—he was cleanly academic, bloodless about the details, putting Robert's things into boxes in the attic, paying the funeral and cremation bills. Alice saw him weeping only once, sitting at his desk, holding a statement from the water company. His fingers were busy with the rhythm of his despair. Alice came into the study, stood behind him, wanting to touch those hands.

He turned to her, then wiped his face with a handkerchief. His face turned soft and plain and he nodded. "Time for lunch, Alice?" He'd closed the room of sorrow, without inviting her inside.

Dr. Mendelssohn was careful about everything when they were children. He'd made it clear at holidays and birthdays that the expense was the same for each child: if Alice's sixth birthday present was a bicycle, Robert's model rockets should cost the same when his sixth birthday came around. He calculated increases for inflation, doing the math in his head with his index finger extended. Graduation from age to age was treated equally in terms of allowances, chores, and privileges, though a few exceptions were made for Robert, because he was a boy and because he created exception where there was none. All was fair in portions of roast chicken served from the pink-and-white plate, where the gravy pooled and made rivulets, oxbow lakes.

That was how Alice thought of her father most of the time, the man with the meat fork and carving knife, measuring out equal servings for everyone he loved. He'd come to every graduation, every school play he could, and all the concerts. The Mendelssohn children were encouraged to be more than just scientists (the assumption being that that was what they'd be).

Had their father known anything really about their lives, she thought, he'd have given up pretending to be fair. He thought he was close to his children, but he never knew how much she'd wanted to give up the violin when Robert quit the piano, how much she'd wanted him to say it was okay to get that C+ in math in eighth grade, when her crush on her teacher had crippled her concentration for the entire year.

Dr. Mendelssohn had never known that Robert slept with both men and women, that for several years he'd experimented with drugs, looking for something that was invisible to the meek, he'd said. He'd called Alice in states of exhilaration, pain, and confusion. Alice had wondered about her brother's life then, about how much he despised himself. Of course everyone had some of that in them, she'd thought; she knew longing for death lay under the thin skin of youthful belief in immortality. But with Robert it was more immediate, as if his skin were transparent.

In his last two high school years, when Alice was in college in Michigan, Robert ran too hard on the edge of things. He was in two car accidents, one when he was drunk but, luckily, not driving; he visited prostitutes, and had written Alice a letter, full of elaborate remorse and a sort of challenge, daring her to hate him for it. Yet he'd always been a successful student, had always managed a dazzling veneer for Dad. And then he'd gone off to Stanford and, as he'd said, "found science." Alice had hoped he'd landed safely in the center of an island of belonging, that he'd found what he needed to keep himself alive.

Leon Goode was on stage with Stanley the twenty-pound boa wrapped around his body when they paged him about a phone call. He was in the middle of his "Snakes are gross and slimy and smelly, right?" spiel, to which the school group, third graders, would mostly yell, "Yeah!" with a few dissenting science fiends or snake lovers yelling, "Uh-uh!" Then he would say, "Well, I've got a secret: whoever said 'yeah,' has been *misinformed,* because snakes are really smooth and cool and nice to the touch. They have no sweat glands, you see, so snakes in the desert . . ." Before he reached this part, right after the resounding eight-year-old screams of affirmation, he heard his name on the loud-speaker.

He ignored the first three prompts. "Leon Goode, you have a phone call on line three, Leon Goode." He recognized the voice, the high-school girl with the green-grape bubble-gum breath and the ponytail on the crown of her head. She teased the tail out like a hair balloon.

"Do you think snakes sleep?"

The kids mumbled.

"Well, they do, just a few hours a night—or day—some sleep during the day—and they keep their eyes open." Leon tried to concentrate; he'd gotten distracted from his normal rap.

He continued, "Now, have any of you ever touched a snake?" A few loud "yeahs," but mostly a low "no" murmur and thirty little heads swaying no, too.

"Well, most of the time, it isn't a very good idea to touch snakes. They're usually busy doing their own stuff . . ."

"Leon Goode, line three, pick up line three." These kids hadn't listened when he'd introduced himself at the beginning of the talk. They didn't know he was being paged; to them it was part of the ambient background noise, the roar of conversations and squeals and sneakers rubbing the floor in passage.

"Um, if you see a snake in the wild—"

"Leon Goode." It was a different voice, now, one of the supervisors, probably. "Leon Goode, please pick up line three immediately. You have an urgent phone call."

"Um, just a minute, guys." The kids started to wiggle, ready to bolt—they knew they were about to get their opportunity to touch the snake.

"Um, hold on, guys."

Leon checked for Stanley's head; the snake was working his way under the microphone wire, poking between lab-coat buttons. Stanley hadn't been fed for two weeks, and tomorrow was rat day, so the boa was pretty active. After feeding, he would laze heavily, like a great wet-clay ser-pent, but today he was feisty. Leon backed away from the stage, felt the hot lights glide off him as he turned for the side door. "Just a minute, folks," he said again, in stage voice.

The phone was at the bottom of the backstage landing; Leon had to descend the steps while keeping his hand steady near Stanley's head. The boas were supposed to be in their cages or carrying cases at all times, except for demonstrations and shedding season, when Leon and the animal guy and the interns helped them shed in the class-room, peeling them like tangerines.

Stanley must've felt Leon sweating—he wrapped tighter. The backstage lights were off, and Leon almost fell at the bottom of the steps. "Bloody—" He gritted his teeth and picked up the phone. Punched at the buttons, hoping he would get the three correct ones. He thought he heard giggling in the audience. He wondered how long before the teacher complained to a guard or decided to gather the whole group and leave.

"Yeah, this is Leon Goode—I'm in the middle of a demo, what's so urgent?"

"Leon, hold on, um, just a minute," said Gum Girl. Two clicks. "Leon? Leon?" Still Gum Girl. "Wait, I have a call for you." A few more clicks.

"Leon? Christ, this damn phone."

"Andrew? Is that Drew?"

"Sorry to bother you at work, Lee, I was having trouble tracking you down." Andrew sounded like he was in the shower, or a rainstorm of polystyrene pellets.

"Drew, it's great to hear from you, but there's a hungry boa on my neck and a glob of kids waiting." Leon definitely heard kids laughing on the other side of the stage.

"Leon, it's Dad."

"Shit, what?" He pictured his dad covered with stinging ants, then his body distended with water, drowned. He wasn't a very good swimmer.

"He's okay. I mean, we don't know. Leon, he's been missing for almost two weeks."

"Missing?"

"I hate to ask, but Mum offered to pay for your ticket. Can you come home and help me look?"

"Um, yeah, um, where can I call you?"

"I'm home. I mean, with Mum."

"I'll call you back in a few hours. Let me make reservations. Is it okay to call late?"

"Yeah, use Mum's credit card, she says, to call, and to get the tickets."

"Is she looking, too?"

"No. I mean, he could be with some woman or something. But I'll tell you more later. Didn't you say you're wearing a snake?"

"Yeah. And—shit." Leon looked down. Stanley was unwrapping from him, curious, straining for the backstage bulletin board. Leon was sure he heard laughter. "Shit," he said again. "I've left the microphone on."

Part II

Eight

Three stops into the outskirts of Townsville, the bus to Malanda was empty except for Annabel and the driver, a small wrinkled woman with a face snapped shut like a purse. As they rounded the road curves into the thick green mountains, Annabel stretched out on a seat, looking at her *Tower Karst* book, trying to read the jumping letters of her research notes as the bus slammed her up and down against the vinyl.

I won't be much good if I'm sick before I even get to the bats, she thought, as the words blended into moving smudges. She gave up and looked out the window, where the forest was a blur. She remembered John Goode's eyes; he could be in that forest, or taking a quick trip to Magnetic Island, or Utah, or he could be back in Townsville—he could be anywhere. It was infuriating, that he could collect her need like that, offer to take her project on, and then disappear. She felt a new shoot of worry in her belly, but then she swallowed and was mad again.

Professor Goode had suggested she might try electronic tracking with her bats, and she'd balked at all the equipment, the expense. She trusted her eyes and notebooks. There was hardly enough time for the best kind of watching, without trying to learn all the gear, without taking her research out of the camp. Besides, she firmly believed it was best to study animal behavior without disrupting the animals. After all, how normal would she act if she were trapped by giant bats, stapled with a heavy piece of metal, and then released somewhere in the vicinity of her home?

On the other hand, some people could use electronic tracking tags themselves, she thought. The professor. He should wear one; then he'd be a flashing light instead of a great empty. Robert. Robert should have worn one. Even when he was present, parts of him had been missing. Annabel tried to imagine Robert sitting beside her, rummaging through her notes. He'd have on a T-shirt so worn it was softer than skin. His quick hands with bitten nails would fan her papers. Probably he'd tell her which ideas were wrong, which plans were inadequate. But he'd lost the right to guide her by dying.

Annabel fell asleep with her face pressed against the vinyl seat. She dreamed blank ocean dreams—speeding along the surface, diving into empty water.

She woke to the bus driver's parrotlike call, "Malanda, last stop Malanda, last stop Malanda." As if Annabel were one of many passengers.

She hauled her gear to the peeling white porch of the Malanda pub and stopped in for a quick soda—*lolly water,* the Aussies called it—before setting out on the three-kilometer hike, with her pack and box of supplies, to her site. The pub wore the pale perfume of old beer. Annabel walked across the clean tile floor, bought her soda, and had a brief chat with the woman behind the bar, whose head was large and pink, like a strange melon, her eyes watery, her scalp visible through thin white hair.

Mike Trimble had told Annabel that the bartender, Midge, was safe—that is, not an anti-environmentalist. The farmers were all right, but the loggers were suspicious of anyone with a backpack. Midge didn't mind greenies, but she wouldn't say so too loudly, Mike explained, since she wanted to keep her job.

Annabel watched Midge mopping the bar. She wanted to touch the white scalp, test it for heat, to comb through the silver strands.

"Here for a visit?" she asked Annabel, shrugging at the huge backpack.

"Yup, I really have to get to work on my—you know, I've got some stuff to do."

"Mate of mine said they're getting pretty tough on greenies up in Millaa Millaa, you know, up near those falls?"

"Pretty tough?"

"Just that the loggers don't like them, ya know, the usual harassment."

"Which is?"

Midge leaned in over the counter, and Annabel noticed that three of her four front teeth were the color of weak tea. "Oh, knocking down camps, a fire here and there, some warning shots."

"Nice. Don't tell them where I'm going, okay?" Annabel swirled the last few drops in her glass. She rubbed her forearm; it was sticky from resting against the bar.

"Love, you haven't told me, so I couldn't give you away."

"That sounds like a reasonable arrangement." Annabel smiled. She swung off the stool and picked up her pack.

"Good on yer," said Midge.

Annabel stopped and turned on her way out. "Oh, you haven't heard from Professor John Goode, have you, or seen him around?"

"Nah," said Midge. She was looking at the glass as she drew a beer from the tap. "What a spunk, though, eh?"

"Um, yeah, I guess?"

"Means he's a looker." Midge grinned her full brown smile.

"Ah, yes," said Annabel.

When she reached the edge of the woods by her site, there were pebbles in her shoes, and hot spots that would probably grow to blisters. A lizard assembled itself from road pebbles, darted over her toes, and was camouflaged again. She could smell the bats, a rich scent of mango and musk and guano, from the road. Zillie Falls, about a kilometer away, made a low background hum, millions of pounds of water daring gravity.

Annabel pushed her hair behind her ears. Lettucy hair, she thought, not red enough to be red, but not brown enough either, or ruly and shiny like Alice's. She unsheathed her machete and cut away at some young stinging trees that had sprung up where she'd made the narrow entry path.

"I . . . hate . . . waiting . . . ," she repeated as she slashed at the trees. Annabel-in-control, Annabel-at-the-helm. She wondered if other people knew how hard it was for her to be led; she let them, but wanted to have the map in her hands. She wanted to know where she was going.

The bats were making their usual din of screeches and yelps; it sounded like the warm-ups of an elementary-school orchestra, mixed with birdlike howls and human baby cries—wonderfully strange, hungry. She used the machete to hold back brush in her path and went in, watching the ground for snakes as she walked. Wait-a-while vines caught her clothes, and she picked and tugged them off. At the clearing, the bats were fidgeting and grooming; several stopped to watch her progress.

"Hi, bats," she said. "I'll try not to bother you." They looked at her, eyes circled by the gray fur spectacles, wary, but not visibly worried. Do bats worry, she wondered, do they mourn missing bats, the bats who die of age or accident? She'd read about elephants, scattering the skeletons of their dead.

Annabel set up her tent, put down her tarp, and lay on it, binoculars raised to watch the bats as they adjusted to her presence and watched back.

Professor Goode, gone missing, Annabel thought, looking up, watching one bat stray onto another's branch. The dominant bat hissed twice and the intruder backed off. Annabel marked her waterproof log: territorial, vocalization, hiss, not full call. Gone missing is not the same as being gone completely. He could be off taking soil samples, he could have lost track of the days somehow—how did one fall so completely out of time?

She remembered sitting on the island off the Great Barrier Reef with Professor Goode. She had just been making human contact, she told herself, she'd never meant to be playing the game of territory, or mating display. His face, backlit with his own emotions—she'd loved him at that minute, not been *in love,* but she'd loved him for telling her his secrets.

His eyes, brown and blue, like different climates, looking at her, telling her he was a horrible husband. And she'd wanted to kiss him, but it was something else—what exactly had there been between them? A magnetic pull to confide, a sense of urgency, and maybe trust. Maybe.

His quiet, when she'd told him about Robert. Wherever he was now, he knew Annabel had wondered about her brother's death. He'd taken her secret and gone missing himself, as if the hint of mystery were a suggestion.

It was a relief to be alone again; she felt like a chicken freed from a tiny, overcrowded yard. But after a few days, her pleasure with work was interrupted by worry. She wanted to talk with Alice—go back to town, call her maybe—but what could Alice know about Professor Goode? She'd probably have a neat and careful explanation; she'd decide that everything would be all right, and Annabel wasn't sure that was what she wanted to believe.

There was nothing left to do besides work and wait, eat chocolate in her tent at night, review her notes. Three days, five days. Then six days. She was rigorously observing bat behavior, using her chart and symbols for sleeping, grooming, eating, mating, with different notations for position, territorial squabbles, warning screeches when a shadow in the shape of a sea eagle passed overhead. The bats began to make sense to her, their behavior patterns forming shapes on her graph paper.

Each night, as she did her calculations, she drew pictures with her data—the order of the bats, their system, what kept them from falling from the trees and sky. Annabel went to bed when it was getting dark, rising at dawn to watch the bats arrive from their fruit-feeding nights. After the first few days, they'd stopped swiveling to watch her watching them; it was as if she had a one-way mirror now and, with her notes, a crude guidebook to their world.

Pteropus conspicillatus, spectacled flying foxes, used the giant ficus tree branches like rooms in a house: younger bats slept here, here was mating, over there to pee. Entire limbs had been stripped bare by bat feet, so they climbed easily across the branches, small horizontal steps, or big swings from foot to the hook at the tip of the wing-fold.

What amazed Annabel was how rarely they flew once they'd settled into the camp. If there was a territorial squabble, the less dominant bat might fly off in a flurry, the caws of discussion still loud from both participants. And if there was something to be alarmed about—once a sea eagle flew in over the canopy—Annabel saw it after the bats had started a flutter and ruckus, screaming, howling, and shaking the trees.

Mating was more embarrassing than she'd imagined. She was a scientist, this was science, but still she felt like a voyeur: it seemed so private. Sometimes they mated back to front, sometimes front to front, which she started to interpret as a sign of affection, since she'd read that back to front was a more successful posture for conception in bats. So there must be pleasure or affection involved, unless this was an evolutionary appendix. And when they finished, sometimes the male bat wrapped the female in his wings.

G w e n d o l e n   G r o s s

They slept like this, and Annabel noted it in her water-proof log and tried not to think about men.

Their trees were like apartment buildings, their families ordered according to age and strength. The fights, about territory or mating, resulted in a social arrangement as elaborate as any city neighborhood's. And, as they settled to sleep in pairs or alone, they seemed far more comprehensible to Annabel than people.

She enjoyed being alone, most of the time. As the sun slipped below the cracks in the bottom of the trees, the bats woke their sleepers, they careered around the branches like parents packing for vacation. Waking, grooming, chattering. They peed, swinging on their wing-hooks from upside down to right side up so the stream would pass directly down to the forest floor. And then, like a living cloud with many voices, they took off to feed. It was such an argument of motion, the mobilization from trees to air, the sheer croaking singing wall of bat sound, that when they were gone Annabel felt deflated, and hugely peaceful. For a while the other sounds of the forest were inaudible to her. She lay on her tarp, looking up at the empty tree branches, feeling intensely human and alone.

She woke in a sudden panic about leeches. She'd seen Professor Goode covered with them, in her dream, and her body stung with imaginary holes. She felt the itch of anti-coagulant, the blood rivulets. She turned on her flashlight to examine herself, to look around—the tent, a few mosquitoes casting giant shadows, the small hump of her notebook in the corner, her battered but unbloodied legs. She rubbed her scalp, checking there, and her eyes, and inside and behind her ears. She looked at her watch: four A.M. In a few hours she could get up again to look around the site; she'd watch the bats arrive and settle into camp. She'd be full of purpose and surrounded by a society. She'd watch and record; there had to be something true there, something easier to estimate and examine than the inexplicable motivations of people.

Leon had a six-hour wait in the Honolulu airport: short enough that he couldn't safely catch a gypsy cab out to the beach or to get some barbecue and some air, long enough to feel like torture. When he arrived, it was midnight, local time, and he had started to feel unpredictable surges of nervous energy. There was such a strange urgency to this trip, and he wondered if there was any emergency, or whether his family had invented something from nothing. He sat down on a concrete bench in the open-air hallway to the terminals. Every ten minutes there was a hot wave of jet-fuel stench, but otherwise the air had a fruity flower smell.

What was he supposed to feel? When he'd called for the tickets, he'd said, "Bit of a family emergency," as a reflex, to the agent.

"If it's a funeral, you'll need a copy of the death certificate for the special fare," said the agent.

"Oh, no," said Leon.

"Those are the rules," said the agent.

No discount without death in writing, Leon thought. His dad hadn't given enough advance warning—he'd even picked an ambivalent form of crisis to impose. Dad could be anywhere: he could be waylaid in a hotel with some woman; he could be staring at a road-cut with fascinating striations. He was always distractible.

Once he'd missed a choir concert Leon was in, and Leon had missed it, too, because there was a great swimming hole only five kilometers off the directions to the school where Leon's choir was meant to be singing. Even at thirteen, Leon was anxious about his father's diversions, but thrilled. He'd been nervous about the concert anyway; his voice was starting to crack, and he didn't always match his alto section anymore. The director was impatient, flinging his baton on the floor when the choir was rowdy or incapable of the desired pianissimo. The baton tip broke off once, struck a girl's knee like a dart. So when Dad turned off from the directions, Leon knew there was a possibility of missing warm-ups. Then, when they parked in a dirt lot behind an Aborigine reservation, he knew he might not be there for the first set. Mum was meeting them there; Mum would notice there was no Leon in the alto section. But after about a kilometer's walk through scrub woods and then a muddy track—Leon was carrying his dress shoes over his head by then, thinking maybe they'd still be needed—there was a wide fast river, with white-water slides and clear eddies. His father stripped to his underwear and so did Leon, sighing. There was going to be fun, swimming. There was also going to be another family *discussion* when they arrived back home.

At the Kingsford Smith airport, Sydney at last, Leon stopped being tired. He was alive with energy as he waited for his luggage so he could get through customs, alert as a hunting cat. A set of golf clubs passed, matching leather trunks with gold-tone rivets. A battered cardboard box with an address and HI, JOHN! drawn in purple crayon on the side. His father could be arriving in Sydney at the same time, on the same plane, Leon thought. He ought to watch for the familiar sagging suitcase, listen over the din of motors and mumbles for his father's thick chuckle. Then his duffel bag spun around on the belt, one strap more torn than it used to be, and Leon heaved it onto a cart and wheeled through customs.

"Welcome home, mate," said the official, pounding a stamp onto his passport.

"Thanks." Leon looked at the man. He had a brown birthmark the size of a quarter right by his lip. He was already opening his mouth to greet the next citizen.

In the arrivals lounge, Leon scanned for his brother. Somehow he'd expected sirens, an urgent parade of investigators, papers to sign. He'd expected to do something. Instead he was hugged by his mum. She smelled of vanilla, and she held on for a while.

"My boy," she said, leaning out of the squeeze to look at his face. "You look exhausted."

"Where's Drew?" He didn't mean to sound thankless, but he'd expected his brother, the cavalry. He'd expected to saddle up, and here his mum's vanilla scent made him want to sleep instead.

"Drew drove up to the beach for the day—Warriewood. He went shopping first—"

He shouldn't ask whether the beach was part of the search. It wasn't right to ask his mother about it, he thought. He pictured Dad with Lila Wallard at the beach, carrying water up from the ocean to splash on her as she lay, bony and giant-handed, on a big blue towel. A towel Mum had picked out at a department store before a family vacation. Lila Wallard starring in *Breaking Away,* Lila's husband cleaning Lizzie's teeth.

Leon leaned against his mum as they walked down halls and across the road to short-term parking. He fell asleep in the car and dreamed of blue-bottle jellyfish, squishing and stinging beneath his feet.

Nine

The package arrived before the funeral, when Alice was at her parents' house. Packed up by Robert's assistant, it included holey T-shirts, worn almost translucent, a small spiral notebook full of notes in a private shorthand and equations, two beautifully carved, clean hashish pipes, a pair of pants with pebbles in the pocket.

Alice had taken the notebook. Her father sat in his chair, pretending not to watch as Alice and her mother touched the things. Her mother was crying quietly. Alice took the notebook and looked at it that night, in her old attic room. A sun-bleached red cover, the spiral bent out of shape by fiddling fingers. After the notes, water-blistered and stained with a salty green, there were blank pages. Then, between the blank pages, there was a postcard from Grand Cayman, a blue blur of coastline and palm trees. The card was addressed to her, and in the message square Robert had written, "Don't worry about me, Alice. I know exactly what I'm doing." Robert's handwriting slanting slightly to the left. Alice touched the words, smeary ballpoint.

He wouldn't make a mistake with his tank; he had to have died on purpose. He had been studying the flashlight fish, an animal with pouches of light-emitting bacteria living under each eye. His assistant had said it was a routine evening dive, that Robert had signaled for her to go up a half hour before, that he did that all the time and stayed down by himself, following the zigs and zags of the fish, who turned their lights on and off to elude predators. He hadn't come up for a half hour, then another ten minutes, and then she'd tried all their signals, because he'd start to run out of oxygen in another twenty minutes.

When they brought him up, the tank was empty.

Alice sat on the narrow bed with the notebook shut. Maybe he'd taken too much medication, maybe he'd sabotaged his own tank. *Alice, did you ever see objects melting, did you ever notice that objects are no more solid, really, than liquid?*

She'd wondered why her parents hadn't asked more questions, why they hadn't insisted on an autopsy, why they seemed numb and sad but almost unsurprised.

Because they knew, too, they knew Robert was susceptible to accidents, but that this wasn't one of them.

Sometimes she thought about showing the postcard to her mother, or to Annabel. She'd left it in the drawer of her nightstand at her parents' house, so she wouldn't turn to it night after night, two small sentences like accusations. But it was as if Alice and her parents had a pact not to tell each other too much, not to talk about what each must know. And Annabel, who probably wouldn't believe it if she was told, Annabel was somehow too young, and even though she knew it was a lie, Alice let herself think that not telling her was a kind of protection.

The road seemed dustier after a week in the rain forest. Annabel had washed in the falls before she started toward town; she'd felt clean, but after less than a kilometer she was thinly coated with silt and sweat. Two cows in a field leaned their heads together, brown gossiping with black. A school bus passed, kids staring out the windows in pairs. Best friends. Second best. Sworn enemies. She had almost forgotten how people moved among each other.

She needed to get batteries for her head lamp in Malanda. She needed to refill the propane canister for her stove and get dental floss, she needed to throw out a bag of waste, and she supposed she ought to call Townsville again, to ask around town for any word of Professor Goode.

A blue pickup headed in the opposite direction stopped as she walked down the road, dust flowing over both truck and Annabel like water. The window came down and Mike Trimble grinned out at her. Sabrina was in the other seat, clean and groomed. She was wearing lipstick.

"Greetings, bush woman," said Mike, sticking out his hand.

Annabel looked at his hand for a second, then put down her trash bag and shook it. "And to you, oh captain of civilization. What brings you to my wilderness?" Sabrina waved meekly, then picked at a spot on her jeans.

"Sabrina's still tracking down a platypus," said Mike. "Have you got a platypus?"

"No. Have you got a Professor Goode?"

Mike stopped grinning. "God, I haven't heard any-thing—I honestly thought he'd have shown up by now." He turned to Sabrina. "Did you hear anything at the uni?"

"Once someone said there was a message from him, but I think it was from one of his sons," said Sabrina. She took a few seconds, still picking, then looked up from her lap. "Everyone was sure he'd come to you first, Annabel."

"Not a word. All I've seen is bats."

"We're headed toward Millstream, and I'm supposed to be back in Townsville by tomorrow to teach." Mike shrugged. "Or I'd offer you a lift. Maybe on my way back through town."

"That's all right," said Annabel. The weight of waiting for the professor sunk further in her throat. "I like walking, except for the dust. Hey, this isn't a company van." She tapped the truck.

"Mine," said Mike. He looked as pleased as a kid with a new bike.

Annabel leaned her head in the window to address Sabrina. "Well, good luck with platypuses."

Mike touched her shoulder. "You keep going with those bats. If John doesn't show up soon I'll get up to give you approval. Though you're starting to look rather batlike, so I'm sure you're all right."

"Gee, thanks."

Annabel stepped back as the truck pulled out. She hoped Sabrina would find some platypuses; at that moment, she hoped Sabrina would learn a secret language, would lose herself in watching. It could happen to anyone who let themselves go, and even Sabrina deserved that wondrous, intense pleasure.

In town, she sat in the pub again, waiting for Midge to come in for her shift. Annabel ordered a chook sandwich: oily chicken, a hot-dog bun, a scrap of lettuce, and too much mayonnaise. She sat on the bar stool chewing. It was delicious, and she thought she ought to bring something interesting to eat back to her site; noodles and powdered soups were getting dull. She should get some fruit, she decided, if she could get a ride back from town.

Midge appeared behind the bar, interrupting Annabel's food reverie.

"There's a message for you, love."

"A secret coded message with colors and numbers, or something from Professor Goode the Absent?"

"Sorry, didn't take the call, just brought it from the post office, so I haven't had time to decode it and broadcast results to the movement."

Annabel looked at Midge's watery eyes, surprised by the tone of the joke.

She unfolded the paper. It read, *Doctor Janice says she'll be by your site next week. Meet at pub Wednesday.* "Wednesday when?" she said aloud.

"Did your mate show up?"

"Uh-uh, no sign. Someone else is coming to see me, though, the greenest of the greenies. But at least she'll approve my project. That is, I hope she will."

Midge drew a beer for herself and sucked the foam off the top. "Have one?" she asked.

"No, thanks. Must get back to my bats." She wadded the message in her hand. Doctor Janice, like the long arm of the law. Annabel imagined sweeping her site paths and dusting the vines. Janice might swipe a finger on her tent, come up with grime, unacceptable.

Back at her site, she was out of powdered potato again, and her three unused rolls of film had molded in spite of the silicate packets. She tried to scrape off the mold, but it grew back again even as she pulled her knife across it. There was a similar mold on her water jug, and a pastel blue one at the corner of her tarp that sprang up like carpeting. She scrubbed with leaves, then she soaked the tarp in rubbing alcohol from her first-aid kit, but though the flattened out and seemed to dissolve, it rallied in the night and sprang back, blue shag.

Her bats were spending more and more time mating. There was still grooming, sleeping, and arguing over who ruled the tree branch, but the mating line on Annabel's graph had gradually taken the lead over the other activities. More sleep, also, than before. All that love tires a bat out, she thought.

At first, she'd talked to herself all the time. She had to make notes on her chart to remind herself not to disturb the bats. After a while, she wasn't sure whether she'd said what she thought out loud or in her head, so it became harder to regulate herself. But the bats seemed to get used to her, and then to ignore her almost entirely.

Annabel started to know some of them, too, learning their distinguishing features and territories—markings, shapes, voices, even their eyes were slightly different in shape or size. She named one pair: a large male with a broken spot in the gray fur that made the spectacles around his eyes became Tristan; the female with whom Tristan mated and groomed and, in the downpours, wrapped, was Isolde. Annabel used the couple as her starting point when she recorded behavior. Tristan and Isolde dominated one branch, but they didn't have to defend their space—the other bats rarely challenged them, leaving a little extra distance between their roost and common space. She guessed from their size and fur color that they were older. Isolde had flecks of gray on her black belly. They looked gentle to her, a loving couple—when she was thinking of them at night, she couldn't help personifying, wondering what they'd say to her if they could speak. But during the day she tried not to let emotion cloud her work.

When the bat camp made its operatic departure in the evenings, Annabel noticed how alone she was. During the day, she was almost part of the colony, even if they were swinging around on wing-hooks and she was taking notes.

On Tuesday evening, the night before she had to go into town to meet Janice Martin, Annabel tried to follow her bats after they took off. They didn't all take the same direction, but there was some consensus. Tristan and Isolde flew off with their wings close, as if they were strung together. They called to each other, to the group, as they became hovering pin dots in Annabel's vision. The rain-forest floor route was far too slow; she'd never keep up with winged mammals, but she followed her impulse—after they screamed and fluttered their way out of camp, she kept trekking through the forest.

Annabel had her compass, and her machete, and she had walked out of her known territory. She could hear the river, but she couldn't hear the bats. She sliced through stinging trees and tugged through vines until she could see the water. There was a thick vine hanging in a U, a perfect bench-swing from which to watch the sunset. The orange sky was quickly growing dark.

An early-waking sugar glider leapt from a tree, spreading the membranes between its fingers and toes and gliding about twenty meters to swoop and land on a patchy eucalypt trunk. Another glider joined it and they chattered over the sap spot. Annabel swung her boots out in front of her, bits of torn green wrapped around them. A leech strained upward around the ankle. She was no longer startled by them; they were predictable. She let the leech climb onto her finger, then flicked it off, hard, with her other hand. "Into the river with you," she said.

The shadows of branches and stones in the river made her think of Professor Goode, his floundering in the river at 40-Mile Scrub. "That shadow is not a body." She said it to herself, to the river, to the leech she'd sent flying.

She refused to believe it had been on purpose. Dying was easy, and Robert wasn't looking for the easy way through anything; if there was a more strenuous route, he'd take it. Alice acted like it was a secret, painting tiny dark dots of suggestion in her messages. Of course Annabel knew what they thought—her sister, her mother, and maybe her father, too. But they didn't have to discuss it, or hide it from her; she didn't agree.

She pushed the rope swing forward again, watching the river make its slow motion, infinitesimal grinding away at the shores, silt shifting grain by grain. Annabel wished she had a drink, some alcohol to numb the evenings without her bats. She imagined Maud, sipping wine with her William, full of the normal events of a day outside the field—a day in the world of people's petty interactions. She touched the green earrings in her lobes and wondered what it was like to give up, what it would be like to be *able* to give up.

She pulled a leaf from her vine bench and tossed it toward the river. It wasn't shaped for flying; it dove and lifted in a wave pattern and fell a few feet away. It was almost dark, and Annabel had only a tiny pocket flashlight; her head lamp was still in the tent. She began walking back the way she came. Since she knew where the river was, she'd be all right. The river is west, she thought, all I have to do is go east and a little north, and I'll find my site. Nothing to be nervous about, she told herself, then wondered why she was nervous.

No one would hear her if she yelled. It was comforting, and it was terrifying. It had been that way the whole time she was here, but suddenly it seemed more important, as if she'd just realized she was naked. Naked, inaudible, and lost. It would be embarrassing to die lost at your own research site.

A stinging tree struck the side of her face, the tiny bristles penetrating her cheek. Soon it would start to sting and burn, but it was only a small patch. Maybe Professor Goode had gone into the rain forest alone, like she had, maybe he'd fallen in stinging trees, maybe he'd been swimming, and walking around barefoot in his careless way, and now his body was coated with sting. Maybe he'd gone into shock; maybe he was lost somewhere. Or could he have gone after a woman—his wife, or his affair? It seemed unlikely. The John Goode she knew was too distracted by the details of the world, the science, to go after humans, to try to fix anything, even if it mattered to him. But how well could she know him?

Annabel used her machete to hold back the trees, and picked up a stick to sweep the ground for snakes. It was much harder without her neat little path at her research grounds. It was much harder at night. Not lost, she thought; then: lost? Probably it was still light outside the forest, but among the trees, she was in a pocket of darkness.

The animals didn't care. In fact, they were busy changing shifts—diurnal to nocturnal. Some spiders were sleeping, some would be getting up to spin traps for insects and birds. The assassin spider would emerge and start her new nightly web. All the forest rats would shuffle out now, night workers punching time cards. Annabel stopped for a second to listen, but all she heard was birds and wind. The kookaburras that woke her in the morning were finishing off a good sunset laugh. Laughing at her, maybe; silly woman, thought she was a field scientist. She could hear her own heart beating.

Annabel smelled the gingery trumpet flowers and heard a quick, light hoot. An owl, quite like a New Jersey woods owl, only it looked different and ate rain-forest rats and infant snakes. Annabel felt a surge of confidence and energy. If she held up her penlight at the right time, she might see a green possum, a tree kangaroo. She stood on a log and swept the ground with her stick.

"No snakes here," she sang.

Then she tripped slightly and grabbed at a vine. The

vine was thick and muscular. The vine tugged against her hand. Annabel held on for another second, thinking maybe she ought to scream. Then she let go and fumbled for her penlight. The birds were silent, and she could see it in the flash of her tiny lamp: an amethystine python, maybe ten or fifteen feet long, who had not wanted to be grabbed by a careless field scientist, but had wanted to ascend the tree unmolested. Fool's dapples, the pattern on its back, approximate black diamonds on brown. She wasn't scared, though her body flushed with adrenaline—maybe she wasn't communicating very well with her body. Instead, she was thrilled by how beautiful it was—the snake, who moved up the tree now, like water poured upward.

After the snake, Annabel felt a miraculous confidence, a powerful sense of direction. She would get back to her site as surely as if she knew where she was going, as if there were marker flags and it was daylight. Her hands were still slick from the encounter. The remnants of light had drained from the spaces between the leaves, green had faded into the gray of the world after sunset. The machete was perfect for holding back branches and vines, and Annabel dropped her snake stick. The snakes on the ground were worse than the ones in the trees, venomous instead of constrictors, but she firmly believed she wouldn't step on one. When she saw the first orange tape and her hunch of tent in the small clearing, the confidence drained and left her wobbly.

Annabel didn't bother to cook dinner but sat inside her humid tent, eating muesli, wrapped in her sleeping bag, wasting battery power to keep the inside lit up green to ward off the demons of experience and irrational fears.

The python wasn't interested in her; it wouldn't come after her like the villain in some horror movie.

Tonight she'd stop thinking about her brother, even Professor Goode. Instead of focusing on the dead and the missing, she wanted to think about the things and the people she could reach. She opened a notebook and started a letter to Alice.

March 19, 1996
Dear Alice,

Tonight I got lost in the rain forest and grabbed a snake. It wasn't a venomous one, only a constrictor, and it didn't strike. In fact, I never even saw its head, but it gave me an unexpected sense of death. Alice, I think it can't be as bad as we think, that is, I think it must always be a surprise.

Probably the fact is nothing like the anticipation. I don't think Robert looked for death, I believe it was as unexpected as a vine that becomes a snake. I know you suspect otherwise, you've been hinting at it in your quiet way, instead of just telling me what you think. Sometimes you're so much like Dad, hoarding secrets like strange bitter candy.

You and I, Alice, we have to stop worrying about what it was like for him, we have to get past this. I wish we could just say it and be done. It was an accident. It must have been.

Alice, tonight I want to talk with you, feed you some of this muesli, sit on your couch, stay in your house with the warm running water, with the food smells, tomato sauce, garlic sautéing, apples softening as they bake, and the noises you make, you and Kevin, shuffling through drawers for the right kind of spatula.

I know I'm never going to send this letter.

She didn't rip up the page; there was nowhere to put it except her carry-out garbage bag. Annabel closed the notebook and curled around the knob of root that pushed up from beneath her tent floor. She went to sleep with the flashlight on, defining the walls of her green nylon bedroom beneath the vines and trees and the empty bat camp.

T e n

Too much light, Leon thought as he woke. Too much light and someone's poking me. He pulled the cotton blanket over his head. A familiar smell, pale vanilla, and his mother's detergent. He was home and he was sleeping and if someone was poking him, it must be his brother. If he didn't open his eyes, he wouldn't have to remember who he was.

"Lazy bag," Andrew whispered in his nose.

"That's my nose, you bugger." His own voice. There was no denying it, it was home and he was Leon. Then he remembered the rest: his father was missing. He pulled off the blanket; the light blasted his eyes. Leon felt as raw as a de-shelled snail.

"So, what do we have on Dad?" He squinted, holding up his hands as blinders.

"Fine greeting that is," said Andrew, sitting down on the bed and poking Leon's shoulder, his stomach.

"Stop poking." Leon sat up and grabbed his brother. He was too slow to really wrestle, but this is what they did, they tugged at each other, this was their ritual of recognition.

Leon leafed through the local paper and sucked down Andrew's viscous coffee. His brother knew about the affair—he'd found out from their mother. But Leon had details, and he wondered if they ought to start looking for Dad by contacting Lila Wallard. Lila and Lizzie, forever linked in his memory by the theater. He wouldn't call Lizzie while he was home—he was here for his father. Leon felt like he ought to get out a file folder, gloves, netting, a clipboard, binoculars.

"If you must know," said Andrew. "I went to his office. Found three things."

"Oh." Leon put down the paper. "That *is* why I'm here, so yes, what were they?"

"I thought you might need a dose of good Sydney sun first, paleface," said Andrew. "His wall calendar, the one with the moon rocks on it? Well, there was something written on Wednesday two weeks ago—it said 'The Gorge.' Though I wouldn't make too much of it, since the only other things on the month were Mum's birthday and 'change oil.'"

"Okay. So what else did you find?"

"A scrap of paper that said 'Annabel Mendelssohn, Cathedral Fig,' and a photograph of someone who looks an awful lot like Dr.—you know, the dentist's wife—Dr. Wallard. She's wearing a dress with such a low-cut neck you'd think there was something to look at—"

"Shit. I never told you it was Lila Wallard, I guess."

"So that *is* her. God, I can't believe he'd cheat on Mum with that stick insect."

"Drew—"

"No, he's an asshole. I'm not sure why we're bothering to look for the bastard. He's probably cheating on Lila Wallard with this Annabel Mendelssohn at the Cathedral Fig Hotel or something."

"I think he took us to Cathedral Fig once—a park with those big strangler trees—it's in the Tablelands or something. Queensland. Big buttress roots."

"Lila Wallard has big buttress roots."

"Come off it, Drew, we're going to have to look for him somehow."

"I don't know. I don't know if I want to. And how did you know about Lila?"

"Saw them in a movie theater together."

"What were they doing?"

"Drew, I don't know if we should keep on—"

Andrew stood up from the table. He was so tall, Leon thought, he's been growing again while I was away. "I want to know all of it, Leon," he said. "I want to know everything our father's been up to, so I can decide whether it's worth looking for him at all."

"Okay, okay. They were just necking, and that's all I saw, Drew."

"So I guess we ought to call Lila Wallard."

"Okay, how about we make a list."

"This isn't a shopping expedition."

"Yeah, but let's do it anyway. Lila Wallard, Annabel Mendelssohn, Cathedral Fig. Can we borrow a car?"

"I've got a car. Mum gave me hers when she bought the new one."

Leon's mum made pork chops and applesauce. He cut his meat small and ate it fast, not wanting to say he'd stopped eating red meat. It tasted wonderful, but he tried not to notice. Cucumber salad.

"Grew the cukes," said his mum. "Great garden this year."

Usually the garden was Dad's domain. There'd been experiments with corn kernels dipped in tar to keep away crows. The corn didn't germinate, and the garden reeked of tar all summer. And Dad tried grafting, which hadn't quite killed the apricot tree, and cross-breeding lettuces. The harvests had been spare and bitter, but interesting.

"Mum, I don't want to talk about this much, because I know you probably don't want to hear—"

"Leon," his mother interrupted. She chewed her salad carefully, sipped her wine, then continued. "I paid for you to come home, and I'm going to pretend you're here to visit. Please do whatever you think you ought to, but I can't promise to help you look for him. I think I ought not to look for him. That is, your father always made me wait, always made me search. I can't do that right now, and I don't want you two to have to go crazy looking, either. But you can't help being his sons, and you shouldn't—" She looked weepy. She hardly ever cried, and when she did, she tried to keep it hidden from them. "Leon," she said, her face on the edge of crumpling. "I'm glad you're home."

"Hey." Drew laughed quick and hard. "What about me?"

"You eat too much," said their mother. And she leaned across the cucumbers and kissed Andrew's cheek.

.　　　.　　　.

After tea Andrew went out again, destination unan-
nounced, but a female friend referenced. Leon felt the
distance he'd enforced by moving away—a tug more
sentimental now, when he was home, than when he was in
Boston. He didn't know what Drew was reading, who he
was dating; he hadn't even known he'd inherited the car.

Mum said she was going to bed, and Leon sat in the living room as alert as if it were morning. He pulled the atlas
from the shelf and traced a route from Townsville to
Cathedral Fig, in the Atherton Tablelands. Drew had written down the number for the office of the field-studies
program at James Cook where Dad was teaching. "Dad
Siting Central," he'd written next to the number. "They've
seen him latest," he'd said.

Leon pulled a slip of paper off the notepad by the
phone. He wasn't sure what he was going to ask, but
wrote "When last seen? Appointments? Who is Annabel
Mendelssohn? Lila Wallard?" on the paper.

Even if Drew wasn't going to stick around, he was going
to call. Leon lifted the receiver to dial and heard his
mother's voice. He started to hang the phone up again, but
then he held on, listening.

"I didn't want to call you," she said. "It's really for my
sons, they are rightfully worried. I'm not asking you to tell
me too much—I don't want to know too much—I just
wonder if you know where he is, whether he's safe—"

"I'm sorry, Mrs. Goode," said a familiar voice. It was high,
slightly nasal. "He and I are not—that is, I'm back with
my husband, and John, well, he said he had to be faithful
to you—"

"Faithful?" He could hear his mother growing fierce. Her voice became quiet and pointed. "I don't want to know about that." Each word was like a period, full stop.

"No, then, I'm sorry. I haven't seen him in months. I have no idea where he is."

Lila Wallard, Leon realized. The other voice was Lila Wallard. He eased the receiver back onto the phone, pressing the button first so hopefully the women wouldn't notice. He crossed Lila Wallard off the list.

Leon faded in and out of sleep, tangled up in jet lag and the few thread ends of possibility about his father. Andrew wasn't looking, he was mulling, he was encapsulated in his own world; Leon would have to be the director. He fell into a brief, hard sleep, dreamed that Ursula was trapped beneath the floorboards of the house, that he had to pry off the right one to find her. He woke, sheets strangling his legs and damp with sweat. Three-thirty. Leon reached over to the table by the bed and touched the only evidence he had: the list with that name, Annabel Mendelssohn. He traced the letters by the light of the digital clock and then tried not to search for anything other than sleep.

On Wednesday at noon, Janice Martin was not in the pub in Malanda. Annabel, who had walked hard and fast to get there, was inspecting her blisters on the front step, trying not to be annoyed. She hated waiting, and she felt the anticipation of Professor Goode again, a flood of frustration she'd forced back and then stopped noticing while she concentrated on her bats. And the free-fall sensation from the night before, when she'd grabbed the snake, still filled her with a mild adrenaline. Thrill and fear diluted only by her heart's continuing since then—she was alert and exhausted, she was ready for a fight.

Annabel put her sneakers back on and walked into the pub. Pretty busy for noon, she noticed; almost all the bar stools were occupied, and there was a game of darts in progress in the corner. She noted the swivel of eyes to the door as she walked in; she was tempted to yell "Yes, I'm a greenie!" Instead, she walked to the bar, aware of the squeal of her sneakers on the tile.

The man behind the bar had a melanoma scar on the side of his face, a stitching-in like he'd been patched, the thread pulled too hard.

"What can I get you?" He looked down, at Annabel's throat.

"No Midge today, eh?"

"She's gone to Sydney." The man's eyes shifted up to her face. Maybe because she knew Midge, she thought. "Family business. Friend of hers?"

"She's the best," said Annabel. I don't really know her, she thought, but she is the best friend I have in town. Annabel realized she was the only woman in the bar, that the eyes were still on her, quick glints. She knew she looked suspicious, though she hadn't seen any more than half her face in a hand mirror for so long she didn't know just how bad it was. Probably she had twigs in her hair, dirt smudges on her face, and she guessed she smelled of bat, despite a quick wash with a dirty bandanna in the river that morning.

I'm growing dull to human signals, she thought. "I'd like some Milo," she said. "Do you have any Milo?" When she'd first drunk it, it had tasted fake, but she'd grown to like the drink.

The bartender winced. "You'll be wanting the *milk bar* for that, miss," he said.

Annabel knew there was a can of Milo behind the empty lemon-slice bowl. She'd watched Midge make it for herself, but she didn't say anything. She swung around on the bar stool and watched the darts game, feeling unwelcome. Maybe Robert felt like this when he left his diving and deep-ocean vehicles for the outside world. The inside, really. Stingy with words, closing up, squirt, like a clam when the flippers of other people brushed.

Annabel refused two offers of beer and finally took the third, because it was almost one o'clock and she thought she was pushing her luck by keeping a seat without ordering a drink. The bar was air-conditioned, though; sweet cool was worth the risk.

At two-thirty, Janice Martin pushed open the door to the bar like a gunslinger and yelped, "Sorry, cracked windscreen!"

Someone missed the board completely at darts and swore. Annabel slipped from her stool and led Janice back out the door. Her legs were cold from the air-conditioning now; she was through sitting and waiting.

"Can I get you a drink?" asked Janice.

"No, let's get going."

Janice was a few steps behind her, then half a dozen steps. Annabel thought the van would be right outside, but it wasn't.

"We'll have to walk to the petrol station." Janice's voice sounded abrasive. "They're making sure the new windscreen's set. So there's no hurry."

Annabel turned around and looked. Janice was pink-faced but calm. She was probably only five or six years older than Annabel, and she was a single woman, a scientist. Annabel wondered if she'd been sleeping with Mike Trimble, what kind of romance the two of them had. She was still peeved for having to wait so long.

"How long do you think?" asked Annabel.

"Let me buy you some chocolate or something at least." Janice didn't sound generous somehow; she sounded demanding.

Annabel sighed. "Okay."

Two hours later, Annabel was in the passenger seat of the van, looking down at the road of her regular trek and thinking how short it was, riding instead of on foot. There was an electrical energy in the car, a crackle of not having much to say.

"Still nothing about Professor Goode?"

"We've been in touch with the family," said Janice. "And Dr. Sutherland—you know, the program director—will be in touch with the police about it soon."

"Police."

"It's been weeks, Annabel. That's a bit late even for John."

They parked in a muddy spot by the entrance to Annabel's site, and Janice stuffed her backpack with a notebook, potatoes, a box of tomato puree, peppers, and oatmeal. She pulled a sleeping bag from the back of the van.

"Sleepover?" asked Annabel. She'd thought this would be a quick inspection, that she'd be alone again in a matter of hours. The sleeping bag made her anxious. "My tent's pretty small."

"It's getting late, so, sorry, you're stuck with me for the night." There was no question in her voice. "And besides, I thought I'd take you on a little field trip tomorrow, and then back to Townsville if your project can stand a few days' rest. You can come back again with Mike—"

"Field trip?" Annabel heard her own voice, edged with suspicion. "Are we off to search for Professor Goode?"

"Not exactly." Janice heaved her backpack on, tucked the sleeping bag under her arm, and walked into the woods.

My path, thought Annabel. She's leading me down my own path. And where does she get off being so elusive about taking me somewhere? I'm not a five-year-old who wants a secret surprise.

Janice wrote a lot. She scribbled in her notebook at dusk while Annabel watched her bats lift off for foraging, relieved to see Tristan and Isolde at the front of the pack. Janice stopped stirring the stew to jot something down. The stew smelled awfully good. Annabel was impressed by fresh vegetables and Janice's quick inventiveness. But when she said so, Janice murmured, "Mm-hm," and kept writing.

The flashlight on Janice's side of the cramped tent stayed on after Annabel had said good night, twice. It was like having an adolescent child, Annabel thought, so secretive. Noisy presence, but retreated into the privacy of her own berth. She wanted to ask what Janice was writing, but felt that would be giving in somehow. It couldn't all be about her project, could it? It couldn't all be this supposedly straightforward approval procedure—after all, Annabel thought, her notes were thorough, her site measurements and markings all according to standard form. Maybe it wasn't about her, maybe Janice was writing about Mike. Or her secret life: maybe she had children living on Tasmania or maybe she wrote poetry. Annabel had watched her undress, the method of a woman used to hiding herself: Janice pulled her bra out from inside her shirt, slipped into her sleeping bag, and slid out her jeans. She even turned her head when she brushed and rebraided her hair, as if her face might reveal too much.

I'm probably reading too much into this, Annabel thought. Her stomach talked to her, tight and uncomfortable. She pulled out her water bottle and tried to remember how she usually fell asleep. She'd been alone long enough that another person breathing beside her, not to mention scribbling secretive notes, was distracting. How had she ever slept in a room with Sabrina? It had only been a few weeks, but she'd evolved in that time, lost some of the skills of a social being. I'd rather be a bat, she thought, sighing loudly.

"I'll be done soon," said Janice.

Annabel tried to tense and then loosen her muscles, starting at the toes and working up. When she'd finished her knees, Janice turned off the flashlight. Somehow, the dark made her more restless. Finally, Janice was sleeping, hard, her inhalations long and loud, as if she were slurping the air. Annabel willed her to be quiet. It was too warm inside the sleeping bag; she thrashed herself out of it, hoping the movement would make Janice turn over, Janice inside a double-thick bag, zipped up to her neck. She didn't stop. Finally, Annabel matched the breathing with her own.

In the morning, Janice was up before Annabel. She was outside the tent door, as if she hadn't ever been inside, asking, "You up?" in a singsong voice.

"Oh God," said Annabel. "I didn't get up to watch them come in!"

"Want breakfast in bed?" Janice was unzipping the screen door, proffering oatmeal. Real oatmeal, not muesli, with raisins and cut-up apple.

"Um, yeah, but my bats—"

"Don't worry, you can take a day off." Janice put a Sierra cup by Annabel's feet. A trick, she'd been tricked into this somehow, oversleeping. Her sleeping bag was balled in a corner; all she was wearing was a T-shirt and underwear. She felt exposed, undercooked, all her naked flesh in the tent's green light.

Janice wasn't looking at her; she was zipping the tent back up.

"You're approved. And besides, I thought we'd go see my friend Gretel today. A few of the other students are meeting us there—we'll have a potluck, and she might have some ideas about John."

It sounded like a dinner party, something domestic humans who lived in houses did. And like an unorthodox agenda for the university program. Why hadn't she

explained that before? "Um, thanks," said Annabel, thinking about another dateless day. She sighed.

"You might want to take down your camp." Janice's
voice circumnavigated the tent. Annabel could see her
shadow already, so it must be late. She looked for her
watch.

"It's already ten," Janice said.

"Fuck." Her bats had been back in their trees for hours.

"What?" Janice was yards away now. What was she
doing? Peeing?

"Nothing," said Annabel. "Thanks for breakfast." She
projected her voice, flat and loud, out into the forest.

In the van, Annabel felt herself shrinking. She wasn't a
woman in the world, who chose where and when she
went, who was learning the secrets of *Pteropus conspicillatus*.
Instead, she was a lowly student, not even allowed to drive.
She'd needed Janice's approval to keep watching her bats,
and after all the fuss, was she really going to learn anything
original, anything applicable to the body of science? Or
was she just a voyeur, someone who watched fruit bats
mating for her own perverse pleasure?

Her hands became tiny as she shrunk, feet like dried
seeds rattling in the pods of her boots.

She wouldn't ask again where they were going, though
not knowing was as itchy as wool underwear. Janice turned
the radio on and started singing to a Beatles song. Her
Aussie accent was absurd, Annabel thought, but then she
realized the Beatles had British accents, and American
didn't match, either. It was a gentle voice for such an

aggressive woman, thin, wavery, but happy in its minor variation from the actual notes of the song.

She glanced at Janice's arm—the elbow dimpled as she gripped the wheel. Hand clenched more than necessary. Annabel almost wanted to touch Janice, that dimpled skin, to tell her what she'd seen in the bats, to show Janice how they wrapped each other, how safe they were together; even squabbling over a branch, each bat belonged. And at the same time, she wanted Janice to go away, to drive her back to her site and leave her to her private looking.

"I had a good look at an amethystine python the other night," said Annabel, staring out at the tunnel of green as they passed through forest. The road folded back on itself like a paper fan, and the van's brakes whined as they pumped downhill.

"Through your binocs, I suppose?" Janice asked, during the instrumental and sound-effects part of "Yellow Submarine."

"No, really, it was a more tactile encounter."

The song ended and Janice turned the volume down on a commercial for Cadbury chocolate.

"If it was on the ground it probably wasn't an amethystine—"

"Not on the ground." Annabel was growing again, her seed-feet sweaty as they pressed against the rubber of her boots. She was taller than Janice, she noticed, at least her torso was. Janice was hardly tall enough to drive; in fact, she was pressing the accelerator with an extended toe.

"Fill in the mystery, then, girl—just where was this snake?"

She isn't such a crab, Annabel thought. "I grabbed it, thought it was a vine. It was almost dark, actually, and I slipped a bit. I was doing the whole snake sweep." Suddenly it occurred to her that Janice could misuse this information, could say Annabel wasn't ready to research alone. But it felt so good, telling.

She continued, "Didn't even see the head, but I knew what it was from the pattern."

"Gorgeous," said Janice. Her eyes were steady on the winding road. "Good luck it wasn't a taipan."

Annabel fit her clothes again. "Thanks," she said.

"Did I ever tell you about the time I lost two of my best rat subjects to a python?" Janice smiled. "I actually climbed into my canopy stretcher to try to rescue them. So much for scientific method. But I'd been out a month without seeing another human, and I didn't want to start all over again—"

Annabel scratched at the colony of insect bites on her arm. *Gorgeous,* she thought. It had been, too.

Eleven

It had been years since he'd driven this far up the coast. Drew was obliging company, singing loudly with the radio, driving when Leon grew blurry. They went to drive-throughs for food, chewed their way through the figs and sandwiches their mum had packed for them, and stopped only for food and gas.

As they drove past the ghoulish form of the Newcastle Steelworks, Leon tried to tell Andrew about Ursula, as if there were something to tell. When he mentioned women, though, Drew spoke with the vagueness of a real-estate advertisement; each had some euphemistic feature. Leon wondered whether his brother was a jerk with women, whether the parental model of fidelity had had a bad impact. But this was only now, he thought; up until the affair we knew Dad loved Mum, they were a given, cohesive. He wondered what it was like never to lose that faith in the alliance between your parents. Naive, maybe, to think they would always stay passionate, but comforting all the same, as if there was some hope in the world for a stable connection. Not static free, but stable.

"Sounds like quite a handful," said Leon. Drew had just described a woman who wanted to have sex while he was driving.

"So to speak." Drew emitted a barklike laugh.

"Is there anyone in particular you really care about? I mean, really think could be special?"

"Gad, you sound like a gran." Drew tapped the steering wheel. He looked forward, then into the mirror. He passed a truck, car engine straining.

"Drew, just because Dad's being a jerk—"

"Fuck you." Drew drummed his fingers on the wheel.

Leon heard the words again, hard words, unfair. He felt as if one of those desiccating bugs had landed on him, injected its bilious stuff, and sucked out his liquidated innards.

What had happened to Drew? It wasn't his fault, maybe. Maybe it was only a stage. Maybe he hadn't yet found his *thing*, what he was drawn toward. He'd found what repelled him—he'd told Leon he would never be a scientist, and he'd passed through his university science requirement by taking the easiest geology course. He was a literature major, but that didn't seem to be about passion. Leon wondered whether it was fair to expect career goals of his brother; after all, he'd been the one who quit graduate school. He tried to remember himself at twenty, what he thought about women. Leon breathed on the window and wrote a "U" in the fog. He waited for his heart to stop pounding with frustration toward Drew. His brother hit the wheel with his fingers, harder, thumping, thumping; then he stopped.

"Sorry." Drew touched Leon's shoulder.

"Yeah." Leon wiped the "U" away.

"What about you? Is there someone in Boston, maybe? Someone whose name begins with 'U'? Uvula?" Drew giggled. "Ukulele? Ural Straits?"

"U-Are-a-Winner?" Leon joined in. He hadn't thought Drew had seen him writing. He hadn't thought he'd guess what he was writing, either.

"I'm not an asshole, really. Or at least, I don't want to be."

"Ursula."

"Nice name."

"Nice woman." Leon braced himself for Drew to say something crass.

"Serious?"

"No. That is, we aren't. I wouldn't mind it, but for now, well—she's someone I think about a lot."

"Sounds like very safe sex."

"Hah hah."

"Nothing wrong with that," said Drew. He rocked his neck and sat taller. Leon thought he didn't look at all like Mum, or Dad. He looked like an unfamiliar man.

They passed the silver towers and high-rise-shadowed beaches of Surfers Paradise, where Leon had spent several spring breaks working at Sea World and surfing on the wide sweet beach. They had surfing in common, though Andrew was fanatical about it; Leon liked it, but he hadn't minded giving it up when he went to the States. Now Andrew held out that Hawaii and California were the only decent places to live if one had to go to the Northern Hemisphere. Hawaii was almost respectable, he said with a smirk.

After they entered Brisbane, Andrew took the exit to go into the city.

"Hey—what're you doing?"

His brother sucked a milkshake through a straw, his hollowed cheeks making him look goofy, and also old. At this point in the projection, Leon thought, Drew would be a bony old man. Leon hoped his face would soften with age.

"Got some friends here," said Andrew.

"Will they help us look for Dad?"

"You know . . ." Drew was avoiding looking at him again. His glance flickered around, mirrors, road, his own lap. Leon suppressed the urge to say *Watch where you're going.*

"You know, maybe I'll do some research here for a while. I mean, maybe I'll make some calls or something."

"Are you wagging out on me, Drew?"

"Not exactly. I mean, you can stay, too. Call that field-studies place at the uni, check out the beach."

"I didn't come home for the beach," said Leon.

"Yeah, you said." Andrew looked down again. He squashed his milkshake cup and rolled down the window.

Leon tugged the cup out of his hand. He'd foreseen it flying out the window, filling the roadside with more debris. He's trying to piss me off, he thought, throwing crap out the window.

"I wasn't going to toss it. God, Leo."

Leon put the sticky cup with its straw tail in a plastic bag in the back.

"So, do you want to hang out for a while?"

Leon sighed. "I think I ought to keep going now. But if you want to stay, stay." Did Drew actually think he'd left his job, his cusp of dating Ursula, and flown home to hang out with Leon and his testosterone-saturated friends at the beach?

"You can take the car—just bring it back and pick me up."

"Yeah." He wanted to hit his brother; he wanted to scream at him—*Dad's missing, you idiot.*

Andrew steered through the city, past Victoria Park, to a cluster of crumbling apartments a few blocks from the river. He left the motor running and pulled the brake.

Leon watched him wrench his duffel bag out of the back, pick a fig up off the floor and pop it into his mouth. "So, do you have a number here?"

Andrew dug in his pocket, pulled out some laundered lint, then a five-dollar bill. He took a pen from Leon and wrote a number across Queen Elizabeth II's face. "Be good to my car, and let me know if you find the bastard," he said.

"Call Mum and tell her where you are," said Leon.

"I always do."

Leon wasn't going to fight—he couldn't afford to lose Drew, too, but oh, how he wanted to smack him then.

Clamping his teeth together, Leon bit the edge of his tongue. He drove into downtown Townsville, past a stationary parade of tourist shops selling T-shirts and kangaroo-hair stuffed koalas and didgeridoos made of cheap materials and items imported from Asia. He had to circle around a pub and drive about a kilometer toward the university before the streets cleared out and he could park. Maybe Dad was unfaithful here, too. Chapped cheek against some woman's shoulder, the light and dark eyes focused on an unfamiliar body.

Or maybe he was dead. Maybe he'd died of guilt. For a minute Leon wished it. Then he thought, no, missing wasn't the same as dead. He wished he could be Andrew, could quit looking and take back his own life after no more than a surface dive in search of the wreck.

There was a bookstore wedged between a milk bar and a Reef Trips shop where a saleswoman leaned out toward him, one front tooth crooked, like a half-open door. "You looking for a *good time*?" She chuckled at her own innuendo. Leon pushed past her into the bookstore, wishing he was.

He bought maps of Queensland, the Atherton Tablelands, Magnetic Island, the Reef, and a National Parks topo. He threw a compass on the pile at the last minute, and a local guidebook. Then he took out his credit card, wondered how long he could last by borrowing.

"Long in Oz?" asked the man behind the counter. He was wearing a tank top, white, to set off his leathery red skin, and his armpit hair tufted out like epiphytes.

"Just since I was born," said Leon, sick of being taken for a tourist.

"Oh, sorry, mate. I'd have taken you for a Brit with those clothes—" He gestured with the card, but looked down at the pile of maps. "And maybe a greenie besides."

"That I am," said Leon. He examined his reflection in a glass case—he was wearing a pair of cutoff shorts from home and a T-shirt from a bar in Austin, Texas. The shirt had been his roommate's, traded for one of the Aborigine-pattern ones. They'd been drinking beer before Harvard's classes started. Back then, Leon had talked about home as if it were a foreign place. Now he wondered where he belonged.

At James Cook University, Leon walked down the long, dry hallway of the administration building. It smelled like school: a mixture of mold and rubber. The secretary for the department of the field-studies programs was out. There was a note to that effect—a torn paper scrap with a research paper reference in bibliographic format showing through from the back. It was taped to the window and curled up with heat. It said GONE TO LUNCH, and appeared to have been there for months.

Leon wandered around the corridor, looking for someone to talk with. He didn't even know what to ask. There had been some books he'd loved when he was a kid, a detective series. At a crucial point in each plot, the detective reviewed the six keys to a mystery: who, what, when, where, why, and how. He could ask that, Leon thought, he could find some harried professor of agriculture and quiz him, "Who? What? When? Where? Why? How?"

The Why seemed most pressing, but then, least likely to lead him to his father. Why was he here, Leon Goode, live-animal and physical-science demonstrator, education specialist, when he should be on stage with the owl right now? What was he hoping to find—his father hiding in his office? Camped out at Cathedral Fig with soil samples and a backpack, going mad from guilt and longing for Mum?

A woman with thick blond hair came down the hall, stared right at him. She was seductive, Leon thought, wondering why. Maybe it was how her eyes were set slightly

too far apart on her face, or her lips; she was wearing lipstick, he realized, and rather a lot of blue and brown eye
makeup. It seemed like a trick, to wake him in a certain
way, when he didn't will it.

"Hello," he said, to make her stop.

"Hello." She didn't look at him; instead, she looked at
the secretary's door.

Leon thought she was bluffing, that the note must
always be up. "I'm Leon Goode," he said. "I'm looking for
my father."

"Oh!" She turned to him and took his hand in hers.
Cool skin. "I'm so sorry!"

"Does that mean you've heard something?" Leon's face
flushed. "No, no, I mean, I'm sorry he's missing." American accent.

"Me too." They stood in the hall, useless.

"I'm Sabrina Sellis. Let's see if we can find one of the
profs."

She was businesslike, cool. Leon could see the makeup
painted over her skin. Too bad, he thought. Up close the
light revealed her and the trick was lost. She'd look better
without the mask.

Janice Martin's friend Gretel lived in a lumpy wood house
at the edge of a rain-forest patch. Annabel wanted to climb
in on the branches that slouched into open windows. Gretel
herself was almost six feet tall, and effusive. She squeezed
Janice hello, yelping delight. Then she squeezed Annabel,
who felt a surge of pleasure from the hug—uncomplicated
human contact.

On the house tour, Annabel sloshed in her damp clothes, listening to the ring around Gretel's voice. There were rooms full of books, clothes folded into piles, almost no furniture. Sometimes, Gretel explained, her sisters, two triplets of whom she was the third, came to stay with her when they weren't in Yugoslavia or Antarctica. They were journalists, one a writer, one a photographer, and they worked as a team for the A.P. Annabel tried to picture three Gretels with haloed voices filling the house.

Gretel supported herself by working at a medical lab, examining cultured samples through a microscope. What she did mostly, though, was collect salvageable road kills as samples for science and perform basic veterinary procedures on rescued wildlife. Her samples were most often snakes: death adders, tree snakes, brown snakes, rock pythons, and even a snake lizard, most of them squashed in only a few places, which she kept in a giant freezer in her kitchen. She used them for lectures at the local elementary school, and for visitors.

The house was open to guests, human and animal; at night green possums entered like residents, walking along the branches that grew through the windows. They were fed in the kitchen, waddled their way down the stairs to a bank of feeding bowls. Birds came in, too, magpies and currawongs, iridescent blue-green riflebirds, and other birds of paradise. She was also visited by squirrel-like sugar gliders and an occasional prehensile-tailed rat, and there were recovering rescuees in cages in the backyard, or wandering the premises, including a giant cane toad named Lolita, who liked the kitchen best and reportedly ate fried chicken.

Janice and Gretel finished each other's sentences while they started work on tea. Annabel sat by the fireplace, a round in the center of the huge living room, snapping the ends of homegrown string beans.

"Mike should be here soon." Gretel nudged Janice, and Janice swatted her friend.

"Anyone else?" Annabel asked, her mouth full of string bean.

"Don't wreck your appetite," said Janice.

"Don't be such a mum," Gretel hooted.

"Anyone else?" Annabel asked again. It was so warm by the fire, and she was on a soft shaggy rug; she could easily sleep if she wasn't so hungry.

"Sabrina, I think. And if we've *any* luck, they may have found Professor Goode. Mike went up to three of John's sites to see if he was mucking around in dirt, making his soil scientist's way." Janice was shucking corn now.

"John Goode has his own special ways," said Gretel.

"Meaning?" Annabel wouldn't let the innuendo go this time. After all, the man was missing, and since he was supposed to approve her site, she felt inversely responsible.

"Meaning that he's a very charming man," said Gretel. "I'd have asked him to look at the trees in my bedroom long ago if he hadn't been so relentlessly in love with his wife."

"Enough," said Janice. "Remember, she's his student, and besides, he's *missing*."

"Lighten up. She's an adult, not a high schooler."

"Missing almost a month, Gretel."

Janice stepped away from her friend, and Annabel noticed

the weight of concern on Janice's features for the first time. We're lounging around, she thought, fussing about our daily lives, and he's fallen *out,* somehow.

Annabel brought her beans down to the kitchen as Mike Trimble jogged through the doorway, yelping, "Hullo, hullo!"

He hugged the women, all three of them, and Sabrina straggled in behind him. Her hair looked clotted, her jeans were muddy to the knee, and she smiled at Annabel.

"No John?" Janice asked, looking toward the door as if he might appear.

"Not even a shred of him," said Mike. "The office has tried all the hospitals in Queensland, too."

Annabel pictured that pinkish flesh, shredded. What if someone found an arm, a bloodied bit of clothing—would it feel like discovering death, or just what it was, a piece?

"There was one lead—a park official said he'd written a permit for John to remove some specimens, but he signed it a few months ago, effective through April, so the timing's vague. Besides, that would give us all of Porcupine Gorge, not the kind of area you can skim over in an afternoon. . . . I've talked to Townsville—the wife and sons are already looking," said Mike. "And the Search and Rescue said they'd start. I made a report at the police station in Charters Towers." He swept his hand toward Sabrina, who was sitting by the fire, rolling up her muddy jeans. "Afraid I left this one out for an extra hour or two, digging up her soil organisms while I filed all the papers."

"An hour or five, actually, Mr. Mike," said Sabrina, but she wasn't scowling.

"What happened to the platypuses?" Annabel asked. Sabrina had come a long way from her sworn interest in plants, she thought.

"They weren't interested in making an appearance," said Sabrina. "Bugs in the mud are much easier to get hold of."

They had spaghetti for tea, and corn and green beans and thick coffee, which Gretel said was Belgian, from one of her sisters. Lolita the cane toad came and begged for spaghetti, opening her mouth and approximating a hiss. Gretel swore Lolita had a vast vocabulary of croaks and raised toad eyebrows.

"Toads don't have eyebrows," said Mike.

"They aren't hairy," said Janice. "But the ridges still count as eyebrows."

After they ate and washed the dishes, they lay around the fire like drowsy bears. Janice and Mike touched each other's faces, then Mike lay back in Janice's arms. Sabrina was the first to fall asleep.

Annabel felt as if Professor Goode was in the room in relief, like the shape left in a thin layer of cookie dough after the cutter. They'd stopped talking about him, though, and she wanted something else, a tear in the waiting. She remembered how he'd sauntered up to the campfire at 40-Mile Scrub, how he had seemed to practice vanishing in the river.

Gretel had been reading by the firelight, and she looked up, saw only Annabel still awake. She put her finger to her lips, grinning at Annabel, and went down to her freezer. She unwrapped a plastic package and brought a frozen death adder to the fire, then set it in front of the sleeping Sabrina. Annabel smiled at the joke, but when Gretel went upstairs she switched the thawing reptile so it faced Mike Trimble instead.

Gretel woke Annabel by lightly pressing her shoulders. Annabel had been dreaming of snakes, death adders dancing to Broadway tunes, boas wrapped around each other in a musical number about hibernation. She felt pleased by her own silly unconscious, but guilty for forgetting the professor in her sleep. She remembered the first time she'd dreamed of anything other than Robert after he died, a week after they found out. Until then she'd only had surface sleep, lucid dreams where she remembered him, imagined him losing breath as he drowned. She dove with him, trying to feel it, too. But then one night she dreamed of sex, a deeper sleep, a pleasurable dream. She didn't even remember who the lover was, but she felt guilty for the release, for betraying Robert by moving past grieving for him so soon. She hadn't even started mourning in waking life, but her mind betrayed her, electricity of her dreams continued an active living.

Gretel tugged her hand, helping her up. There were two green possums and a melomy rat snacking in the kitchen. They looked up with bright eyes, backlit, even in the dark room. She led Annabel upstairs to a bedroom where a branch grew thick through the window. A tree kangaroo was eating from a dog-food dish outside the window frame.

Gretel whispered, "Tree roo, thought you might like to see it."

Annabel nodded, whispered, "Oh, yes!"

Then Mike Trimble screamed. It was a shard of panic, his throat resonating with raw fear. He'd heard them walking down the stairs, and then he'd seen the snake.

Janice yelled, "What?" as Mike's scream slipped down a register, and then he began to laugh. He'd lain flat as he screamed, not wanting the adder to strike, but now he leapt up and ran over to Gretel and Annabel. He hugged them a bit too hard, so that Annabel couldn't breathe. "You bugger!" he said to Gretel.

Sender: (Annabel Mendelssohn)
AMendelss@ausnet.jcooku.tvl.edu
To: AEMendel@biosci.com
Subject: quick stop
Saturday, March 23, 1996

Dear Alice,

I'm back in Townsville for a few days, though it seems foreign to me now, all this civilization, running water . . .

I'm sorry I left you hanging about Professor Goode. We're all still hanging. Sometimes it seems like he'll simply show up any minute, but it seems less likely as time passes. He could be somewhere in Porcupine National Park, according to some ranger. It itches at me almost as much as all the bug bites, leech holes, and stinging-tree spots on my poor battered self. No one has started any rumors, though, about his intentions. And I've always been a stickler for evidence before I start writing up conclusions.

Okay, some less heavy stuff, Al—Lars showed me a gross thing they do with leeches at the porch near the library; they put salt on them, dissolve them alive. Yuck.

Thank you for looking into a visit—oh well, I can't believe how expensive tickets are! Now, back to laundry.

Love, Annabel

Twelve

Connecticut was smeared with the sudden greens of false spring. Alice was walking Pavlov without a raincoat. She wanted it to rain, to drench her, for the water to pass through her skin and make her grow green, too. Annabel's message left her lost—maybe she ought to tell her sister what she knew about Robert, maybe she knew something already. Somehow it was important to make things clear now, just when it was impossible.

Alice felt like she'd lost Annabel in time. She missed her sister's phone voice, the quick clipped consonants, the way she elongated her vowels, made them liquid, like their father, and Robert. Alice forced herself to think of the missing professor, as if she could find an answer by thinking hard. It nauseated her, because she didn't even know what he looked like; all she had were clues like height and hair, and he was gone. She couldn't see Robert dead either, though, his body. All they had was ashes and living photographs, and her image of him drowning was manufactured. Alice pressed her fingers to her nose, trying to feel panic. She held her breath, listened to her heartbeat slowing, but then she let go, inhaled. She wanted to feel the quickening, not the dull thud of her well-fed heart.

The last time Alice had seen her sister was at Annabel's graduation from the University of Chicago. It was a thick wet day, and her face and throat, framed by her black gown and a sliver of color from her violet sundress, were as powdery smooth as a dinner mint. Alice's skin blotched in the heat; she'd felt old, watching Annabel hold her mortarboard hat and bounce up to the platform to take her diploma.

It still pulled at her, when they'd said good-bye in Annabel's apartment-complex parking lot. Good-bye like a string threaded down her throat, through her belly, into her veins, a string tugged taut. She'd wanted to *guard* her sister, to keep her safe in a way that was impossible, across distance, time zones.

It wasn't only the distance, it was the pause in the dialogue. There'd been a picture before, of the made-up roommate, parrots and mangoes, of the bright-eyed Professor Goode. Now it was hard to imagine a moment in her sister's day. The truth was, nothing was like being inside a project, questions that drank your concentration and made you lost to everything but searching for answers.

Alice thought about the professor's family, the search. What happened when you looked for someone and there was nothing? Or what about finding them, evidence of the end of them? She thought of the diving partner who'd had to bring up Robert. How bizarre that people became scientific matter, remains, when they were finished living. A body, a corpse, the creature with evidence of its former function.

Robert, for all his selfishness, had just been a person. Alice could imagine it: being trapped so deep inside her own sadness she couldn't see anyone else. But still, it was selfish. His dark hair, his hunched back, his soft dangerous mouth—while he hadn't belonged to any one person, he had belonged to her, to them, the family. And he'd stolen himself from them to live inside his own darkness. To die there.

He'd described the animals he followed—a shark that blazed bright green, firefly squid dotted with lights, sea worms that flashed bright to find mates, a squid that squirted a luminous stream to distract predators while it slid off into the dark. Maybe what he'd been after all along, studying the bioluminescent animals—those he could dive to and those too deep for a human body to bear the weight of the water—maybe he had been seeking his own internal light, something to guide him, to keep him bright in the darkness of the world.

She had to believe it wasn't that he wanted to take himself away from them, that perhaps he'd remembered them at the last. Maybe that was why he'd made it look like an accident—so even the people who knew him best could choose to believe it was a misadventure, instead of a theft. Annabel certainly had. And Alice had been tricked in the past, when he had needed her in high school, in college, tricked into thinking she could help him somehow.

That was the worst part, that he'd chosen, despite all the ways she waited and listened, to be entirely alone.

The light dimmed; Alice could see the degrees of change, the tree-fingers growing darker, shifting out of color and into the black-and-white texture of a storm.

Each of them sought a place to burrow—to lose themselves: her parents, Annabel, Robert. Robert went in all the way. That must be what they were after, the suspension of self in the science. Constant pursuit, concentration on the motions, not the ends. And she'd believed Robert, that because he was looking, he was done trying to test the boundaries of his mortality. But under the water, he'd still been testing.

The dead might have secrets, she thought, but there were no secrets kept from the dead. Suddenly the wind was wet, and then it was pouring. Alice's feet were soaked, her hair became wet strings, and she started running. The dog was gleeful, bounding beside her, and Alice pounded down the center of the street, thankful for the rain, which let her cry without any evidence.

Markos White had stowed his tray of epiphyte samples, books, his backpack, and the long, flat case containing his microscope in the trunk of Leon's car. Leon's mother's old car that was now his brother's, to be exact. Markos had been in Daintree, and was telling tales of mold on the equipment, of the birds, and what he had identified in the cells of the epiphytes he'd collected. His voice was calm and gentle, but he'd kept it up for hours, as if fending off the inevitable conversation about why Leon was there. Leon's head hurt.

They drove up the Palmerston Highway; Markos would stop at Cathedral Fig with Leon, then go off to Yunga-burra to get on with his work. Leon had imagined Cathedral Fig the whole time they were driving and Markos was performing verbal plant dissection. They'd reach the park, ask the ranger, and be led to a campground where his dad had set up camp and hadn't bothered to let anyone know. He'd be unshaven, covered in mud, and he'd be making a bolus to test some soil, a wad of mud in one expert fist. When Leon called to him, he'd look up, gleeful, as if he'd been surprised on his birthday. It could happen. He could also find nothing.

There was a small wood sign by the road: CATHEDRAL FIG, and an overgrown track. He could hear grasses tearing as the underside of the car caught them. Too bad for Drew, his car might be dirty. And too bad he hadn't stayed on—Leon had replayed his brother's departure in his mind, embellishing with the right words; in his head he'd convinced him to come along by saying "I need you along, Drew, we'll find him together," or by grabbing Andrew's arm, keeping the car on the highway, and passing by Brisbane.

Leon pulled into a parking lot, beside a minivan from the Palmerston Schools.

"So, shall we take the tour?" asked Markos.

"I thought there'd be a ranger." Leon looked at the keys in his hand, still sitting. He was tempted to start the car and turn around and go home. Home. He'd drive to the airport in Cairns, catch a flight to Sydney, stop only to change planes for Hawaii, Denver, Chicago, and Boston. To hell with his father, to hell with Drew. Maybe Mum would move to the States.

"Oh, no," said Markos. He stepped out of the car, came around, and opened the driver's door. "I've actually been here before—there's just the Cathedral Fig itself, quite huge, and a nice path."

"It's almost all I have left on my list," said Leon.

"Your list?"

"Of leads." He followed Markos down the path.

The Cathedral Fig was an ancient tree with buttress roots more than twice as tall as Leon. It was a strangler, climbing up another tree until the host was starved for light. It could have been a building, a church, he thought, the bands of green at the top: colored glass. They passed the school group, kids about seven years old, Leon guessed. They were sitting on the ground, off the trail, having a lecture from a very tall woman. As they passed, she pulled a snake out of a paper bag. Half the children screamed; others sang out with the joy of surprise.

"This guy's not alive enough to strike," said the woman. "But what would you do if you saw one near your house or in the school yard?"

"Kill it!" yelled a boy with a crooked haircut. "Shoot it, *bang, bang*." He aimed his hand like a gun.

"Well." The woman was waving the snake as she spoke. "Since this is a death adder—"

"Deaf adder!" yelled a little girl with a lisp. "Deaf adder!"

"Yep, since that's what this guy is, or *was*, until he was smashed by a lorry—"

"Deaf adder!"

"You'd mostly find him in cane fields—"

Leon interrupted her. "I'm sorry," he said, aware of all the kids turning their beams of focus on him. The woman was taller than him, which made him feel strangely safe. "I'm sorry, but I was wondering if you're familiar with this area. You see, I'm looking for someone."

"Mrs. Kata, could you take over for a minute?" A tiny woman with silvery blond hair stood up and led the group away, toward the Cathedral Fig, which two kids started to scale. Mrs. Kata corrected them, tugging down, hard and fast, like a snapping turtle.

"Now." The tall lecturer put her snake-free hand on Leon's shoulder. Markos hovered close, then drifted off as if he'd been interrupting.

"My name's Gretel Macquarie, and you are?"

"Leon Goode."

"Leon Goode, I believe you are looking for your father—" She smiled, illuminating her face.

Leon could feel his own hard pulse, in his neck, in his face. "Do you know where he is?"

"No, love, I'm sorry. I know some of the folks from James Cook, that's all. Have they told you which sites to check out? He had a student up in Malanda, and he was recently in 40-Mile Scrub, and do you know about the permit for sampling in Porcupine Gorge?"

"Oh God," said Leon. His hands were tingling. "Let me get this down."

"Love, I'm sorry. Let me finish this lecture, then I'll take you home for lunch and we can talk this over."

Leon wanted to grab onto her, his first clue, to keep her from going back to the children. "I'll check around here and meet you back at the bus," he said, watching her walk away.

Markos White was fingering a vine wrapped around another cathedral fig tree. He cupped his hands and turned to the woods. "JOHN GOODE!" he yelled. "ARE YOU OUT THERE?"

Leon almost shushed him, surprised. Then he yelled himself. "DAD? DAD! DAD!" No one answered. The kids chattered by the big fig, the galahs squawked. It was hollow and terrible to call so loudly and get no answer.

Leon remembered hide-and-seek with Andrew; once, as a teen, he'd driven off from a game without telling his seven-year-old brother the game was done. Drew kept looking, Mum said, for over an hour. When Leon came back with a friend and chips from the market, Drew wouldn't talk to or look at him. The punishment had lasted three days—Drew didn't take the treats Leon offered, or even a long-coveted rock-band T-shirt. No peace offering could cool his anger, until he let it go himself.

"C'mon," said Leon, trying to smile at Markos. A kookaburra laughed.

"I really don't know much," said Gretel, handing Leon a dish of sliced mango, star fruit, and papaya. They'd emptied a huge bowl of salad with cucumbers and boiled eggs.

She told him about Porcupine Gorge on the drive, and about Mike Trimble's line of search. His father would love this house, Leon thought, noting the muddy possum tracks on the bedroom floor as Gretel gave him a tour before lunch. His mum wouldn't. What had happened to their compromises—to half-tent, half-hotel family vacations? Why did his dad have to destroy everything, when he could have just looked and not touched?

Now, eating at a big round table, he said, "The gorge, that sounds promising. What else? Anyone else?"

"I'm sorry, love. I don't think anyone else has seen him.

He used to get pretty wrapped up in his own work, your father."

"Wouldn't argue with that," said Leon. "What about other women, do you think there might be other women?" He heard the edge in his own voice.

"Other women?" Gretel held a mango slice between her fingers. Her lips were wet with fruit juice.

"I don't have any illusions that my father is Mr. Faithful."

"God," said Gretel. She leaned across the table to touch his shoulder with her sticky hand, but stopped short and took a napkin off the table instead. "He always seemed entirely dedicated to your mother, to me at least. Not that he wasn't attractive—"

She was using past tense. "Well, he isn't—anyway, if you don't have any other clues, I do thank you for the wonderful lunch." Leon could picture this tall woman kissing the top of his father's head, leading him up to the tree-shaded bedroom.

"You can stay here if you'd like." She kept eating fruit with her fingers, a slice of the star.

"Thank you, but I think I'll head for Ravenshoe—he liked, that is, he always *likes* to go to Millstream Falls. Then maybe Malanda, and then the gorge."

As Leon settled into the dusty car he looked back at her house. He loved Gretel for an instant, for believing in his father's fidelity, for feeding him, for acting like this whole mess was unfortunate, but not separate from the world. His father was just missing. If only she hadn't used the past tense that way, as if he were completely gone, nothing left to look for.

As eager as she was to get back to her site, she didn't mind
riding with Mike and Janice now; she was growing used to
company—in conversation, eating meals, sharing the ill-
fitting clothes of the professor's disappearance. Janice sat in
the van's back seat and broke pieces off sugar bananas, passing up chunks of sweet fruit to Annabel's mouth, to
Mike's, without partiality. When Annabel asked for her
binoculars, Janice roused herself from her recline and rummaged in the gear boxes.

"Like a talisman, eh?" said Janice. She held up a frayed
piece of rope. "Not this."

"Nope, hard to see bats through that," said Annabel.

"Or this." She waved a bottle at them, full of greenish-
yellow liquid.

"Hey, careful, that's mine," said Mike, looking at her in
the mirror.

"You must get more vitamin A," said Janice. She chuckled at her own small joke and handed Annabel her binoculars.

They stopped in Ravenshoe, where, Janice said, the
environment minister had been roughed up back in the
'80s, when he came to propose that some land be put aside
for World Heritage.

"Not much for greenie slime like us here," said Janice.

"I have a hunch about the campground," said Mike. "I'd
like to find out if they've seen anything."

This was Professor Goode, implied but unspoken.
Annabel felt guilty for wishing they could drive directly to
her site—she pressed her fingers against the window glass.

When they stopped the van at a rotted red-striped tent that was the campground and caravan park office, no one had seen a man with one blue eye, one brown, who liked swimming holes and examined dirt as if he could read the future in it.

Mike kicked at the ground as Annabel and Janice were getting back in the van. His face looked young to Annabel, etched with dark frustration. For a second he looked like Robert, and she realized it had been several days since she'd thought of Robert, since Gretel's. It was as if she'd tricked herself, the way she'd done to learn to ride a bike, to swim—concentrating on everything except the thing you are most afraid of. She was most afraid of losing him, but she wanted to let go. It wasn't entirely bad.

The green blur as they wound up the Palmerston Highway was barely visible from the van, all the lives inside the forest—lemuroid possums, stick insects, mosses and vines—secreted from the time tunnel of the highway. She was so relieved to be back at her site, unloading her gear from the van, that she didn't notice that the bat chorus was no longer audible from the road. She wanted to be alone, she told herself; she could slip into watching that way, become sheathed in science. But this time she'd miss the company.

"Well, bat girl, see you soon," said Mike. There was a smudge of banana on his shirt.

"Good on yer," said Janice, smiling. Annabel grinned back, trusting each of them, pleasantly sorry to see them leave.

After the van pulled out, trailing a plume of stirred-up road, Annabel noticed the silence. Maybe they're quiet today, she thought, her pulse hard in her temples. Not a sound as she started in. Grabbing her gear, she pushed into the overgrown path without watching for the stinging trees. They kissed her as she passed, leaving the burn on the back of her hand. Annabel followed the orange tape markers.

The camp was a hole in the forest, the ficus trees stripped bare by bat feet and mouths, the terrible blank blue sky visible from below, the trees empty. They looked dead. Annabel started to run, pushing around the perimeter where she'd marked bat territory on the trees below, listening, hearing only the sudden cracks of the plants she stepped on, her own heart beating harder, as if trying to escape from her body. When she looped back around to her tent site, still believing the bats might appear, she noticed a wooden board nailed into the ground. She lifted it as if it were one of Gretel's frozen adders.

GREENYS OUT

She would refuse to cry, she thought, sitting down on the ground. The back of her hand where she'd brushed the stinging tree began to throb, persistent and increasing, like someone sobbing.

Thirteen

In the morning in his rented room in Ravenshoe, Leon noticed all the objects around him, things that had surrounded him while he slept. He hadn't noticed, when he lay down last night, the nubby off-white bedspread, the comma-shapes in burgundy on the wallpaper. In the corner, there was a three-legged table with an assortment of boarding-room accoutrements: a silver-handled hairbrush with yellowed bristles, two crusty-looking hand towels, and a cracked water basin with a rose pattern filled to about a third. A matching pitcher, filled to the brim, sat squat on the floor. There were waterbugs on the surface of the basin, as if it were a pond, and beards of green algae growing out into the water from the sides.

Leon imagined his hostess or host assembling these objects, then leaving them there for decades, until the whole table was covered with a thick soft moss. He wondered who else had slept in this bed, whether there'd been sex where he was lying, whether his hosts had bothered to change the sheets or smoothed them over unwashed, to be frugal.

Of course they changed the sheets—they hadn't seemed perverse at the door. Still, he hopped out of the bed and dressed quickly, imagining he could avoid something in his last hour in this room that he hadn't been aware of for the previous nine.

At breakfast, there were eggs and bangers, toast with the crusts cut off. Sausage smell filled the house, and Leon licked orange marmalade off his finger. He sat alone in the steamy dining room on a crickety wicker armchair. The husband-and-wife team attended him like he was a grand-son, bringing more cream when he poured a little in his tea, an extra pink paper napkin when he crumpled his after swallowing the last of the eggs.

"So, here on holiday?" The man was hovering in the corner of the room; he wouldn't sit down. Leon imagined he'd had his own breakfast, fast and gulping, in the kitchen while his wife cooked. Maybe he'd eaten two biscuits fat with butter; he had a crumb hanging at the corner of his mouth.

"Not exactly." Leon noted his host's disappointed expression, and stopped pushing the sausages around his plate. He cut one and bit, sighing. Vegetarianism was on permanent hold now—like the rest of his life. "I used to come here all the time with my family," said Leon.

"*Really?* Not many like that around here. From Mel-bourne, are you? I try to guess by the accent."

"Sydney, actually." Leon tried not to speak with his mouth full. He put butter on his toast, bit, and let the bread press against his palate.

"And what's your father's business that he comes up here? If you don't mind my asking, that is."

Leon looked at the man, his pink eyes downcast, asking and then retreating. "Sells logging equipment," he lied.

"*Really,* I might know him, then, but you signed in your name—" He wandered off into the hallway, checked the guest book. "Goode, nope, not familiar."

Leon bounced up from his chair, not eager to keep on this course. He couldn't make up more—that one lie alone made his tongue feel swollen. Or maybe it was the sausages.

"Well, I'll be off, then."

"There's a waterfall circuit. I've a brochure somewhere."

His host tagged along after him, but Leon made as quick an exit as he could without being terribly rude. He *hoped* he wasn't terribly rude. As he pulled back onto the road he realized he was still gripping his crushed pink paper napkin.

Leon missed the first turnoff, for Malanda, and saw the small sign for the Millaa Millaa waterfall. He parked in the lot above the falls and thought about stripping and swimming. There was a group of squealing schoolchildren in red bathing suits and blue; they threw water at each other in the shallow end as if they were throwing mud. Did he think he'd find his father by acting like a kid? Maybe that was the best way, after all, since John Goode acted like a kid all the time—maybe the best way to find him was to act like him, instead of being responsible and searching.

After a good swim, Leon drove to Millaa Millaa, where he called his mother from a phone booth. A logging truck pulled in as he dialed, then idled beside the booth. Leon smelled diesel fumes and sawdust; there were great logs maybe ten yards thick bundled up on the truck bed. He got his mother's answering machine; he could hear her voice, but not her words, over the idle. Then the beep, he was pretty certain he heard the beep.

He cupped the receiver with his hand and said, "Mum, everything's fine, this is Leon. I mean, I haven't found— that is—everything's fine with *me,* but I still have some looking around to do before I come home. Just wanted to let you know. Do you remember coming to a town called Millaa Millaa? Waterfalls? That's where I am. Gotta go. Love you."

Leon felt as if he'd sent a postcard. His mother was as distant as that to him now, accessible only by words in one direction. He thought of her insistent voice on the phone with Lila Wallard, her private face. He'd imagined her eyes closed when she spoke, to keep them from tearing.

On the road to Malanda, something starting dragging on the bottom of his brother's car. I'll have to check, thought Leon, but he kept driving, through deep puddles, past cows huddled together in the field though the day was sunny. Probably there'll be rain, because cows know. He could see scraps of dark green where the rain-forest remnants abutted the fields. Clouds hovered over them. There would always be a few clouds as long as there was a little green left.

Leon stopped at the pub in Malanda. His T-shirt was still wet, stuck to his postswim skin. He was cold; he hadn't noticed—he'd driven with the window open, and a membrane of dust had adhered to his face and arms. He'd have a drink to warm himself up. It was a fallacy, he knew, that alcohol provided warmth, but something he wanted hard to believe now, nonetheless.

The telltale X's on the Foster's sign looked so festive on the building, and inside, behind the bar. He used to think those meant kings, he'd called them the king's marks, and his father had let him say it. Mum asked him what he meant, one of the few times they were in a pub as a family. One was not supposed to bring kids to pubs in Sydney, but John Goode strode right in, impervious to disapproval. Drew had a lolly water and Leon had a glass of ice, which he cracked in his teeth so that his molars ached with cold. "They don't mean kings," his mother had said, her face completely straight. "They mean kisses."

There was a man in the corner at the Malanda pub, leaning against the wall as if he were a weight-bearing beam, another man fondling the darts, not throwing. The woman behind the bar had a huge head, that typical pale thin hair of the oversunned. She smiled expansively at Leon, as if he were a dish of ice cream.

"G'day, love, what'll you have?"

"Foster's," said Leon, relieved to be recognized as an Aussie. He couldn't bear another misguess.

Beer at two in the afternoon—Leon imagined he could make this a habit. He pushed a five-dollar bill across the counter—noticing his brother's Brisbane phone number as the money went in the till. He took the change.

The bartender had gone back to her chair by the television. The volume was off but she was rapt, watching staticky soap-opera stars gesture at each other. The beer was bitter and good, and he shivered as the chill filled his body. Leon felt the ache in his jaw—he always got a jolt like this when he drank.

A woman in damp clothes walked into the pub; she had
a sturdy lope, like a sure child; she had a strong smell, too,
like crushed leaves.

"Annabel!" The bartender abandoned her TV.

"You're back, Midge," said the woman, as she slung an
enormous backpack on the floor—rope and flagging tape
were tied to the top, a knife strapped on the front. "Welcome back." She sounded so dispirited Leon could have
hugged her, but the name stopped him from moving. He
watched her for clues: Was this his father's second secret
lover? Could his father pursue this woman, Leon's age or
younger, her hair wet and dusty, her crumpled work shirt
and wader boots? Her eyes were green, he noticed, and her
teeth were even. Was that an American accent? She
sounded like an American.

"Annabel *Mendelssohn*?" Leon asked, daring to look into
her face.

The woman balked, stepped back as if she'd been
shoved. Her face was lit with fight. "What the hell do you
want?" she snapped. She slid her hand down her bag
toward the hilt of a machete.

"Easy, Annabel," said the bartender. "He's not a logger—loggers don't dress like city tourists."

"How do you know my name? What do you want?"
She was still holding the machete handle.

Leon drank his beer, the ache spreading along his jaw.
He tried to look calm. "I'm Leon Goode," he said. "I'm
looking for my father."

Part III

Fourteen

Annabel kicked the sign, a thick piece of plywood. She could bring it in to the police as evidence, but of what crime? They'd done something to make her bats leave, but she'd searched the camp, the perimeter of the bats' cacophony of daily activity, and she hadn't found anything else—no dead bats, which she'd imagined among the vines and mud, no slashed trees, no fire. Even if this was official World Heritage property, no one here believed in the rights of bats. Bats stole fruit, they scared children, their seed-dispersal and cross-pollination skills didn't concern most people.

At that minute, she hated people: foolish, oblivious people. The loggers' hatred of environmentalists wasn't a game; it was dangerous stupidity. How could she have been so blithe—had she mentioned the site to anyone in town? Stupid, stupid, trudging into the woods and leading in the pestilence of idiots the way Europeans brought disease to the New World.

Under the sign, Annabel found three spent buckshot shells. So they'd fired at them, scared them off. Bastards, she thought, kicking at the sign again. It hurt her toe.

She hefted her pack back on, dragged out the box of extra food supplies she'd bought, when she'd been oblivious, contentedly planning, imagining it could be a week or even two before she left her site. Out at the road, she tucked the food into a ditch under a palm frond. She could come back for it if she ever found her bats. There were big footprints dried in the mud near her path; Annabel sketched them in her notebook—there may have been no real crime, but she wanted this evidence anyway.

She started back toward town, jogging slowly, her toe throbbing. She pictured herself, as if she were in a movie, cheerfully waving good-bye to Janice and Mike, not even noticing the silence. Where did bats go when they were shot at? Did they travel for kilometers, or just down the road to a new spot, where they could squabble and strip the trees again? Sometimes when they exhausted their branches, they moved about fifty meters. But after human attack? It wasn't information she'd read in any journal article. She stopped her jog every so often to listen, her anger keeping her strong and fast, enhancing the span of her senses. She heard the stones crush under her feet, parrots, a kookaburra's laughing call, the wind clicking the stiff palm leaves together. She kept hoping for bat song, but even if they could come, they wouldn't be searching; Isolde wouldn't fly overhead, crying, looking for Annabel.

There was a low hum from the road—Zillie Falls. Maybe the bats were by the waterfall, choosing the sound for cover. Annabel scrambled through the scrub at the edge of the forest. More stinging trees struck her, cheek and wrist. She held up her machete but didn't slash; enough damage done.

At Zillie Falls there were no bats—had she really thought there would be bats? But there was the real path opposite the one she'd improvised, and the parking lot, with two parked pickups. Annabel could hear the splashing of swimmers in the little lake at the bottom of the falls. There was a man sitting in the bed of one truck, cleaning a gun. He was bare-chested, and his skin glowed pinkish brown. The man was almost hairless, with a thin line of blond down the center of his chest, his belly. Annabel thought: you're pathetic, not as well protected as an animal, except for your stupid cowardly gun.

She'd ask him if he knew anything about the bats—she'd stay calm and she wouldn't aggress him. As she walked toward the truck, the man looked up, hazy blue eyes. He half-smiled, and suddenly Annabel was scared, though still furious. He could be some ordinary guy, cleaning his gun, or he could be a rabid antigreenie, the bad speller who made the sign. He was armed; she wasn't.

She froze, no longer wanting to confront him. Look at me, she thought, some woman with a backpack and mud on her face, a waterproof notebook, wader boots. I might as well be wearing a big sign that says "Rape me, shoot me" on my forehead. She didn't even feel safe crossing over to the path, but when she started back she realized how loud she was, sloshing along in her boots, her huge messy pack. He might shoot her for the fun of it. Yesterday she'd have come to these falls alone, she'd have skinny-dipped if no one was around. They could be ordinary people, friendly even, but today she'd lost the thin coating of bravery that kept her safe in the world.

Annabel waited them out, standing at the edge of the clearing for over an hour. Gun Man finished cleaning and went in for a dip. The other truck owners, two tired-looking wet men, came up from the lake, dried off, and drove away. People looked more dangerous than death adders, that delicate skin, malevolent intent. Her own skin flamed where she'd brushed against stingers, her feet throbbed wet and hot in the boots.

Finally, Gun Man stepped back into his truck cab and drove off; she could see a piece of plywood in the bed, and the silver glint of something metal, perhaps cans of spray paint, perhaps a hitch or a toolbox. Either way, she felt relieved and idiotic as she washed herself, the stinger sites more painful in the water, then changed into sneakers and walked back on the path to the road, and on toward town.

About two kilometers before Malanda, a round old pickup pulled up beside Annabel.

"Need a lift?" asked the man inside. His face was leathery, his voice wobbled.

"No," said Annabel. She was incensed at him for asking.

"Sure?" he asked again, smiling. Two brown teeth, one gold, one missing.

"No." She wouldn't flirt and she wouldn't say thank you. Her teeth cut into the insides of her cheeks.

"You sheilas," said the man. He pulled out hard, clouding Annabel with dust. Her hands were shaking, and her knees felt soft, unpredictable.

Finally, town. Annabel didn't want to call the university in Townsville, announce failure. She could stay in town for a night, then go back and look. Maybe she had enough credit left to rent a car, though she didn't even know if she could rent a car in Malanda. Stupid Malanda, where the bat-shooting bad speller could be anywhere. She'd go to the pub; maybe Midge could help her out.

The place was practically full, men in the corner playing darts and wasting time, another on a stool, chatting it up with Midge. She'd never seen him before, a tourist maybe, or maybe he was the man who hated greenies. She was pathetic; they were all becoming him. And of course it had to've been a man. The big boot print. She walked as tall as she could, filthy from the road dust, and stood at the other end of the bar. Midge was watching TV now, and she looked small and slumped. But she turned when Annabel thumped her backpack to the floor.

"Annabel!" said Midge. The smile made Annabel safe, at least for a second.

"You're back, Midge. Welcome back." She kicked at her backpack, disassociating herself.

"Annabel *Mendelssohn*?" The man stood up, beautiful blue-green eyes, a touristy T-shirt. He was scrubbed and wore jeans, had a familiar look, but she didn't trust him. Hate sometimes hid in pretty forms.

"What the hell do you want?" she asked. He looked so eager, hungry almost. That lovely mouth, a tentative smile. She picked up her pack, ready to leave.

"Easy, Annabel," said Midge. "He's not a logger—loggers don't dress like city tourists."

"How do you know my name? What do you want?"

"I'm Leon Goode," he said. "I'm looking for my father."

Annabel let her pack slump off her shoulder onto the floor again. "God," she said. "I'm glad to meet you. I mean, I'm sorry you have to be here, because, I mean—" She wouldn't cry, she wouldn't. Her eyes burned.

Leon Goode stepped closer. "How do you know my father?" he asked.

She couldn't help the liquid spilling over onto her face. "He was my professor," she said.

"Ah," said Leon.

Midge was leaning over the bar. She looked ready to say something, but was silent.

"You look like you could use to wash up," said Leon Goode, watching Annabel cry, his hands moving in the air as if he'd like to comfort her, but his voice stayed hard. "I thought I might stay at the caravan park. Where are you staying?"

"Nowhere, anymore," said Annabel. "Maybe I'll come with you." She picked up her pack and glared at him. He stood still by the bar, looking puzzled. "What?"

"I guess that's okay," he said.

"Midge," said Annabel. "Someone's been shooting at my site."

Midge nodded. "Don't go back, love," she said. "I'll pass on the word."

Annabel felt like part of a secret network. She didn't want to be a spy. She only wanted to be a scientist.

Annabel woke in her tent, but the shadows were unfamiliar, and the sounds—not the scrape of leaves against the tent fly, birds' call and response, but motors grinding, a family bickering over breakfast. The caravan park smelled of exhaust and cut grass. Heavy wheels rolled over the pebble road. She remembered that her bats were gone. She remembered Leon.

She wasn't sure why she'd left the pub with him, but after the shells and the sign, and her trip back to town through the territory of trucks and guns and men, Annabel hadn't really had anywhere else to go. Driving to the campground in his rattley car, Leon had been generous about everything, kind even, while she explained why she'd been so hostile at first. But still, he acted wary, keeping more distance than necessary between their bodies as they walked from his car, as she stirred hot cereal on her small stove for dinner. He contributed raisins, and a lump of chocolate that had assumed liquid form in the glove box several times during his journey. Rehardened, it looked dusty and was impregnated with foil, but still tasted good.

He'd started quizzing her about his father at dinner, questions streaming out of his mouth like endless ribbons from a magician's hat.

"Do you remember anything he said? About going anywhere?"

"Well, he said a lot, though I honestly don't remember anything about going anywhere before he took off that last time. We had lectures. I don't know." She spooned a hot raisin into her mouth.

"It's important."

"I know, and maybe I should have paid more attention, but I didn't expect him to disappear."

"Tell me again, when and where you saw him last— maybe that will help you remember something. Did he act in any *particular* way?"

"At school, he was packing up his car. But it was just a few boxes." She didn't say *The last time we talked on campus he winked at me and offered me some of his mango.* She didn't say, *I had a silly crush on him.* It was unimportant, and she was foggy now, her face heavy with exhaustion.

Finally, Annabel said, "Hey, I'm really tired. I'm going to my tent."

"Sorry, I just thought you might know where to look," he said. She was already unzipping the tent door.

"Sorry. But what about Porcupine Gorge, have you been there yet? There were the permits."

"Yeah, Gretel told me—have you been there? Did you go there with him?"

"No."

"Did he say anything—"

"Tomorrow," said Annabel. She had to pee, but she was too tired to move anymore, and he might follow her. She shuffled into her tent and slept.

Peeing was more urgent in the morning. At first she started to step out as she was dressed, in T-shirt and under-wear, but then she remembered she needed to wear more clothes in a caravan park. The pressure in her bladder made dressing excruciating: shorts, sandals, so slow.

Annabel sprinted to the concrete bathroom bunker. Then she washed her face and looked in the mirror. Her hair was light from the sun, and her face looked tough and brown from exposure. Her legs itched, her arms itched— perhaps she was finally drying out from the constant shower of the rain forest. Annabel gave herself a makeshift sponge bath with the liquid soap at the sink and her dirty bandanna. She was covered with dry patches and pink welts, scabs and scrapes. The stinging-tree spots startled her as she washed: her wrists and hands, her cheek pulsed from the firing spines.

She started to giggle. "I'm a greenie," she said aloud, touching the reflection of her finger in the mirror. "See how green?"

A toilet flushed, and she remembered that she wasn't alone. How did anyone survive such constant exposure to other people? My bats are gone, she thought, disappeared like the professor. She thought of Leon. She had to help if she could, tell him everything she knew about his father. But what was there, really, besides Porcupine Gorge? He swam with crocodiles and was a flirt, but he hadn't ever crossed the line of play with her. He said he still loved his wife, he loved his sons, he feared he was losing them. But saying all this would sound like he was dead already. Maybe he was. Maybe he'd been bitten by a redback spider, struck by a brown tree snake, maybe he'd been shot. Tick fever. Food poisoning. Torture, someone could be torturing him because he was a scientist. He could be sitting under the brush, wounded or dead, wherever his site was, at a road-cut, that gorge. The world was full of accidental hiding places. Stick with facts, she thought, and keep away from the family stuff, it's not your place.

Leon had slept in his car. When Annabel returned from the bathroom he was stretched across the dusty hood like a cat, eyes closed to the sun.

"Sorry if I was a bother last night," he said. "I was a little excited—you're really my only lead. But it wasn't very nice of me to grill you."

He stood up and faced her; his eyes were very nice, the bluish-green. He had his father's broad chest, but not the belly.

She thought of John Goode's face and hands—how he'd let her in, how he'd mentioned this man, his son. He'd given her secrets of sentiment, like samples of his true heart.

Annabel could go back, look for her bats, or she could give up one search for another. Professor Goode had become more important, somehow, while she slept in this caravan park.

"Porcupine Gorge," said Annabel. "Get out your map, that's where we're headed."

"We? What about your research?" Leon inspected his own fingernails. They looked clean enough to Annabel. John Goode had filthy fingernails. He said he stored soil samples under them. Annabel wondered whether Leon had heard that phrase all his life, or whether it was invented for students.

"I don't know where my bats are, and I don't think I want to search around alone right now," said Annabel. "Besides, I have enough data for my project, though maybe not enough for a real paper—" She wouldn't pass on her worries to him. She wasn't giving up, though a lump of doubt sat in her throat. Maybe she'd have enough for a paper, maybe the bats would return after she found the professor, or maybe it was all gone, research, Tristan, Isolde, the whole idea of being a field scientist. Right now she had to leave them, she thought, but there were bats to be researched all over the world, if that was what she was going to do, and only one missing Professor Goode. "And

I'm tired of spiders shitting on me from above," she said, "and skin rot."

"There may be spiders in Porcupine Gorge," said Leon. He was looking at her in a funny way, his head tilted, eyes intense, as if her face were a painting. Arousal spread from her belly to her knees, her skin grew alert for touch. She didn't want it, it wasn't right, but there was something beautiful about his similarity to his father, and something compelling about the two of them having lost the same person.

"That's all right," she said.

"Were you lovers?" He looked straight at her. Now the look was unnerving.

"Shit, no," said Annabel. But she could feel her face pinking, the heat of it.

"Sorry, but I don't trust him." He turned away, toward the line of trees bordering the caravan park.

"I'm his student, Leon." Her face would give it away, she thought, that she'd imagined kissing John Goode, that she'd tingled where he touched her. But no, of course they weren't lovers. He hadn't offered, and she didn't think she would've accepted.

There were two likely places to stop on the way to Porcupine Gorge, Leon said: the butterfly park near Charters Towers, because *he* might stop there, and a place just north of Hughenden, where they could find a quiet campsite. Then they'd take the notoriously bad Kennedy Developmental Road up into the park. Porcupine Gorge itself had a campground and a hiking trail down to the gorge. Annabel traced the route on the map with her finger: she

felt like a phony, as if Leon had found her in a fortune-
teller's shop and she was expected to guide him. She
wanted him to trust her—not his father's lover—and she
wanted to take some of the burden of the disappearance
from him.

Leon seemed to have a grudge against his car; he drove it
too far into parking spaces, let a branch drag underneath
for the last few kilometers on the road to Charters Towers,
and a pebble was caught in the oil pan, so the scraping
sound was punctuated with a high rattle. While he drove,
she watched him surreptitiously. He was easy to be with,
like John Goode, with a quick smile even under the dark
wing of their circumstances.

She watched him scratch an insect bite on his leg until
the skin was raw, the lump rubbed off, and tiny dots of
blood domed. What had he pictured when he thought
she'd been his father's lover? Had he seen kissing, his hands
on her thighs? Annabel was embarrassed by the pleasure of
imagining him imagining her. She studied the landscape
out the window, turning drier as they drove southwest,
scrubby fields like bad beards, the pale green of reluctant
growth. Then she saw something huge, running almost as
fast as the car through the field.

"Jesus, what's that?" she said. She pointed, then rolled
down her window to see better through the dust. Leon
stopped scratching his leg and looked over.

"Can't see. Is it brown?" The car meandered toward the
center of the road as he strained to look.

"Careful," said Annabel. She rolled up the window and
rubbed dust from her eyes, lost the moving thing, then saw

it again. "More yellowish," she said. "And it has a very long neck. God, it's fast. A bird? Could it be a bird?"

"Emu," said Leon. He stopped trying to see.

"Of course, an emu," said Annabel. Some scientist. She thought she'd seen the Loch Ness monster sprinting through the outback.

"Do emus eat meat?" she asked. She was suddenly silly. "Will a chicken eat chicken?"

"I've tried that one," said Leon. "If it's in a sandwich, they'll eat anything."

"Will a fish eat filet o' fish?"

"Only on fish night at the pub," said Leon. He smiled. It was a beautiful smile, thought Annabel. I'm not going to fool around with this, I'm not going to get stupid for some man, especially one whose father I've dreamed of undressing.

The butterfly enclosure was a mesh tent full of flowers and thousands of butterflies—tiny ones and ones the size of pie tins, in tiger patterns, iridescent cerulean, foil-bright red. They landed everywhere, filled the air with mating flights and newly hatched drunken meanders. Almost as wild to watch as bats, thought Annabel, with no faces to reveal expressions, to help her guess the meanings of their flight. Their silence seemed appropriate, paired with the noise of their colors.

Annabel stood still and two landed on her red shirt. "They think I'm food," she said. Leon was walking ahead, looking at the people as if they were as interesting as the insects. He'd shown a photograph of John Goode to the attendant, who hadn't seen him, he didn't think, no, he wanted to look again, what was he wearing, he'd asked. When Leon didn't know, the attendant shrugged and asked for the entrance fee, interview over.

"You look right for it," he said to Annabel. "Tasty colors." He walked around the loop path and came back behind her.

"I could watch them all day," she said. Hundreds of butterflies, yellow and black, with scallop-edged wings or false eyes filled the air, landed on the plants and tourists, dipped at hummingbird feeders.

"So could he. He used to take us somewhere to try to spot the birdwings—they're really rare now, but there were more around then. It was somewhere near here, probably. Drew and I dueled with our nets, but Dad always found something good for us to see, and we had to drag him off or he'd sit staring all day."

"Sounds nice, looking for butterflies. My parents were a bit drier about family outings. Though my brother collected anything dead—" She stopped. Annabel could easily imagine John Goode, lost in the world of the minute— one small insect, the soil striation.

"Do you remember where that was, that you went?" she asked.

"I wish I did—I'd check there, too. Isn't it odd?" He reached toward the tiger-striped butterfly on her shirt, but didn't touch. "I mean *weird*,"—this he said with an exaggerated American accent. "That we have these whole lives with our parents we don't even remember? I mean, places they took us in infancy, and then, the places we remember going, but we don't know exactly where they were?"

"Very *weird*, really," said Annabel.

"Once I called up my dad from uni, said I was going on a field trip to Tasmania, and he said 'You've already been.' He meant when I was two or three, but I didn't remember. And even America, they took me there before Drew was born—have you got places like that?"

He was so polite, he wouldn't forget she was there like someone else in a reverie might. His face was gentle as he let a black-and-red butterfly land on his finger.

"Atlanta," she said. "I was apparently conceived in Atlanta, if that counts. Oh, and they took us along on a conference in Boca Raton when I was one. That must have been great for them, juggling sessions, baby-sitting, and diapers. I don't remember anything, though, so I know what you mean."

They bought lunch at a milk bar, chook sandwiches and chips in red-and-white paper boats, which they ate on a picnic bench in the tiny town square. Annabel itched; she felt as if she was patched with rot and dry. She scratched, wondering whether it would take her body years to re- cover. Maybe there were permanent residents already, molds and algaes that would never leave, even if she showed them a real Chicago winter. Chicago was like an imaginary place to her, and even her bats seemed far away. This landscape was what seemed real, the eucalyptuses, the elegant black swans and Egyptian ducks in the pond, a piece of chook gristle between her teeth, which she took out and threw to the ducks. They fought for it, and one duck ate it.

"See," said Leon. "Anything in a sandwich."

And Leon Goode, he seemed very real.

Fifteen

The campsite was breezy. Boulders like great cracked eggs
rose up above the river. There was a smell, too, damp rock,
like a cave. Annabel had assembled her tent, but she was
spreading her sleeping bag out on the rock beside his awkward pile of blankets, his makeshift pillow of dirty clothes
wadded into a rain slicker. Leon was growing used to her
quickly; he imagined it would be easier to sleep beside her
than alone in the car. Lately, he'd been more awake at night
than during the day, tormented by places he should have
looked while he had the chance. Why hadn't he asked
Gretel more, where *she'd* be if she were missing, whether
his father had mentioned *anything* the last time she'd seen
him? When had she seen him, were they lovers? Of course
not, she'd been so sure of John Goode's fidelity. It wasn't all
that important, probably, whether he had slept with anyone else besides Lila Wallard—even if it was important, it
wasn't enough to make him disappear, sex.

Then again, Leon's own experience of sex had made
him feel lost sometimes. The first time, with Lizzie, he'd
wanted to cry after they separated. It wasn't an enduring

sensation; it was a quick rift at the end of pleasure. And it got easier as sex became a habit between them.

Leon believed in fidelity; he was sure he'd be able to stay faithful to one woman, once he found her. Sex was important, too important to misuse. Not that he wouldn't imagine other encounters—even when he was with Lizzie he fell in love with the way a woman in a suit rubbed lipstick around the edges of her mouth, engrossed in her car mirror at an intersection, when she thought no one was watching.

Leon took that woman to bed when he was trying to sleep, climbed into her car and slid his hand up her skirt, between her thighs. He made that woman, who he knew only by her lips, arch her back with pleasure as he pressed his tongue into her. But it was all imaginary; he was safe in the real world because he discharged enough electricity in his imagined world. Leon believed in the ability of love to make him trustworthy, and he believed he would have the right kind of love, though he wasn't sure when he'd find it, whether it was something to look for, or whether it would be automatic. He didn't think he was naive; instead, he believed in it, faith.

Knowing about his father's love life was a torment, but still Leon was fascinated, as if that was where the clues lay. He should have asked everyone for more: Gretel, with her strong hands slicing cucumbers for lunch, her thick voice when she said, "John—that is—your father." There was that woman with the makeup, Sabrina. She'd been a flirt. Perhaps she spoke that language, knew something more about his father. He should have interviewed her.

He was being ridiculous, suspicious in all the wrong ways. Gretel was probably right—his father probably believed he was being faithful the whole time, even when he was with Lila. Maybe it was the delayed shock of his own betrayal that had sent him off—wherever he was.

Leon sat in his car, steaming up the windows he'd closed against the mozzies, as he rummaged for supplies. He saw his own path, his temporary blindnesses during each day. Why hadn't he asked for the names of other attendants at the butterfly enclosure? Why hadn't he checked all the pubs in Charters Towers?

Annabel had blushed when he'd asked whether she'd been his father's lover, but after his initial attack of suspicion, he believed her. There was something in her nature that inspired trust—maybe it was the way she went along with him as soon as they met, despite the horrible turn at her research site. Even with her hand on her machete at the pub—perhaps it was her self-sufficient confidence that made him trust.

Annabel took the car to go to the pay phone in town. She had to call her sister, she said, and Townsville, and her mother. She suddenly seemed to remember the rest of the world. Were they really looking, Leon wondered, or were they just half-heartedly following leads, using his father as a chance not to be who they were before he disappeared? He hardly knew anything about Annabel, just that she was American, that she had been scared off from her research site, that she managed a brave grin whenever Leon was ready to give up on his father. And that he didn't want her to go, that something about her kept him awake, her voice, her gestures, her eyes on his face like light.

She'd asked for the car like this: "Leon, toss me the keys?"

And he thought about asking why, looked at her arms curved around her body like parentheses. Instead he said, "Yes," and tossed them to her.

"I have to call my mom, and my sister, and Townsville," she said. "I'll ask if they've heard anything, of course."

When she turned to go, Leon felt desperate. She could drive off forever, she could decide the search wasn't hers; maybe that mother she was calling would want her home. He thought of Andrew, and Mum, and shut his eyes to keep from worrying about them, too. He needed her as she left, needed someone to keep him from giving up, because looking for his father was too big—right now, he wasn't sure he even wanted to find him.

When Annabel came back, Leon was lying back on the cool smooth rock, watching the sun chalk orange into the sky. The mozzies had left when the breeze picked up. This was familiar, too, lying out on giant boulders as stars punched pinholes through the dusk. There were no other campers, so the car crushing gravel seemed as loud as a jet landing in Leon's quiet.

He sat up and saw a dozen or more wallabies by the stream, fussily grooming their faces.

"My sister wasn't home, and neither were my folks, or else they were all screening their calls. I talked with Dr. Sutherland though—he said your mom gave official permission for the army and police to search for your dad. But nothing else from there." She paused and looked at the wallabies. "I brought stuff for s'mores, an American specialty. You've invited dinner guests?" She handed him a box of graham crackers and a wrapped meat pie oiling the paper.

"Tourist wallabies," said Leon. "They'll be wanting directions to Ayers Rock."

"Maybe they've seen a man with one black shoe," she said. "Or better yet, one with one blue eye. They can share our supper." She sat down and unwrapped her meat pie, then tossed a crust toward the wallabies. They came up the rock like a swarm.

"Very unscientific, feeding the subjects."

"Eh. This is a holiday, right?"

"Um—" He raised one eyebrow.

"Not really."

"First they'll surround us," said Leon. "Then they'll ask us to take their photograph in front of the sunset." He bit into the greasy meat pie as Annabel brought hers toward her mouth. It tasted good.

He woke early, because there was nothing to filter the light. The wallabies were all around him, watching his face, like alert waiters. Leon looked at Annabel, a cocoon with one arm pressed to the rock. They could be sleeping on the moon; the planet could be empty except for them and the wallabies. The sky was a radiant pink, and Leon felt like singing.

Maybe he'd invented Ursula. She seemed much less real than the woman beside him, with twigs in her hair, sharing this rock bed. He wondered how his father had seen

Annabel, why he'd written her name and Cathedral Fig on that paper scrap. She'd said she thought it was just about approving her site. Maybe there were other bats he thought she might like to study, maybe he was noting things he had to attend to when he came back to the program. Attend to Annabel Mendelssohn. Her forest scent, so much sureness in her small body. She was much too young for him, Leon thought, and they weren't lovers, but that didn't mean his dad hadn't noticed her, considered. His father was more thickly confusing to him now than he'd ever been, not only because he had disappeared, but because now Leon had to think of him as alone in the world, as someone who traveled and made choices regardless of his family—regardless of Mum. His dad was a composite of images and memories for him, but for John Goode, his life was his own particular movie, the version he chose to step into each minute, how he turned, what he touched or moved away from.

"Too much light," said Annabel. She pulled her sleeping bag over her head.

They made more s'mores for breakfast, cooking marshmallows over the stove, since it was already too warm for another fire. The road to Porcupine Gorge was dotted on the map, the symbol for ungraded dirt. He hoped the car wouldn't be too damaged, that it would get them there and back. Andrew could find another car—it was all he offered in his place for this search. Leon imagined coming back down the dotted road, triumphant, his father riding in the back seat, asleep from his ordeal, like a child. But what if they didn't find him in Porcupine Gorge? He looked at the map, dropping graham-cracker crumbs onto Cloncurry and Julia Creek. Wrong direction, he thought, hoping the food wasn't giving him clues.

"Let's do a sweep of the grounds," said Annabel, saluting.

"Hah," said Leon. He helped her pack up, and they followed the small network of trails in the campground, yelling, "John Goode, Dad, Professor!"

It would have been faster if they'd split up, but Leon didn't suggest it; he wanted company. He didn't like Annabel leaving him alone. He felt like a kid who was too old for a baby-sitter but hated being left in the house by himself.

Leon did take one path by himself, though, a path that led to a small cluster of trees on the side of the boulder field. He had to pee, and he didn't need Annabel along for that.

"Oh fine," said Annabel. "No girls allowed." Then she smiled. "I'll meet you back at the car."

Leon looked at the acacia tree as he peed on its roots. A basket fern like a green gift clumped on a rock at the base. He started to think about all the ways his dad could have died, wishing he had some sort of mental link, like in the movies, that he'd know he was alive somehow. He could have stepped on a venomous snake, he could have drowned. He could have been in a car accident, or met up with some unfriendly person. Some angry anti-environmentalist, some crazy. He rated drowning at 80 percent likeliest, since his dad was always swimming. He tried to picture those pruned fingers, with soil still under the nails, but still it felt fake. Terrible, but fake.

As Leon turned from the tree, he saw something whitish protruding from a small pile of stones. It looked like a seashell, and Leon reached for it, pulled part of a pelvis out from the pebbles. It was baked brittle and dry, but there were still some small scraps of something on the bone. A human pelvis. He put it down, swearing in a whispered stream. Then he picked it up again and brought it to Annabel.

"So, ready to chase porcupines?" said Annabel. She was sitting on the hood of the car, writing a postcard.

Leon held the bone away from his body. There were ants climbing along the powdery edge, big ants, the stinging kind.

"Found a souvenir?" asked Annabel, flashing a glance at him.

"More than that," said Leon. "I've got something I'm not sure I want to identify—"

Annabel jumped up. She took the pelvis from him. "Shit." She fingered the shape. She could be touching my father, thought Leon, this could be him—

"Well, at least it can't be him," she said.

"How do you know?" Leon watched her face. He didn't want to look at the bone.

"Didn't you say you used to operate the invisible woman? Look at the curve—it's female, Leon."

"Transparent Woman." He said. He sat down on the ground. "Of course. Female." He had never fainted, and he wasn't going to let this be the first time, but for a second the world narrowed until he had only a cone of vision. He remembered to breathe. Slowly, slowly, he thought, as the world widened again. "So who is *that* then?"

"I guess we'll leave that up to the authorities, won't we," she said.

She laid the pelvis on the back seat of the car and took

over the driving. Leon was amazed that they'd found something, some great piece of evidence, but it belonged to someone else's mystery, someone else's tragedy. He tried not to think about what could have happened to the woman—how and when did she die, was she murdered? Was her buried body dug up by dingoes? He looked at Annabel; she was holding the wheel with one hand, though the road was bumpy. She was humming, even though they'd found a piece of someone's body.

"It's really old, you know," she said. "It's not your father."

She was detached and calm, precisely what he needed to keep him moving forward, to keep him from looking down into the abyss of possibilities, to keep him from falling.

They drove back down to Charters Towers and left the bone at the police station. After they filled out the forms and answered questions, Annabel told the officer, "We have to get back on the road, we've got a missing person to track down."

"That would be Professor Goode?" said the officer.

Leon shivered. Air-conditioning chilled the room, and he'd sweated during the questions. "How do you know?"

"Report's out, of course," said the officer. "We've been keeping an eye out for him at the pub."

"Great," said Annabel. "We won't need to stop there, then." She turned to Leon. "While we're here, let's do a quick sweep around town," she said.

Leon nodded, wondering whether she agonized over their path in the same way at night or whether her conscience was as clear as it seemed—light, scientific.

Sixteen

The bone had troubled Leon, she thought—he looked dazed, closed inside his own thoughts when they reached Charters Towers. She led him around the town like a child, asking questions in the post office, the bank, the Stock Exchange Arcade, where there was a mining museum. It wasn't horrible to be looking, as long as she was organized—the work was another research project. And something about Leon made them a complete enough world by themselves, so she didn't long for her lost solitude, or for any additional company. It wasn't right to notice, but the shape of his eyes belonged to his father, the square chin, though the mouth was different from the one she'd imagined kissing. Softer somehow—interesting, but less dangerous.

She kept thinking of Maud, how when she'd said she was leaving the program, Annabel had thought she could never just quit like that, shift priorities. But she'd done just that when she left her site. This search was most important now, keeping on some kind of path, even if the scent had long since faded.

She'd developed her photographs at the One-Hour while she was in Charters Towers with Leon's car. She hadn't shown them to him: blurry shots of giant clams, Lars and mudskippers, the line of faces leaning out of the train at Chillagoe. Her bats. Her site was thick and green and the bats turned toward her inside the frames of warm, developer-scented prints. She sat in the plastic white habitat of the photo booth at the back of the milk bar. Bird-eating spiders. Then there were three shots at the end of the roll: John Goode packing up his ratty little car.

In one he was lifting his huge box, bent badly so his back would hurt. He was wearing his Forest Preservation cap, the one with the patch of a green tree on a red background. The cap itself was white, smudged with sweat and soil. She remembered the weight of it, warm with his sweat, when he'd put it on her head back at the reef island. The smell of the sea.

The next shot was in profile as he leaned against the car, cap off, looking toward the university. In the last shot, he was turned to face Annabel, squinting against the sun, looking past the camera at something invisible to the frame, holding up one arm as if waving good-bye.

Annabel wanted to go back to that moment, to sprint out of the grass and stop the mistake of his departure, change the time line, or, at the very least, ask him where he was going.

The man in the railway office remembered Professor Goode, because he'd been working at Chillagoe when the professor had organized the field program's train expedition, the special arrangements for the van.

"Has he been through *here* then, you think?" the man asked Annabel.

"That's what we're trying to find out," she said. Leon was fidgeting with the train schedules, restacking the pile. "We'd hoped you could help."

"Sorry, love, but let me take your number—I'll keep a lookout," he said. Annabel wrote the Townsville program number on the back of a schedule.

They walked away from the station, past several gorgeous lacework-detailed houses that gold had built. Annabel pictured sitting on the veranda of the bright blue house they were passing, with John and Leon Goode, laughing over his disappearance, drinking iced tea.

"Can I buy you an ice cream?" Annabel wanted to do something to wrest Leon from his shell. "Or a vodka?"

"Let's get on to Porcupine Gorge."

"Let's just look around a bit more," she said.

She led them to a small shop that sold opals, jewelry, postcards, and a one-dollar, self-guided tour of an opal cave. Annabel paid two cave-tour admissions and asked the woman behind the counter whether she'd seen a man with one blue eye, one brown, a professor with wild hair and an attractive smile. She looked at Leon as she said "attractive," hoped he wasn't listening hard, because he'd been so suspicious earlier. Leon was letting silver chains on a circular rack slide through his fingers.

The woman had seen someone like that, she thought, a few weeks ago. "About my age, love?" she asked.

Annabel looked at her, assessing: maybe a hard-lived late fifties. Her hair was dyed an orange color, but Annabel could still see gray at the roots. Yes, she thought, that old, your age. "Uh-huh, that's about right."

"I think he was looking at something for his wife, could that be right?"

Leon dropped the chains and stepped over to the counter. "What did he say?" he asked.

"I think he said he was looking for a peace offering—hey, you two aren't private investigators or anything, are you? Like on the telly? I saw this show—"

"No." Annabel reached out, touched the woman's sleeve to ground her, to ground herself. "What else did he say?"

"He had rather dirty hands if I remember it, cracked nails. I said he ought to get a manicure, maybe that would please his wife. And he laughed." She looked at Leon. "You his brother or something?"

"Son."

"Oh, dear, guess he was about my age then." She smirked, waiting for something, a compliment, perhaps, denial of her age.

"Did he buy anything?" Annabel felt calm with possibility. It could be him, but it could also be this woman trying to gratify. Would a man buy an opal and take it back into the field? How could anyone predict what someone would do, their order—a normal person even, let alone a scientist, let alone Professor Jump-out-of-Boats-and-Swim-with-Crocodiles Goode?

"You know, I think he decided to wait. Though he could have put something on layaway—"

"Could you check your receipts? In case he did? His name was Goode, John Goode." Annabel felt Leon stiffen beside her. "That *is* his name," she said.

"Maybe I'll call home," said Leon. "Though I'm not sure she wants to know. Maybe I'll call the university." He leaned on the counter, not going anywhere.

Annabel put her hand against the small of Leon's tense back and led him to the cave entrance at the end of the shop. "Let's spelunk first," she said. "We have the tickets."

He hovered at the entrance, holding back. Annabel took his hand—it was sweaty and warm. He smelled good, lemony, and she thought for a minute she might like to touch his face, too, she might like to taste his skin, to offer comfort with something other than words and hand-holding. She wanted to press him against her, to tell him everything would be all right. She wanted to believe that, too. John Goode's son, she thought. Everything wasn't all right and she wasn't here for romance. She led him down the rusty metal stairs to the opal cave.

It was as cold as a walk-in freezer, ceiling and floor adorned with stalactites and stalagmites in some places, and bald where they'd been cut away to create a path. There were signs bolted to the walls and a running extension cord for caged bulbs that lit up the path. Annabel didn't pause to read the tour signs as she strode down the walkway. Not a real cave, she thought, no bats. It smelled of paint.

Leon held her hand tightly, and the walk was urgent, in the cold dark, neither of them knowing what the woman in the shop would say. Leon was shivering now, but she didn't say anything. She led him past the signs and out again; the exit deposited them in a lot outside the shop.

"We could leave," said Leon. "We could just go home. I don't see how it can make any difference. What could she possibly know?" He sat on a parking barrier in the sandy gravel of the parking lot.

"I want to get a look at the porcupines," said Annabel. She took both his hands and pulled him to his feet. Then she let his hands go and put her own inside her pockets.

Walking back to the shop, she realized she hadn't thought of Robert for so long she felt as if she'd fallen inside a dream, feet trying to step on the blank space of bedsheet as she woke without landing. But the lurch passed, and it was all right, it only ached a little.

Letting go, this is what people meant when they said it; she'd always imagined releasing Robert's hand, letting him fall, but he was different now—he was with her, but not gripping so hard. Annabel wondered whether Alice had done this, too, or if she couldn't because of her suspicions, if that was why she never really wrote or talked about him, changed the subject or kept him safe in the ancient history of childhood stories.

Annabel looked at Leon. Perhaps he would have to let go, too. Perhaps his father would show up dead, they'd find the body, abruptly stop the forward momentum of a search.

Leon was still shivering.

They hadn't found anything yet. "Okay," she said. "Next stop, Porcupine Gorge." She kept her voice even and energized.

"I don't think you understand." He was looking at his feet. "Maybe in the States you always find what you're looking for—who—but here people just go missing."

"I don't think he wanted to," said Annabel, thinking of her photographs, of John Goode packing his car to go—

wherever he was going, without explanation, without leaving instructions or telling anyone. She'd been a voyeur then, too, watching as her subject made his inexplicable migration. Wherever he'd gone, he'd been full of intention. Maybe he'd been thinking about rocks or soil samples, but he wasn't thinking about his students, his colleagues, or his family. Someone who recognized the constellation of people who mattered to him, to whom he mattered, would've told someone where he was going. But Leon probably knew this. He probably knew it as deeply as knowing love.

"I don't, either," said Leon. He leaned his hand on her shoulder as heavily as a tired man might lean against a tree.

At the opal shop, the woman was waiting for them. Annabel brought a handful of postcards to the desk and handed over a bright Australian bill.

"So," she said. "Did you check your receipts?"

"No Goode," the woman said. "He must have just browsed. And you know, I think he said he was a dairy farmer, not a professor."

"Oh dear." Annabel looked at Leon. He looked at the floor.

"One more question," she said, putting the change in her pocket and taking the small paper bag. She ignored the sensation that her throat was closing. "Do you remember him saying *anything at all* about where he was going?"

"Sorry, love. Not a thing."

The road to Porcupine Gorge was rougher than bad seas. Annabel started a postcard to Alice right before they hit the first ungraded section, but she surrendered after smudging ink on both the blank part and the side with the photograph of the opal cave. They gave up trying to talk, because it was like coughing when they tried, air pushed out hard, words incomprehensible. Annabel watched Leon as he drove, worried that he was drifting somehow. The opal shop had been exhausting—the charge of possibility, the drain of disappointment. Could you keep someone from falling, she wondered, from losing themselves in loss?

Her molars rattled as if they were loose. There was a ringing in her head—from the motion, she supposed. Leon turned on the radio and tried to tune, but found only static with occasional music. He laughed. She was glad to see the quick flash of pleasure on his face.

"Do you mind driving a little?" It sounded like he was yelling though a fan.

"Do I what?"

"Mind taking over the wheel?"

"Did you say something about bread? What?"

"Tuuuuuuuuuurrrrrrrrrnnnn tooooooooo driiiiiiiive?" sang Leon. He stopped the car in the middle of the road and laughed. "Oooh, it's quiet now," he said. "I like that. We could camp here."

"Tuuuuuuuuurn toooooooo drive," said Annabel. She unclipped her seat belt. "Don't mind if I do."

The mozzies were relentless at the park, so Annabel parked herself inside her tent with the food. She asked Leon to come, too, thinking it was comfortable with him. And that she liked having him close, that his shoulders' slope was beautiful, and that she ought to do nothing at all about it. Just help him look for his dad. She sliced the mango into their bowls of muesli and licked her fingers; sweetness spoiled by the faint taste of bug spray.

"So," she said, as Leon sat eating beside her. "Do you have the map? I want to go at this like scientists."

Leon put down his bowl of cereal, mango, and the last fresh milk they'd have for a while. He opened a crinkly new map. "We're here," he said, pointing to the edge marked by the gates. "We've got to search here—" He swept his hands over the rest of the map and tried to smile at Annabel, but it was more like a grimace.

"Do you mind if I write on this?" She took out a jackknife-sharpened pencil.

"Be my guest."

Annabel used the edge of Alice's cave postcard to draw straight division lines, making approximately equal plots. "We can mark them out tomorrow." She pulled the orange marking tape from her day pack. "And then check out two to four per day, depending on whether we split up, and how dense the terrain is."

"Some of those squares are vertical scree." Leon pointed to the gorge section, thickly lined to indicate elevation.

"So that makes them easier—we'll go here." She pointed to an adjacent plot. "And we'll yell in that direction. I know it's not perfect, but what do you think?"

"We can split up after the first few days," said Leon.

"If it takes that long."

"I don't want anyone else getting lost."

"He really might be here."

Leon sighed and picked up his bowl. "I checked the log by the gate—it's beside the water fountain and a bunch of warning signs about hiking alone, and packing in water, and bringing a compass."

"And?"

"He didn't sign in here, but that doesn't mean anything, really. Dad was never very good about signing in. Or bringing water. Though he does pack a compass, thank God, since his sense of direction is often a bit off."

Annabel looked at the scabs on his knees. There was a new mosquito bite on his arm, one on his neck.

"But he always found his way back," Leon said.

"You can sleep in here if you'd like," said Annabel. She hoped he wouldn't take it the wrong way, that she wouldn't mumble too much at night, or find she'd rolled over into his arms while she slept.

"Thank you."

"I've got a local newspaper out in the car—we can waste batteries reading about the logging accidents in Atherton and who's bought a new tractor. Do you think there's a crossword puzzle?"

"Maybe you'll get a scramble," said Leon.

Back in the tent, Annabel watched as Leon folded and refolded his gray wool army surplus blankets on the tent floor and picked up pine needles and pebbles and slid them out a crack in the door zipper. Fastidious, thought Annabel, so careful. He hadn't mentioned any women in his life, but she didn't know how to ask the right way.

"So, any scramble?" He stretched out on his blankets, calmer than she'd seen him all day. He looked almost happy.

"Jesus," said Annabel, as she opened to the third page of the paper. "No, but it does say SYDNEY PROFESSOR MISSING."

"It what?"

"According to this, your dad has been spotted consorting with Aborigines, living in a cave. He's 'gone bush,' it says. Damn, this paper is a piece of crap. They didn't mention this when I called Townsville."

"What else?" Leon was lying on his back, still, eyes closed.

" 'I don't want to be found.' It's a quote. Some beer factory worker on holiday says he spotted your dad, dressed dramatically—maybe this guy found Sasquatch—"

"Who's Sasquatch?"

"Bigfoot? You know, any mythical man-beast. The paper says 'wild hairy bushman,' so I interpreted," said Annabel.

"Bigfoot?"

"He's a giant man-beast, mythical?"

"Oh, the bunyip."

"What?"

"Bunyip."

"Oh. So your dad, apparently, is a hairy bush beast—a bunyip—who doesn't want to be found."

"That last part doesn't sound entirely untrue."

"Sorry, Leon."

"No need to be—we have a plan, we'll look for him tomorrow. Maybe we'll find Bigfoot. Big Foot? Is the rest of him big, too, or does he just have one set of cucumber toes?"

Annabel laughed and turned off her light. "We won't waste any more batteries on that thing," she said, tossing the paper aside.

She listened to his breathing in the dark, waited for it to slow and deepen. If he didn't fall asleep, she could ask him if he was all right. She imagined their voices in the dark, at the edge of the gorge, by the empty spaces of the woods. Full of animals, vines, and the possibility of Professor Goode. She could tell him about Robert; maybe it would help, she thought. Robert, who was beginning to be finite, complete in his death. John Goode was amorphous; he threatened her cautious peace. Annabel listened to Leon's steady breath, a sweet and solid sound, and fell asleep without saying anything.

The anticipation of the first few days had passed. Leon had plunged through the woods at first, calling, half expecting to discover his father by a campfire, cooking a porcupine on a spit, that bright boy face. Looking through trees and vines, at the crooked horizons of the gorge, he had been imagining his father as younger than himself. It was as if, as the time he'd been missing grew, he lost years. He became a young man, impatient, strong. Leon realized that he'd always thought his father could handle any physical challenge—until he'd seen him in the movie house with Lila Wallard. That weakened his father, to Leon, made him not only bumbling but also vulnerable.

After the scrambling and scratches of a few days, the food and water Leon and Annabel had packed in was running low, and Leon no longer expected Porcupine Gorge

to produce his father. In fact, while he searched methodi-
cally, dogged, he stopped expecting John Goode's slouched
form, his shoulders. Leon's shouts became routine, and he
didn't anticipate an answer.

Annabel was stubborn in her method; she'd mapped out
squares for them to search and she kept him to it. When he
thought one of her plots, a viney tangle of thorny acacias
and stinging trees, was best explored at the perimeter, she'd
insisted on breaking the square into its own grid, plowing
through, searching as if his father were as small as a lost
watch, and as quiet, ticking.

At the camp, on night three, it started to rain hard, and
their small fire was muted into wet coal glow. They took
their remaining provisions: crackers, a plastic tube of peanut butter, and beef jerky, into the tent. She was so easy
about this, too, about sleeping in the space together. At
night sometimes Leon woke, incredibly horny, and watched
her sleeping shape in her bag. He couldn't do anything
about his state without making noise, and he couldn't wake
her with evidence that he thought about her that way. On
another night he'd gone outside, walked away from the
site, worried that she might wake up too and call for him
and, even for a second, have someone else to look for.

It was too muddy and wet to leave the tent. His sleeping
bag was slick with damp where he pressed against the side.
His toes were damp inside his socks. Leon listened to the
rain's percussion, still searching with his eyes closed.

On the fifth afternoon, the rain paused and sun splintered
through the trees. Trekking through his assigned section,
Leon found a gorgeous emerald tree frog, pulsing green

on the side of a ficus trunk. So tiny, so visible, so alive. It stood there, the sides heaving for breath, the jewel eyes unblinking. Leon addressed the frog: "Are you my father?" He could be, he thought, charmed, waiting for my mother to kiss him and bring him back to human form. Leon chuckled and the frog scrabbled up the tree with suction-cup toes. Leon felt guilty for his moment of silly pleasure, as if he could jeopardize his father's safety with laughter.

"Hey!" It was Annabel's voice, the first time he'd heard it since morning. The sound was muted, hidden some-where in the ficus trunks and palms and vines. Leon turned and shoved through the wet green, jumping over the bod-ies of fallen trees without sweeping for snakes.

"What is it?" he yelled as he ran toward her.

Her words blurred over the sound of his running. He tripped, falling through thorns that shredded his shirt like giant cat claws. Finally he found her on the slant of a hill, standing and staring at something they hadn't seen on the map. A thin deep line of water cut a cliff below Annabel. It was invisible until you were almost on top of it: a drop of thirty or forty feet into a fast-flowing river. Annabel was pointing at an eddy.

"What? Can we get down there?"

"I tried from the other side, but it's really too steep," she said. She pointed upriver, and Leon saw a fallen tree spread across the fifteen-foot span of the hidden gorge.

"I thought I saw something," she continued. "But it's only a river. I thought you should see it, though, so you'd be careful." She smiled at Leon, and he let his breath slow. The adrenaline had stopped and his muscles ached with the acid of flight. Annabel stood there, a small bossy

woman with bright eyes and a muddy shirt who didn't
know anything more than he did. He wished she hadn't
yelled. He wished she'd yelled for something real. He
wished they were finished, that he could stop being bereft
and get on with things. A shower, real food. That she'd just
leave him alone and stop leading him around. That they
weren't looking for his father. That he could kiss her.

She almost fell into it, despite her careful footing. Annabel
stopped at the edge of the gorge because she had a desperate itch inside her boot. As she stood up from scratching, she heard the water; it was a sudden sound, in a
narrow envelope of space. She couldn't hear it standing,
only crouched, and then there it was, a cut in the earth like
a deep wound.

There was no way down. Maybe with ropes, she thought
at first, but the edges were loose; any pebble could be a
keystone. She followed the edge, careful not to step too
close. The earth could collapse anywhere. She was walking
out of her square, maybe into Leon's. She needed to warn
him, so he wouldn't fall. But first she should investigate for
herself.

A tree lay across the gorge, a silky oak, wrapped by a
strangler fig. It was still living, roots upended by erosion
where the stones and soil had slipped into the cut. But
when she pressed her weight against it, it held. Annabel
tightened her pack so there was no gap against her back,
tucking in the straps so they wouldn't catch on anything.
She leaned harder, then shimmied out onto the bridge, legs
and arms wrapped in a tight hug around the damp bark,

looking across instead of down. All I'm doing is climbing a tree, she thought to stay calm. She inched along, pulling hard to cross over a strangler vine, her hair pressed against her face and her hands working for continuous holds.

About halfway across, she paused. The tree sagged slightly under her weight. Annabel imagined the bend, the tree folding more and more, invisible motion until it let go and slipped into the crack, taking her down in a quiet slump. The pressure of possibility felt good, the sap sticking to her wrist and a wait-a-while vine tugging the fabric of her shirt as she rested her cheek against the trunk. It smelled of moss and rot. She looked down. A blur of water, a thin white-and-gray line, a secret passage under the skin of the forest. The tree was too narrow, and suddenly her breath was fast. She shimmied the rest of the way across without looking down again.

After searching the other side, Annabel crossed back over, quickly this time. She lay at the edge of the gorge by her tree-bridge, scanning the bottom with her binoculars. There were the dots of data: stone, water, stone; and she sought something significant in the pattern. In the first eddy, there were glints like a handful of coins, but then she realized they were stones with silvery deposits, maybe mica, made bright by sun and water. Dead leaves spun in languorous circles where the current was caught in the eddy's bowl.

In the second eddy, she saw a scrap of red in the leaves. As the water moved, the red looked unnatural, the red of human invention, of thread and cloth. She refocused her binoculars and rubbed her eyes. Maybe it was a parrot feather, she thought, watching the water move. The red scrap surfaced for a second before it slid out of the eddy like a fish, set free. As it skimmed across her binocular vision, Annabel thought she recognized the shape of a green tree stitched on a red background, a shape she'd seen before. The patch on Professor Goode's hat.

Then it was gone, slipped down the waterslide of the river. Annabel scanned, but she couldn't find it again. She looked up at the tree where she'd crossed the gorge. Maybe it was a parrot feather after all. A red scrap of cloth, the light fooling her eyes. It could have been anything.

On night six, the rain returned and evolved from tentative fingers to pounding fists. "Three more squares," said Leon, spreading peanut butter on a cracker. "I could do them myself if it's still raining—you could head back to the entrance and get some water."

"No." Annabel was staring at the map again. It was folded into sections; some of the marks around the edges were worn off from refolding. "I put an empty bottle out in the rain. I'm with you."

Leon thought she was too stubborn sometimes, and sometimes she was selfish in her selflessness. She'd told him she found the other students hard to relate to, and he'd laughed and called them wimps, but now he wondered if maybe part of it was her dogged approach to work, her explicit selflessness, her drive. It was hard to be around her without feeling inferior. It was getting hard to be around her without wanting to touch her, too.

"You don't *have to*." He said this without looking at her.

"I do."

"He's my missing father."

"Oh." Annabel put down the map. "I know that, I'm not trying to claim him or anything, Leon. I just want to help you finish the job here. I hate leaving a job unfinished."

"And your bats?" He knew it wasn't fair of him, but he felt the pleasure of released steam; he could want an argument if he wasn't careful.

"Gee, thanks," said Annabel. She shifted to the corner of her tent. Clammed up. Just the sound of rain on the nylon roof.

Leon let it thrill him for a second, the fight. Then he felt awful. He lay across the tent floor, facing her. "I'm a jerk, sorry," he said.

"Just don't *be* a jerk in the first place," said Annabel.

Damn, she didn't like to make things easy. But then he did something he had never intended to—it was like his dream-life taking over: he sat up and kissed her.

"Oh," said Annabel. But she had kissed him back, he was sure of the pressure.

"Annabel." He lay back down again, head on her thigh.

"No, Leon," said Annabel, but she touched his hair, made his scalp electric with pleasure. "We shouldn't do this now." She clicked off her flashlight, leaving them in the dark.

"You're right," he said. He didn't mean it, though. He was afraid to ask why not—maybe she wasn't interested, maybe she thought it was wrong. Leon waited in the quiet and dark, his lips delicious from the touch. He didn't move his head from her lap.

"Leon." Annabel touched his hair again, and every bit of his body pulsed with the torture of wanting to hold her, taste her, press against her.

"My brother died."

His body cooled a single degree as he tried to concentrate on her words instead of her touch.

"He was a marine biologist, and he drowned on a dive."

"Oh, God," said Leon. He sat up.

"Wait," she said. "I have to say it. He died by accident. For a while, I thought maybe it wasn't—that he'd killed himself—"

Her voice was wavering, and Leon wanted to touch her face to test for tears, but he thought it was better not to touch. She took a loud breath, and her voice evened out.

"But now I know he wouldn't do that—that it wasn't on purpose. And I'm starting to get used to the idea that he's dead." She reached out for Leon, found his hand.

"This isn't the same thing," she continued, her voice strong now. "You know, looking for your dad."

"I know," said Leon.

"But I had to tell you," she said.

"Annabel, I'm very sorry." Missing could be permanent, he thought. That's the part she hadn't said. Missing, for all its shadows and clues, could be as permanent as dead.

"Thank you," she said. She moved forward, kneeling on the tent floor, and sighed. Then she kissed him. He put his arm around her back, surprised by her scent as he pulled her close, the smell of woods and ferns.

Annabel's sleeping-bag zipper was biting an impression in Leon's side. He wanted to see her, now that the taste of her mouth was on his, her skin, the perfect indentation at the small of her back.

"Wait," he said, sitting up, groping for a flashlight.

"I know," said Annabel. She was whispering, though there was probably no one around for kilometers. "We shouldn't."

"Oh," said Leon. "No, I just—"

"I mean, I want to, but I wonder whether we, I mean— I don't think we should, yet."

"Annabel." He lay back down and tucked his arm behind her head. He wanted to, but he thought of how alone they were, why they had come here, and that he couldn't afford to lose her now. Or to lose himself.

"I'm happy to wait," he said.

"Oh. Okay." She relaxed against him. They kissed again, then lay together, each pretending to sleep. He still wanted to see her in the light, but he'd have to wait until morning.

Seventeen

Sender: (Annabel Mendelssohn)
AMendelss@ausnet.jcooku.tvl.edu
To: AEMendel@biosci.com
Subject: Hello Alice.
Tuesday, April 16, 1996
Back in Townsville.

Alice, I hardly know what to write. I've been
searching for Professor Goode with his son, Leon,
since god, I guess it's been three weeks, though
it feels like a million years. I left you that
phone message so you wouldn't worry about me, and
don't please, I'm safe. The police are looking
now, and SAS, an emergency rescue group. A big
search crew met us at the entrance to Porcupine
Gorge when we were on our way out, and we looked
with them for another six days, helicopters and
bullhorns and infrared. A few days before we left,
a volunteer group found his car parked on a small
path off the Kennedy Developmental Road, a few

kilometers from the gorge. We went to look—and the
car was fine. It had rock hammers in back, a box of
rotted food, and a collection of partly labeled
soil samples. The camping gear was gone. There
were no notes, or anything. The police said "No
evidence of foul play."

I don't know what else I can say. The rescue guys
are still using helicopters, but there are tricky
places in the park they might never see—unexpected
gorges, rock fields with landslide scars. We found
someone who saw him when he got the permit, a
ranger guy at that park, so we know he was there
sometime, but who knows, he could've fallen in the
gorge, he could have found a venomous snake. It's
awful not to have anything, so we still don't know
whether he's alive.

Leon is wonderful. Really truly wonderful. And I
am okay.

Love, Annabel

It was like a date, walking up the creaky wood steps to
Maud's boyfriend's apartment. Maud and William's apartment. Leon was dressed in a new T-shirt and his jeans were
washed; she almost didn't recognize his smell as he walked
beside her, lint and soap over the musky scent of his body.
Annabel had dug a skirt out of her storage pile in the dorm
house. She'd shaved her legs in the shower, noticing her
body, its bruises and scrapes, and how lovely it seemed to

her, the body Leon touched, the curve of her calf into her ankle. It was like gaining secret powers, having someone appreciate your body like that.

Sabrina would come back tomorrow from her last work in the field. She would spend a few days packing up and then she'd go home to Syracuse, where she was interviewing for a lab job. Annabel imagined her twirling the straw in her diet soda at lunch in some food court, saying "When I worked in the field—"

Until Sabrina came back to the house, they had the room to themselves. It felt clandestine, sneaking a boy back to her room. They'd been sleeping on the floor, because her mattress was too small, and because they'd grown used to a hard surface. Annabel felt too big for the room, too big for indoors now. And it was eerie to be back where she'd known Professor Goode, where she'd first heard him lecture. Looking for him in Porcupine Gorge, somewhere she'd never been, seemed natural. Not looking where she'd seen him last felt awkward, as if the landscape held secrets from his ordinary life.

Maud, standing in the apartment door's frame, looked different than Annabel remembered. Her face was clear and bright, and she was wearing lipstick, but she had deep creases around her eyes. Annabel had thought of her as a colleague, a classmate, but now, beside William, she looked old.

"Hey," said Annabel, falling into a hug. She tried to kiss Maud's cheek, but her lips brushed an ear.

"Hey," said William. He embraced her, too, his body stiff. He had an uneven haircut, and a blond cowlick stood up at the back of his head so he looked like a bird with a crest.

"Leon Goode," said Maud. She looked at him, and Annabel felt a surge of proprietary feeling. She didn't want him to have to talk about his father.

Dinner was a huge fish stew over rice. Sitting at a round, rickety table, drinking wine and using utensils, Annabel was surprised that she remembered how to do all this, how to live in a world of ordered objects. She also adored it, the tastes and the cleanness, that her clothes weren't damp and she had a napkin to wipe her mouth. She watched Leon talking. He was telling Maud and William about the museum, and she could hear the even breaths he took between sentences, pacing himself for the next installment.

"Kind of like your work, William," said Maud, wiping sauce from her mouth. Her lipstick came off, too.

"Not really, though." Leon tilted his head. "I mean, you're building something, you're studying. I just demonstrate."

"Sometimes the kids watch me feeding in the tank," said William. "I'm a bloody clown then." He grinned.

"And I see you eat your subjects," Leon said, holding up a forkful.

Annabel let their accents wash over her, British and Australian. It was Maud who sounded foreign, the American. Maud seemed to belong here, though. As Annabel watched her, in the apartment decorated with a photograph of Maud and William, a knitting project in a corner she assumed was her friend's, books and a fish tank where every fish had a name, the surface of age faded from Maud. She looked loved.

"I've got to go out of the country to refresh my visa next month," said Maud, as if divining Annabel's thoughts.

"How long is it good?"

"For six months at a time, up to two years, as long as I leave in between."

Maud belonged here now. Annabel wondered whether she'd stay.

"And after that?" As she asked, Annabel wished she could will the words back. William was right beside them.

"We'll see." Maud sighed. "I'm trying not to think that far ahead, but the job's good, and William—" William glanced up, then went back into conversation with Leon. "Well, he's good too."

"So, next month, Tahiti?"

"Too far, though we thought about going to Rarotonga. Lots of excellent snorkeling. I don't like to dive, though— so we're going to New Zealand. It's a quick hop of a flight." She almost sounded Australian to Annabel. She could become Australian. What would it be like to give up a place for someone?

Annabel wondered whether it would be strange for Leon back at home, back in Boston, being the man with the accent. She tried to picture him there, watching his mouth as he spoke, as he ate. She tried to picture herself with him there, the fields of belonging reversed. Leon at her sister's house, squeezed in a corner of the big couch. Leon beside her on an East Coast train, passing the white stripes of houses, the thin blue of the northern sky.

The food was delicious: cumin, tomato, wine. Watching Leon speak was even more delicious.

.   .   .

They didn't say anything about Professor Goode until the end, until they were thanking and hugging by the open door. The parrots had long since stopped their chatter. Evening entered the apartment, thick sea air, and an edge of chill. Maud and William like a bank of dunes fronting their domestic scene.

"So," Maud whispered as she held Annabel. "What now? About John Goode, I mean."

Annabel took Leon's arm. "I guess we're going to let the authorities do their work."

"Well, let me know if there's anything I can—we can do," said Maud.

"Thank you." Leon touched Annabel's green earring.

On the walk back to the dorm house, the campus was quiet, the students off for break. A dog trotted past them, sure of its direction, down the road, turning left. Annabel felt the weight of Leon's hand in hers, the weight of this place. It felt like it couldn't be completely right, the bliss of touching him now, the sweetness of being together. Like it might be an excuse, like they'd fallen together out of the frustration of not finding John Goode. It wasn't true, she thought, and the timing wasn't fair. His lemon taste, his shifting walk, the slight comedy of his voice; she wanted to keep him with her, close the small pucker, the space between alone and loneliness, with Leon. An unexpected match. Before now, she would never have chosen him from a crowd, but now she would see only his face among the many, like a single red-lit male cardinal in a flock of dun-colored sparrows. She held his hand and looked at the sky; the marine layer obscured all but a few dim stars.

She wanted to *do* something for Leon, to give him something to fill the hole of looking. She knew this hole; mystery had a special place of discomfort in the human heart. Robert's mystery—this was why she let it fall from her, why she'd decided her answer was accident: because she didn't want to keep dividing him with the possibilities. Annabel wanted to let him be whole in her memory, the history complete with its tenderness and dangers. She wanted to have part of Robert left, and the way to keep him was to believe he hadn't wanted to take himself from her.

Leon, his hand soft in hers, would have to decide his father's history on his own. She wanted to save him from that terrible dive; she wanted to hold him hard enough that he wouldn't have to jump. And she wanted his eyes of forest and sky to look at her, to choose her as their direction.

In the room, Annabel took off Leon's shirt. She could leave John Goode outside, she thought, touching Leon's lips. He carried a veneer of sadness.

"Okay?" she asked.

"Okay," said Leon. He looked at her, and his face was so sad that for an instant she thought it would make her cry.

"Hey." Annabel kissed his neck, breathing in the scent beneath the clean soap smell. "Are you tired? Do you want to talk?"

Leon sat down on the narrow bed, pulled her down in his lap. "No," he said. "Not tired." He slid his hand inside her shirt. The lamp in the corner cast a wedge of light across his face, and the sadness passed like the shadow of a cloud.

Annabel took off her shirt and lay down, pressing against him. She wanted to blend her body with his, to mix and end the sweet and painful separation.

"I think we should," she whispered.

"God, yes," said Leon. He chuckled. "We definitely should."

They pulled the sleeping bag over them on the bed, pulling off their clothing. Leon's zipper stuck on his underwear and Annabel laughed, wrestling with the cotton and metal, pulling the jeans down over his thin hips. They almost fell off the bed, but it was good this way, balancing on something narrow, forced to stay tight and close together.

Eighteen

"You don't have to come to Sydney," said Leon. He slouched against his car in the slanted afternoon sun. Annabel leaned against him. His eyes were green in the light.

"I want to. But I don't know how long it'll take to wrap things up—" She breathed him in. This would have to keep her until she finished her work, sitting alone in the computer trailer, drafting what she could with her data, until she'd seen what was left to see up in Malanda.

"Thank you," he said, kissing her. His mouth tasted of mint.

She watched his car leave without her, painting red dust tracks on the black pavement. After she finished her work, she would go to Sydney, to his family's house, to whatever happened next. Annabel imagined a service, the brother and the mother. Would they cry? Would she? She would go back to Boston with him; she'd bring him to New Jersey to meet her family with its own lost limb. She didn't care what her parents thought of him, though she hoped Alice might appreciate his long laugh. There would be civilized dinners, like the one with Maud. They'd learn to move around a kitchen together, passing cutting boards and pears like ordinary adults. It was worth trying.

Until then, he would be with her, his taste, the imprint of his touch on her wrist, when she went out into the field, now, and later, when she got grants to go to Texas or New Guinea. For once, something mattered more than the picture made by the dots of her data: their possibilities.

Not jumping to conclusions, she thought, watching the dust fan out in the bright light, becoming a cloud, then a pale smear, then nothing. Not imagining too far into the future, just trying. She knew they were possible as a couple, not only because they shared this fresh history, or because he understood that she needed to study, to keep looking for something of significance in the bat worlds, but because she had expertise in *being left,* as Leon's father had put it, in the particular channels loss mined through your surface and deep inside.

And Leon, though he might not know it yet, had been left—not only by Professor John Goode's disappearance but in all the rehearsals he'd staged, as best Annabel understood his history. Some people, she realized, people like Robert and Professor Goode, no matter how they're lost to you and no matter what you find when you search, will always, somehow, be permanently missing.

She conjured Leon's face, his square shoulders, his arm when he slept, crooked around one hip and smooth-skinned in the light filtered by her dorm room's shades. The arm of someone who had been left. It made him belong to her.

A block from their mother's house, the muffler fell off
Andrew's car. The scrape and roar filled the quiet neighborhood, and Leon started laughing.

"Hey," he said. "Since you're driving, does that mean it's
not my fault?"

"Bugger," said Andrew. "Bugger." He shoved Leon's
shoulder but cracked a smile.

"Well?"

"Yes, I suppose that could be true. I also suppose you'll
spot me the cash to have it fixed?"

"What, spent all your savings up in Brisbane?" Leon
looked at his brother as he pulled the brake. Andrew was
tan and thin, but he'd been home most of the time Leon
was gone, only once catching a bus up to Brisbane for a
little surfing. Mostly, he'd been with Mum, helping her
search, meeting with the police and detectives; he'd explained it all to Leon on the long drive back.

Leon's mother had given in to searching. John Goode's
dingy white car was parked in the back of the house, the
soil-sample box and other contents stacked in her office.
The dining room table was full of paperwork, copies of the
police reports, and newspaper clippings on the mad professor gone bush. It made Leon wince a little as he sorted
through them, and sometimes he couldn't help laughing.

They sat in the living room, Drew fiddling with a hole
in the bottom of his T-shirt. Molly Goode had put the
wedding portrait back on the mantle, and Leon looked
across at it, as if it held answers—his father's wide grin, his
thick wild hair. A clue in his face or on his suit.

"The worst was the phone call," said Molly. Leon had read about the helicopter pilot who'd joined the effort after Leon and Annabel left. In the clipping, he swore he'd seen John Goode at a makeshift campground near the river in Porcupine Gorge. The pilot said he'd flown in closer, but the man on the ground—John Goode, he'd said—waved a gun at him, and then fired. He'd called Molly Goode to give her his story in person.

"He was so proud, this pilot," she said. Leon focused on the portrait, still, but he put his hand on hers. "He asked if I wanted him to come visit me in my time of need, and that's when I really didn't believe him. I said there was no way John would have a gun, but he said John didn't want to be found." She looked at Leon, her voice steady. "That he was running away from the world."

"That's absurd," said Leon. Drew was bobbing his head to a private rhythm. He'd heard this before.

"Yes and no," said his mother. "The part about running away. Not that I really think he'd run away *this* way. But he would never have had a gun. And besides, you'd already been there—there was a ground crew searching the same area. I think he said it for publicity."

"Should I go back?"

"The pilot just wanted attention."

"But really, I would go back, check the river area again. I don't know if Annabel would come back—"

"Don't be ridiculous, Leon." She stood up and put her arms around him. "You've done enough already. If he was there, we'd know." Her arms were heavy and warm.

·　　·　　·

They ate supper slowly; even Andrew chewed each bite of his salad—avocado slices, tomato, grilled chook—as if considering the food. They sat at the dining room table with the articles shoved aside in sloppy piles on chairs like dinner guests.

The phone.

Molly gave a quick and nervous stir. "I guess I'll get it," she said. She left them to their plates and went into the kitchen through the swinging door.

"Well," said Andrew. "She's exhausted."

Her words were an indecipherable hum. "Hm," said Leon.

"The phone doesn't stop. It's never anything—or anything good, anyway."

They stared at their salads, then Andrew started eating again. His chin was shiny with dressing. A few minutes later, Molly came back through the door, her face lit with grief like a moonstone. Leon didn't want to know what it was.

"So, what now?" Leon asked.

"Leon—Andrew—" she said. She worked the napkin in her hands. Andrew looked up from his empty plate, but kept his head ducked down.

"The chief inspector says at this point, unless he went on purpose, somewhere civilized, which seems impossible, given the car—" She stopped and swallowed. "At this point, he's presumed dead." She barely paused. "I'm glad John's mother isn't alive."

"So, nothing new," said Andrew.

"No, not new," said Molly. "But finished." She pushed

two stacks of clippings and paper together like halves of a card deck.

Leon looked at Andrew across the table. He reached his hand toward his brother, but Andrew pretended not to notice.

N i n e t e e n

Annabel hadn't *promised* they'd stay together after going back to the States, but she was full of promise—how she'd held him, how they'd decided what was next, together. Cleaving together even as they separated. Lying on his bed in what used to be his father's home office, Leon looked at his sweater sleeve and found a long reddish hair. He held it up to the light, letting the warm pain of wanting Annabel fill his chest. He tried to imagine her sitting in his apartment in Boston, working at his desk while he went back to the museum. He'd be up on stage with a snake, and she'd be proposing a research trip to Texas. He'd have to keep letting her go, but somehow it would be all right.

His mum had started plans for a service, and Leon had said, though he still couldn't believe they were doing this for his father, that it ought to be outside. He imagined mourning by a road-cut, a waterfall. It was hard to think it, work to take his mind there. He saw an invented sun, his mother's face, her lips pressed thin. His father's picture on the mantle again. It was almost as if, by vanishing, his father had moved from the realm of the outdoors, the real world, to the contained and predictable within.

Leon pulled Annabel's hair between his fingers. He'd look out at the crowd of children while she worked at home in his apartment. He'd say "Snakes are gross and slimy and smelly, right?" And even though Mum had said it—*finished*—even though he knew John Goode was gone, he'd look out into the foot traffic and see a brief flash of his father by the owl case, walking in the opposite direction.

Markos White gave Annabel a ride back to Malanda; he'd rented a car and was driving up to Darwin—Malanda wasn't exactly the right direction, but Annabel took him up on his offer anyway.

The rental car had thin doors and tiny tires; it rattled like a broken lightbulb as they drove up the familiar winding green of the Palmerston Highway.

She was thinking about her phone conversation with Alice. She'd finally reached her sister on the phone, but the conversation wasn't the comfort she'd expected. They'd stayed away from Robert, again, and talked about Leon and Annabel's plans instead. Alice had said, "I'm sure it will all work out. I'm sure he's very nice." There was something in her sister's tone—stiffness, doubt—that made Annabel bristle. She was questioning them; she didn't have blind faith in Annabel's choice. As if it had been a choice; Leon was the first one who had simply been the right person, despite the odd circumstances of their meeting. She tried to imagine them all in her sister's white kitchen, holding big-bellied wine glasses; Alice would have to see it, how they fit. But maybe it didn't matter so much what Alice thought.

"Hey," said Markos. "Where'd you go?" He wrapped and rewrapped his fingers around the steering wheel. The mostly static station played on the radio. Snippets of Buddy Holly burst through.

"Home, I guess," she said. "Leon's coming with me."

"Ooh," he said. "Meet the parents. You guys must be serious."

"Guess so," she said. She grinned.

"What about the field?" Markos gripped the wheel with both hands as the road wound around. Light dappled his face as the trees flew by outside.

"Oh, I want both," she said. A small fear crammed her throat, that she could lose one, or the other, that she was risking them both with that desire.

"Good on yer," said Markos, his Aussie accent inexact. "I've never managed to have both." His expression was dark for a second. "But then again, there's never been anyone really worth trying for."

"What's next for you?" She knew he'd already submitted his paper to *Science,* that he had a good shot at a new grant. Markos had been sure from the beginning. She hadn't, she realized, despite her sense of urgency; she hadn't always known where she was going.

"New Guinea," he said, his face flickering with a private smile. "Maybe I'll meet my mate there."

"Maybe." She looked at his profile, the freckles, long lashes, and perfect eyebrow arches. With the pure generosity of the loved, she ardently hoped he would.

They were quiet for a minute. Annabel realized they'd been shouting over the road noise; her throat was dry and sore.

They stopped in Malanda for Annabel to phone Leon. She leaned against the dusty glass and metal of the phone booth, watching afternoon begin its lean into early evening.

"So, that's it," she said. He'd told her everything twice, his mother's clippings, the pilot, the call from the director, the end of the search.

"Presumed dead," said Leon. "Missing."

The phone chunked as it swallowed her coins.

"I'm sorry," said Annabel. "And I'm out of change. And I miss you."

"Soon," said Leon, and the call clicked off.

Annabel stepped out of the booth. Missing, presumed dead. He had to be dead. She saw the red flash in the water at the gorge. No matter how blind he was to his wife and sons, ultimately he had loved them enough not to disappear, to erase himself, deliberately. Though this leaving left a dramatic mark, darker than the smear of erasure. Annabel would believe—she'd be decisive about possibilities. Snake bite or falling or an inhuman human. One day his would be the powdery bone someone would find. Horrible, but it was an accident, and he was gone. This was what she needed to believe, to keep her faith in science, and in love.

Looking at the sky, Annabel found a single star ghosted against the blue. She wished hard, thinking out the words of *Star light, star bright,* certain about what she wanted. She wished for Leon.

.   .   .

Annabel asked Markos to wait while she walked in toward her old orange marker tapes. There was the old food box to retrieve, and she could've left some equipment behind in her hurry; she wanted to take a quick look, then get a ride up toward the falls, where there might be a new bat camp. But once she stepped out of the car and toward the edge of the road, she heard the bat music, loud as the first time she'd ridden up in the van with Mike Trimble.

"Markos!"

He pulled the car to the edge of the road and stepped out. "God, they're noisy," he said.

"And they're back, this is my site—they're back."

"Score one for greenies," said Markos. "Want your stuff?"

"Yeah," said Annabel. "I'm going back in."

If she closed her eyes and listened, she could believe it was the first time she'd come, before the professor disappeared, before the sign and the spent shells. Annabel lay back on her tarp as a rain shower quieted the bats. Tristan and Isolde were gossiping above her. They hadn't mated in the hour she'd been watching; Isolde had chased Tristan away with a hiss. She wondered whether the season was over, whether some of her bats were carrying next year's additions to the camp.

The sudden burst of rain rattled through the ficus trees, tapping on leaves and vines, misting her face with the fine droplets that passed through the gauntlet of greenery to the floor. She inhaled the scent of guano and fruit, the wet loamy smell of the forest. The rain had finished by the time the mist reached her, and streams of sun hit her face. She opened her eyes to bouts of blue.

Annabel wiped her forehead and picked up her binoculars to watch the bats shake off the shower. If she concentrated, she could almost feel Leon's lips on her collarbone, his fingers fitted in hers. The bats' chatter resumed, a school yard of yelling children—high-pitched, incomprehensible excitement. Soon the light would dwindle, the parrots would fill the rain-forest patch with screams and flight. The bats were growing restless, the sleepers waking, preening, getting ready to take off in a great flock of black, departing for their fruit-feeding night. The blue was fading already, and Annabel shivered.

A great cloud of bats filled the sky, wings thumping air, a smear of sound moving with them as they lifted, then passed over Annabel to the west, toward mango orchards and a field of passion-fruit trees. As they emptied from her vision, Annabel sat up and put down her binoculars. She imagined she could take off after them, merge with the living cloud, and, like a single dot of dark on dark, blend into the new night sky.

Acknowledgments

Two enormously talented, generous women guided this book to its home in print—thank you, Elaine Koster and Jennifer Barth.

Armsful of thanks to my writing mentors and friends, Kathleen Hill, Linsey Abrams, Veera Hiranandani, Julie Wiskirchen, Erika Tsoukanelis, Susan Berlin, Amy Beaudry, Pat Dunn, Lori-Lyn Hurley, Cynthia Yoder, Marian Ryan, Judy Reeves, Harlan Coben, Bill Luvaas, Mona Simpson, Harriet Doerr, Tom Lux, Marie Howe, Lucy Rosenthal, my Sarah Lawrence workshops, Moira Bucciarelli, Petra Bauer-Ryan, Pat Alderete, Jeff Matsuda, Gregory Travis, Wendy James, and to John Sterling at Henry Holt.

Thanks also to my students and to all my families who brought me here, especially Edward Gross and Margaret Reid; Paula Herman and Tom Brown; Claudia Rose; Rebecca Gross; Samantha Gross; Alex Gang; Daniel Rosenberg; Harry Rosenberg and Barbara Filner; Herb and Ethel Herman; Ed and Bea Kuntz; Gerta Rosenberg; my son, Jacob; and my husband, Josh, my boat in all waters, my best friend.

About the Author

GWENDOLYN GROSS graduated from Oberlin College, was selected for the PEN West Emerging Writers Program, and completed an MFA in poetry and fiction at Sarah Lawrence College. As an undergraduate, she spent a semester in Australia researching spectacled fruit bats. *Field Guide* is her first novel.